Murder Two Doors Down

Murder Two Doors Down

AN HOA HOMICIDE MYSTERY

Chuck Storla

CROOKED LANE

NEW YORK

Books should be disposed of and recycled according to local requirements. All paper materials used are FSC compliant.

Published in the United States by Crooked Lane Books, an imprint of The Quick Brown Fox & Company LLC.

Crooked Lane Books and its logo are trademarks of The Quick Brown Fox & Company LLC.

Library of Congress Catalog-in-Publication data available upon request.

ISBN (hardcover): 979-8-89242-334-2
ISBN (paperback): 979-8-89242-336-6
ISBN (ebook): 979-8-89242-335-9

Cover design by Yordanka Poleganova

Printed in the United States.

www.crookedlanebooks.com

Crooked Lane Books
34 West 27th St., 10th Floor
New York, NY 10001

First Edition: October 2025

The authorized representative in the EU for product safety and compliance is eucomply OÜPärnu mnt 139b-14, 11317 Tallinn, Estonia, hello@eucompliancepartner.com, +33757690241

10 9 8 7 6 5 4 3 2 1

This book is dedicated to my loving wife. She was certain while I doubted. She protected my writing time better than I could manage. While I worked for this book, she suffered for it. She even laughed at the bits that weren't that funny. I don't deserve her.

Chapter One

I never planned to kill Miss Inga. While the thought had crossed my mind, I didn't dwell on it. I am not a homicidal maniac. And planning to kill someone would require deliberation. It would involve an outline of the necessary steps. Or a drawing laying out the scheme and the escape route. A plan to kill someone is far different than having a fleeting thought now and again. If I were to lean toward homicide, I'm sure I'd do it after thoughtful consideration and meticulous preparation—not maniacally.

Though if I *were* to dwell on killing Miss Inga, I could imagine how easy it would be to spread a fast-acting poison on plants she'd touch when she worked in her garden. Or I could think about how to weaken the gas line on her water heater so it would cause an explosion in the middle of the night. I could even imagine setting a trap so she would trip and fall headfirst down a flight of stairs. That might be tricky, since she owned one of the few ranch homes in the subdivision, but that's just a detail. Those are a few things I could imagine if I *were* to dwell on it. But I don't.

While occasionally thinking of something is not the same thing as dwelling on it, the thought did come into my head when—for the tenth month in a row—Miss Inga came to a meeting of the HOA board for The Estates. The other three Homeowners Association officers and I sat facing a small group of residents in the large open space of our clubhouse. It was decorated in a mash-up of French Colonial and Art Deco that could best be described as Garage Sale Chic. The building still smelled from the previous weekend's "Italian Night" get-together. The social committee's original title for the event had been "Wop-a-palooza." Whatever diversity training these people had received at work, had stayed at work.

Our neighborhood had pretensions of affluence, as we sat nestled between truly upscale developments in the pine-heavy city of Rhodes, Georgia. As an Atlanta suburb, we were living *in* the South while we were not *of* the South. Most residents of The Estates were white-collar transplants from Michigan, New Jersey, Ohio, or some other state with higher taxes and colder winters. They were incapable of properly pronouncing "y'all" as a single syllable, let alone using it in a sentence.

Miss Inga was definitely not of the South and seemed to barely tolerate living here. Her personality leaned toward the naked aggression we associated with the Northeast. She also lacked the layer of sugar that coated the barbs of any true Southern lady.

Miss Inga was inclined to drop a "Screw you" on occasion. Hearing that, a neighborhood belle might respond, "Bless your heart," which meant the same thing with different words. If the conversation continued, they'd follow with something similar to "Miss Inga, you're so brave with all you have to deal with right now. You know. Considering your age and living alone all these years without a man." Miss Inga would suggest they go to hell and that was usually the end of the exchange with each party counting it as a win.

As she had for months, Miss Inga was in front of the HOA board to bring a complaint. I'd prepared for this by chewing a couple of TUMS just before the meeting. The first few times she had come before the board, I felt sorry for her. After all, she was an elderly woman living by herself—just trying to survive in a cruel world. It didn't take long before I decided she was a part of the world that made it cruel for the rest of us.

When the nominating committee needed to fill an open position, I volunteered and put my name in for a three-year term as the HOA secretary. That good deed now felt like a three-year sentence with no time off for good behavior.

On this night, Miss Inga delivered her usual five-minute preamble before she got to the point. "When I moved here, I thought I was going to live in a respectable neighborhood. But I can't be proud of a community that allows people to blow their grass clippings into the street or leave them on the sidewalk. It's unsightly and will absolutely lower our property values."

This mention of the impact on property values was a new addition to her diatribe. None of us had dared dream the day would come when Miss Inga might move. She reminded me of Mrs. Harvey—that woman had been teaching local high school English courses to generations of students. Some speculated she'd loved teaching Shakespeare because they'd been good friends.

"And there is the cost of taking my Shih Tzu, Buttercup, to the dog groomer to remove the grass clippings and to the veterinarian for allergy treatments. I've provided an itemized list of these expenses. I think it is only fair that the homeowners reimburse me."

She delivered her complaint in a loud voice. Each time she paused, the loose skin of her neck continued to shake, which I found to be a minor distraction. A major distraction was the number of broken blood vessels in her eyes. There appeared to be a glow behind the red, but I'm sure that was my imagination. In any case, her eyes blazed in contrast with her dark olive skin and jet-black hair pulled back in a tight bun.

She held her prepared statement in one quivering hand while pounding her other fist on the arm of her chair. Summoning all the moral outrage she possessed—which was substantial—she read through the line items. Not to mention—though she did—the toll on Buttercup's fragile psyche. I found it strange that a woman with the amount of venom she possessed would feel such affection for something that was closer to an animated ball of fluff than a real dog.

On this night, Miss Inga brought an additional issue. "I move that the board of this HOA remove any tree containing more than one bird's nest."

She paused and looked at each board member as if to emphasize the gravity of the situation. We did not return her gaze, as if to emphasize we wished we were somewhere else.

Our president, Marge Peterson, finally broke the silence. "What?"

Miss Inga must have heard the question as "Why?" and said, "There are too many of these nuisance 'songbirds' in the trees near my home, and they create an unhealthy level of noise pollution. I have called 911 several times to request the police do something, but they seem to think the whole thing is funny."

She did not list financial consequences, but I was sure she would the following month.

When none of the others said anything, I felt I had to step in as the de facto parliamentarian. "Miss Inga, our president has not yet called the meeting to order and—"

She held up one hand to stop me, stared at the nameplate before me on the table and continued, "Mr. Brad Hanson, you might be the HOA secretary, but, young man, I'll have you know I studied Robert's Rules before you could count to ten."

"I realize that, Miss Inga. As I was saying, only those recognized by the chair may make a motion at the appropriate time."

At least that's how we interpreted *Robert's Rules of Order*—the manual of parliamentary procedures written in 1876 to be the legislative equivalent of boxing's Marquess of Queensberry Rules. None of us owned a copy of Robert's Rules, but we stuck to our set of procedures unless they became a nuisance and didn't let us do what we wanted to do. Sort of like Congress.

Unrestrained by our shared but vague understanding of parliamentary procedure, Miss Inga left the meeting after delivering her comment. She wanted to be home before the night's broadcast of *The Great English Cooking Show* despite the title's embedded oxymoron.

We still had HOA business to handle, but that was the last any of us saw of Miss Inga. At least that is what I assured the FBI and local detectives the following day.

* * *

After Miss Inga left the meeting, another of our regulars, Mr. Price, stood to have his turn. During summer months, he dressed in shades of green camo. This would last until Labor Day when fashion dictated he switch his camo to fall colors.

For the last several meetings, his issue had been the poop allegedly deposited in his yard by his neighbors' dogs. I say "allegedly" because Mr. Price himself owned three large dogs. When questioned, his neighbors pointed at his mutts and said the blame and the poop lay there.

He started with his usual salutation, "Your Honor."

Marge sighed. "Like I told you before, you don't need to address me that way."

"Yes, Your Honor. I stand before you this day—well, I guess it's night—to ask you to do something about the canine feces that other individuals allow their dogs to leave on my land."

He was among the residents of The Estates who would refer to their yard as their "land" as if it came with a hereditary title.

Mr. Price held up a sheaf of papers. "I have reported to this body on several occasions—the dates listed here if you don't have your records handy—to ask that you correct this injustice."

To the left of Mr. Price and with a half dozen neighbors behind her, Mrs. Okada stood. "Madam President, I don't wish to offend anyone here, but I represent the members of The Estates who have been targeted, both metaphorically and literally, by Mr. Price."

Marge's on-again, off-again drawl came into play. It seemed to pop up randomly, and I doubt if even she knew why. "Dear, y'all've lost me there. Could you back up and tell me just what y'all mean by 'targeted?'"

"I apologize. Mr. Price believes that this group of neighbors, or more properly our pets, have been leaving droppings on his property. Acting on this delusion, he has shot these same droppings into our yards with a catapult."

Mr. Price shook his head in a wide arc. "That is not correct."

Marge lost her accent as quickly as it had appeared. "What part is not correct?"

"First, I do not have a catapult. I have a trebuchet. Second, it does not shoot anything."

Marge asked, "Now you've lost me. What is a 'tre-boo-shay?'"

"Well, I had considered a catapult, but the city's legal code prohibits 'spring, compression, or similarly powered catapults.'" He lifted a small binder full of documentation. "I submit this as Exhibit A. May I approach the bench?"

Marge waved him forward with a sigh.

"Your Honor, as these scale drawings show, my device is a counterpoise trebuchet. It uses gravity and not a spring. As such, I am within my rights to use it to defend my land."

"Then you admit to using this device to shoot dog poop into your neighbors' yards?"

"No, Your Honor. I will stipulate that I used my trebuchet to *fling* specific items onto my neighbors' lands, but I was only returning to them that which was originally theirs."

The proceedings were interrupted when two deputies entered. After Mrs. Okada conferred with them and pointed out Mr. Price, they asked him outside so they could talk. A brief celebration broke out among Mrs. Okada's supporters, which Marge brought to an end by announcing the time for comments was over.

As the spectators cleared out, Marge used her coffee cup as a gavel and tapped the table. She muttered, "Oh fudge," and grabbed a Kleenex from her purse to wipe up the mess. The other two board members and I waited while she did this before using her I-used-to-teach-middle-school voice to declare the start of the meeting.

Scanning the room as if she might find a new participant, she finished with, "We have a legal quorum and can proceed to address the business of the HOA."

Herb—our vice president and Marge's husband—said, "Marge, there's just the four of us. You can lower the volume a bit."

She gave him a wait-until-we-get-home look over the top of her glasses.

He sat back and returned a look that said, you'll-have-a-glass-of-wine-and-forget.

While Marge wore a business suit to emphasize how seriously she took her presidency, Herb wore seasonal attire. For this particular meeting, it was Braves season. In a few months, he would switch to the Falcons, then the Hawks, and back to the Braves. I'd asked him once why he never wore an Atlanta United soccer jersey. He'd pointed to the three team bumper stickers on his Ford F-150 and said, "I only watch American sports."

Marge checked the first item off her prepared agenda and asked, "Will the secretary read the minutes from the last meeting?"

I wanted to point out it was less than a page, they'd all received the email, and had a printed copy in front of them. But it was quicker to read minutes out loud, so I did.

Before Marge had finished asking for a motion to approve the minutes, Edith, our treasurer and staunch defender of the budget surplus, jumped in with, "So moved."

Edith was wearing a light-brown cardigan, which was not unusual. I'd never seen her in anything but a white blouse under some vaguely earth-tone cardigan. She was the only person I knew who wore a sweater in Atlanta in August. She didn't attend neighborhood pool parties, but if she ever did, I was sure she'd have a cardigan over her swimsuit, which would also be in an earth tone. That thought brought to mind an image I regretted.

Edith made the motion to approve the minutes because she loved making motions. When she was not the one to make a motion, she scrambled to second the motion. It served to get her name in the minutes. I'd gathered her manager at work was not generous with recognition, so she sought it where she could. Early in my tenure on the board, I'd left out who-made-what-motion and learned it was quicker to include every petty detail than amend the minutes and reissue them. I faithfully recorded that Edith had made the motion.

Marge waited. I heard what I guessed was the toe of her shoe hitting Herb's calf.

"Seconded."

Smiling, Marge announced the motion was "made and seconded" before calling for a vote. Once it passed, she announced the unanimous decision as if we'd just cured cancer.

Herb raised his right hand to capture Marge's attention. "I think we need to talk about the screwup with the pine bark."

She frowned and looked at her agenda. "That's New Business. Our first item after approving the minutes is Old Business."

Herb sighed. "We decided on the pine bark vendor last month, so it is Old Business."

"If the Vice President will recall, we marked that action item as completed, which means any subsequent issue with the pine bark must be New Business." Marge made another check mark on her agenda. "Will the secretary please read the items of Old Business?"

"Uh. There aren't any."

"Duly noted. We will now move on to New Business."

The next day, under questioning, I declared I had never considered harming anyone in our neighborhood. Later on, thinking back on the board meeting, I hoped if law enforcement got involved, they didn't give me a polygraph.

Chapter Two

I had just finished my breakfast of a bagel, two egg whites, and a cup of Greek yogurt. Research showed these ingredients were part of a healthy lifestyle that increased life span by 2.43 years. While I respected the statistics, my plan was to beat the averages. When I accumulated the benefits of my Modern Healthy breakfasts, Mediterranean Diet lunches, and Mostly Paleo dinners, I had calculated I'd added 7.61 years—plus or minus 1.35 years to account for any variance that I hadn't already accounted for. I needed those years since I was behind schedule. I'd joined GFI, Georgia Federated Insurance, twenty-five years before. I should have been a Senior Investigator by now, if not a department manager. For years, my performance evaluations had been stellar. They did usually include comments on my "inability to take risks," but I never understood what they were trying to say with that. The business of an insurance company is to mitigate risks, after all.

After cleaning up from breakfast, I went down to the basement to work on my weekend project. I was putting up walls to make a small home office in one corner. I had considered setting my desk and computer in one of the bedrooms our kids had abandoned. Between summer internships on campus and full schedules during the school year, we only saw them when they came home for major holidays. After Kate more or less moved out, I tried using her old bedroom, but the lingering scent of perfumes and hair products drove me out within a week. When my son, Luke, decided he too would spend summers at the university, I tried the same thing with his bedroom, but my allergies acted up from the blend of *his* hair products mixed with a smell I'll call incense because I don't really want to know what it was. The basement home office had other advantages. I wanted to encourage the kids to come home as often as they were willing. Keeping their bedrooms waiting for them might give Rhonda and me a few more precious days with Kate and Luke before they graduated and started their lives as independent adults. Granted, I was expecting them to be independent adults who would remain on my health insurance, cellular plan, and Netflix subscription as long as they could.

Eager to make progress in the basement, my task for the day was to drive nails through the bottom of the wall frames and into the concrete floor. Thanks to my protective earmuffs, I didn't hear the doorbell ringing. It was my wife toggling the light switch on and off that finally got my attention. Then I could hear the doorbell and the barking of our corgi, Prince.

After putting my tools down, I climbed the stairs, captured Prince, and placed him in our bedroom. When we got our dog, the breeder told us corgis are "a small dog with a big dog sound." She said it as if it was a benefit. Fortunately for us, Prince had a short-term memory problem that worked to our advantage. Once he was behind a closed door in the back of the house, he forgot there might be an intruder on the front steps and took a nap. Object permanence is not just a thing with toddlers.

With the dog handled, I headed to the front of the house. Rhonda was a wonderful woman, and one thing she had done early in our marriage was to make clear what she expected. For example, when someone came over, I was to receive our guests, so that she had time to prepare herself. After I opened the door, I saw a tall man with dark hair and a slightly shorter redheaded woman. They both took wardrobe cues from *Men in Black.* I expected my two visitors to announce they were Mulder and Scully. I hadn't watched many episodes of *The X-Files*, but I knew such archetypes exist for a reason.

The Mulder lookalike introduced himself as Special Agent Joseph Maloney with the Federal Bureau of Investigation, and his colleague as Special Agent Pamela Stewart. With that, they produced badges that appeared authentic—at least as good as what you can find on eBay.

Pleasantries out of the way, he asked, "May we come in?" though clearly it was not a question.

We didn't use our living room much, but Rhonda was justifiably proud of it. She'd selected Amenable Gray for the wall color because she thought it had a bit more élan than the Agreeable Gray that had become so commonplace. She set it off with a matching sofa and chairs in a deep lavender. I directed my guests into the living room and pointed to the couch as I sat in one of the chairs. Quantico must have drilled into the agents the need to stay standing as neither one took a seat. Perhaps because it would be awkward to draw their weapons from that position.

I felt uncomfortable sitting while they stood, so I rose from my chair.

Scully motioned with open palms for me to sit. "Please, make yourself comfortable."

Realizing the power play of their dominant positions, I remained standing as well. If they were not concerned about prolonged standing leading to varicose veins, then I would show them I could also take risks. "No, I'm better off standing. I've been sitting all day."

Mulder looked at his watch. "It's only 8:30."

I said, "I know. I got up early." It was amazing how quickly and ineptly I found myself lying to these FBI agents. Were they that good at applying subtle interrogation techniques, or was I that bad at fending them off?

I decided it was because I was split between being nervous and excited. I was nervous because I'd never been visited by the FBI before and immediately regretted padding the charitable deductions on last year's tax return. I was also excited because I'd never been visited by the FBI before. At a minimum, I finally had a decent response if someone at the office asked what I'd been up to.

Whenever I'm nervous or excited, I tend to say whatever comes up top of mind. "You said you were 'special agents.' What makes you special?"

The Scully clone made a face like I'd just claimed J. Edgar Hoover was a commie sleeper agent—something my uncle swore was true based on his internet research. With no trace of a smile, she said, "It is merely the title for field agents. We are in no way special."

I said, "That makes sense. If you were special, you wouldn't match your archetypes."

Special-in-name-only Agent Stewart's look made clear who was going to play bad cop if it got to that.

Before I could take us further down that road, her partner got to what I suspect was the point of their visit. "How well did you know Miss Oskarsdotter?"

"Who?"

"Miss Oskarsdotter. She was one of your neighbors. We assume you had some previous contact with her, and we would like to know the nature of those interactions."

I was still cataloging real versus enhanced charitable donations, and it took me a moment to realize he meant Miss Inga. It took me another moment to realize he'd used the past tense to speak of her. "You mean Miss Inga? What happened to her?"

"What makes you think something happened to her?"

"Because when I asked, you both exchanged a look like you'd accidentally let something slip." I tried not to smile when the two agents glanced at each other a second time, confirming it *had* been a slip. The online course I'd taken in interrogation techniques had been the key component in my personal improvement plan the previous month. I considered recommending the course to the agents, but something in their expressions told me they would not be open to my suggestion.

"Unfortunately, something *has* happened to Miss Oskarsdotter," said Stewart. "We are checking with everyone in this immediate area who might have some information to help us. We would appreciate your help here. I'll start again. How well did you know Miss Oskarsdotter?"

I told them what I knew while watching Agent Maloney take notes. He only wrote down select items, so I assumed those must be the important ones in his eyes.

"I barely knew her. To me, she was 'Miss Inga.' She kept to herself for the most part."

He didn't write down anything based on that.

For some reason, it seemed important to me that I make a bigger contribution to his notes, so I added, "But she was a regular visitor to the HOA board meetings and always had something to complain about. Of course, that was her right, and she was well-versed in the covenants. She wanted to ensure they were enforced when she saw what she considered violations."

That earned one sentence in the notepad.

"The only other time I would see her was when she would attend an occasional neighborhood potluck. Everyone loved her fettuccine alfredo."

That earned another sentence in his notes. His partner pointed at one item, and he underlined it. Perhaps they were foodies and getting lunch ideas for later.

It was her turn to ask a question. "Do you know any reason someone would want to harm Miss Inga?"

I considered the dozens of neighbors targeted by one or more of her motions. Not to mention everyone else in the neighborhood who saw their monthly HOA dues increase every time we had to bend to one of Miss Inga's demands.

"No. She was a sweet lady."

Agent Maloney jumped at that. "You said 'she *was* a sweet lady.' Why didn't you say, 'she *is* a sweet lady'?"

"Because you started the past tense thing and then admitted something had happened to her. I wouldn't be much of an investigator if I couldn't work from there to the conclusion she had passed away."

"You're an investigator?" Agent Stewart furrowed her brow as if I had just claimed the moon landings were faked. Another thing my uncle swore he could prove. "We've worked extensively with local law enforcement. Your name has never come up. Which department are you in?"

"GFI."

"You're with the Georgia Bureau of Investigation?"

I felt the need to stand a little taller, so I tried to expand the space between each vertebra.

"Not GBI. G-*F*-I. Strictly speaking, I'm not in law enforcement. At least not in government law enforcement, per se. I'm an investigator with the Georgia Federated Insurance Company."

I felt pretentious for using "per se," and I wasn't even sure if I'd used it properly, but something made me want to make a good impression. I knew the investigator pecking order started with James Bond at the top and worked its way down to mall cops. I liked to think I was somewhere above the midpoint, but I got the feeling these two might not agree.

Their shared reaction to anything unexpected continued to be turning to look at each other. This time, they added eye rolls.

Agent Stewart struggled and failed to keep from smiling as she asked, "Insurance investigator? You track down international art thieves, no doubt?"

"No. Mostly automobile accidents, disability, and workers' comp claims."

They said nothing, but I could see their neck muscles straining as they fought their natural reaction to face each other. I'm not claiming I'd be more stoic, but these two should never play poker.

I said, "There's a lot of money involved in disability fraud. It's pretty high stakes."

Agent Stewart covered her mouth with one hand and turned away as her shoulders shook. I became more determined than ever to demonstrate I was a peer and could contribute to the case I could see unfolding before me.

"Perhaps my expertise can be of use. How did she die? In her age demographic, falls are quite common. In the most recent year we have data for, 28.7 percent of older adults reported falling, and there were over 32,000 deaths." I took a breath, allowing the agents to absorb the details I'd shared. In my experience, most people weren't great with numbers. The fact that I was gave me an advantage at times when dealing with an insurance claim. At other times, my tendency to quote statistics just seemed to annoy the crap out of people. I sensed this was one of those times.

Since it looked like statistics weren't going to work, I fell back on my training and focused on whose coverage would end up with the bill. "Did she fall down inside her house? In that case, her own insurance comes into play. Then again, she complained about her neighbor's cracked sidewalk, so that might be cause for a claim against their insurance."

Agent Maloney stared at me. "The FBI is not in the habit of investigating household accidents."

"Then why are you here?"

Agent Stewart touched the back of her head. "Your neighbor received two taps to the head from a small caliber gun. Just a guess at this point, but we think from a silenced .22. In your experience, anything like that ever come up under workers' comp?"

Like I do with many things in life, I took the question too literally.

"No. Never. Though that is to be expected since most workers' compensation claims involve falls, strains, contusions, or lacerations." Then I hesitated, allowing them to believe I was giving their case serious study, even as I dismissed it—a skill I had used with numerous clients. "Although I suppose it's possible."

Special Agent Stewart sighed and said to her partner, "I told you we should have let someone else take this one. Didn't I say that?"

He was about to respond when my wife walked into the room. She had used the time I'd provided to change from casual clothes to a floral print dress. "Brad, you didn't tell me we had guests."

My back muscles bunched up like they did every time she used what I called her "tight voice." It was the sound her vocal cords made when her neck and facial muscles were all straining to contain her displeasure. Perhaps it was twenty-six years of marriage that had aligned our bodies' responses—irritation in one of us prompted an automatic reaction in the other.

Not that we didn't have a happy marriage, at least compared to most of our married or once-married friends and family. Some people regret their marriages because they believe they could have done better. I thought Rhonda was content in our relationship because she knew she could have done worse.

Still, there were things about me that annoyed her. One of her pet peeves was she did not like surprises—like unexpected guests arriving before she'd had her first cup of coffee and her antianxiety medication. Her condition was self-diagnosed and she said she got the pills from a website recommended by a friend. The bottles were unlabeled, and I wasn't sure if her friend's source was really on the internet or someone in the retail trade for the local college campus.

"This is Special Agent Scully and Special Agent Mulder."

"Your husband is joking. I'm Special Agent Maloney." As he said this, he checked out my wife, as most men did. He spent an inordinate amount of time on her legs, which I didn't appreciate, even though I understood why.

"I'm sorry," I said. "It's early, and I'm still trying to wrap my head around Miss Inga's death. This is my wife, Rhonda."

"Miss Inga is dead?"

Rhonda's voice had lost its barely suppressed tension and had moved to a tone of fascination bordering on delight. I guessed she was anticipating the conversation around Miss Inga's death at the Monday afternoon mah-jongg club. That would be much more fun than talking about who was drinking too much, who was sleeping with whom, and who had been caught stealing bandwidth off their neighbor's Wi-Fi.

When the special agents confirmed Miss Inga had passed, Rhonda shook her head. "That's just terrible."

Rhonda, like me, had been born and raised in Iowa before our families moved south. "That's just terrible" was her variation on "Bless her heart."

I try to be polite and follow social niceties but I was getting nervous as the direction of this FBI visit began to sink in. I wanted to steer the conversation back to learn what they knew and what they suspected. "Yes, dear, it is terrible. The special agents were just telling me Miss Inga was found with two gunshots to the head from a small caliber weapon."

"Most likely a .22," Maloney added. "Not well-aimed, but sufficient."

Stewart turned to me and asked if I had a .22 caliber weapon by any chance.

I wanted to say no but remembered my dad's old pistol out in the garage. I said, "I'm storing one of my dad's because they wouldn't let him keep it in the retirement home."

Rhonda turned to explain to the agents. "When it went off in his room, the bullets didn't even make it through the wall into Mrs. Jenkins's room next door, so I don't know why she made such a fuss."

"It's just an old target pistol my dad used to shoot squirrels in his backyard," I said.

The male agent nodded. "That's fine, but I think it would be helpful if we could examine this gun. Just to simplify matters and rule out one variable."

I didn't know what the variables might be, or the equation, but I didn't want to make an issue by refusing. "It's a waste of time, but I can show it to you. It's somewhere in the garage."

Stewart and Maloney followed me through the house and out to the garage where I had to move a stack of boxes I'd labeled "Sell or give away" ten years before. I made a mental note to deal with these before winter so I could get both cars in the garage. Failing that, I was going to remove the stickers so I didn't feel so much guilt about the piles.

Finally, I uncovered the dusty boxes marked "Dad's." I searched each one but couldn't find my dad's trusty gun safe with the broken lock. I opened my mouth to tell the agents I couldn't locate it when Special Agent Stewart pointed to a half-crushed box in the corner where you could barely make out the "ad's" written in black marker. To get to the box in question, I had to weave between the sedimentary layers of other boxes. When I opened it, there was the gun safe, sitting atop dozens of my dad's terminally scratched LPs of ABBA, Led Zeppelin, and Johnny Cash.

I bent to get the box when Agent Maloney moved me aside and pulled on latex gloves.

"Will you permit us to examine the contents?"

I knew if I didn't allow them to check, we'd sit and wait for a warrant. I also didn't want to do anything to make them suspicious. "Sure. There's nothing in there but his old handgun. It's been years since he used it."

Agent Maloney opened the lid. Sure enough, the pistol was there, but I was sorry the patina was gone. "Dad must have cleaned it up before we took it from his assisted living apartment." When my dad purchased the used gun, the thin film of reddish-brown had made the gun look ancient and somehow more authentic. Now it looked like a cheap imitation of the weapon I remembered.

As Agent Maloney examined the gun, his partner peered over his shoulder, then looked at me and said, "A Ruger with a threaded barrel for a silencer. Your father was serious about shooting squirrels. Was he into guns as a hobby?"

"Not really. But there was a lot of pressure from his buddies. Owning a gun was practically an obligation for someone of his generation living in Georgia. He settled on the Ruger to shut them up and justified it to my mother with the squirrel angle."

"And the silencer?"

"To impress his pals. They didn't think a .22 was a man's gun, but the silencer made it OK 'cause it was cool. Before assisted living, he was in a 55-plus neighborhood that leaned heavily into the 'plus.' They frowned on loud noises."

Under the odor of gun oil, and the ever-present dust, I smelled something pungent and wrinkled my nose. "Smells like cat piss. The neighbor's damn cat must have gotten in again."

"I believe what you are smelling is the propellant of these .22 rounds. It's almost a trademark of certain brands of ammunition."

I forgot the advice I had learned lawyers give anyone under suspicion of anything—keep your mouth shut. "They smell like that?" I asked.

Maloney tilted his head as he looked back at me. His smile didn't reach his eyes. "Only after they've been discharged."

Chapter Three

The agent lifted the weapon and ejected the magazine. He used one latexed thumb to push down on the top cartridges, then looked up at me. "My guess is there are two rounds missing. I don't suppose you can tell us where we might find the spent casings?"

"Probably still on the floor of his room at the home. They don't clean very thoroughly."

The agents exchanged a glance and then gave me a look I recognized all too well. It was the same you-are-so-screwed look that I had given countless potential fraudsters in my years working for Georgia Federated Insurance—chiropractors who padded bills, doctors who exaggerated symptoms, and personal injury lawyers. That last group requires no explanation.

"Mr. Hanson, we'd like to take this weapon for testing," said Special Agent Maloney. "If that is acceptable, we'd also like you to accompany us to our office to continue our discussion."

I hadn't noticed Rhonda had followed us into the garage until I heard her ask, "Why are you taking my husband?"

Since the agents seemed to be struggling to come up with a convincing lie, I took the lead. "Among other things, they want to perform a test for gunshot residue—GSR for short."

Maloney frowned. "And how do you know the specific terminology?"

"I'm also an investigator. Remember?"

He expelled a brief snort. "Somehow that slipped my mind."

"At least let me give my husband a hug before you take him," Rhonda said. With that, she wrapped one arm around my neck and used the hand hidden from the agents to slip something into my left rear pocket. She whispered, "Here's a few of my pills to calm you down."

I thought I was calm until the special agents took either side and walked me toward the door. There was an awkward moment when they realized we could not go three abreast through my garage's side door. The door was thirty-six inches wide, because every external door in our neighborhood was thirty-six inches wide as the Creator and our HOA covenants intended. Apparently, there was some fear that one or more residents might go crazy with a forty inch door—or even wider. The covenants were there to protect us all from the chaos of a universe without rules.

As we stepped one at a time into the sunshine, I could see children chatting as they walked to school. At least, I assumed they were chatting. I couldn't hear them because of the army of leaf blowers scouring yards of anything that was not fescue, zoysia, or Bermuda grass. I thought it might be my last scent of freedom, so I inhaled deeply to absorb the mown grass mingled with the exhaust from the gas-powered lawn tools. I looked to see how many neighbors were going to witness my perp walk but got distracted when I saw three dandelions in one neighbor's yard and the lack of proper edging in another's. I took this as a sign of the general moral decay in society—and perhaps also a sign that my years on the HOA board had not been good for my soul.

I lost any hope of a discreet exit from my neighborhood when I noticed the parked police cars blocking the street at each corner and the tape stretched between trees. It took a moment to read,

POLICE LINE DO NOT CROSS

but the bright yellow tape subtly hinted at its purpose. Off to the side, an older uniformed officer stood with hands on hips in front of two other officers. The two were looking everywhere but at their superior as he yelled, "You had one freakin' job to do. One freakin' job." It brought back memories of the coaching I often received during my first five years as an apprentice investigator with GFI.

But now was not the time for reminiscing. Down the street, even more officers were gathering. Mulder grunted with what seemed like surprise, and Scully breathed a barely audible "What the hell . . ."

"That was fast," I said. "Did you guys call in the police to cordon off the area?"

Mulder and Scully looked at each other, then at me, and then back down the street. As they steered me toward the gaggle of cops, my escorts used their free hands to fish out their badges once again. They waved them as if they were magical talismans, which I imagined they believed them to be. The first officer to notice their badge-waving said, "Captain Dawson, . . . We got a couple accountants with badges here." A tall Black woman with two gold bars on each side of her collar turned toward us.

"I don't need to see badges. Y'all have 'J. Edgar' stamped on your foreheads." She paused. "What're y'all doing with one of *my* citizens?"

Before either agent could answer, she looked past them to where the two younger officers had repositioned the yellow tape. Now the text was right-side up and facing toward the crime scene rather than away. I wondered how our city maintained such low crime statistics. The only thing that came to me was they must regularly lose track of any record of felonies within the city.

"Sergeant, *you had one freakin' job.* Fix that tape now or y'all better hope there's a security opening somewhere since the mall closed."

She turned back to the agents and cleared her throat. "And why're you two doing *anything* in my city without asking my permission?"

Scully spoke first. "We are here investigating the death that occurred last night and have solicited the cooperation of this gentleman as a person of interest in the case."

The captain looked at me. "Doesn't look interesting, but that's not the point. This is my town and y'all don't have jurisdiction." She paused. "And how'd you even learn of the demise of Mrs. Skinner?"

I stepped forward. Somehow two FBI agents showing up and telling me Miss Inga was dead had felt unreal. It wasn't that I was completely callous, but I'd never seen Miss Inga as anything but a pain in the butt. Edith Skinner was also a pain in the butt, but less so, and I'd gotten used to her quirks over time. I realized it was a dumb question when I asked it, but some situations call for dumb questions. "Edith's dead?"

The captain lifted the brim of her hat and leaned into my face. "That's what I usually mean when I say 'demise.'" Turning again to the agents, she asked again why they were in her city—this time peppered with a few colorful expressions.

"We're not interested in an accidental death," said Maloney. "We are here to investigate the murder of Miss Inga Oskarsdotter. FBI jurisdiction includes investigating a murder 'when the purpose of the murder was to promote a criminal enterprise.'"

I had the feeling Maloney was fond of using exact quotes while speaking, and I expected footnotes would soon follow. I was hoping he'd provide a couple to expand on "criminal enterprise." This was the suburbs after all. *Law & Order* was set in New York City for a reason. Major felonies like murder only happened in big cities or possibly in tiny villages where every inhabitant spoke with a charming local accent. Never in the suburbs. At least not our suburbs.

Captain Dawson lowered her chin so she was staring at the agents from under the brim of her service cap. "Who is Inga Oskarsdotter?"

That was not her exact wording. She inserted several obscenities to provide emphasis. I think it also accentuated her perception of the difference between "accountants with badges" and those she considered real police who were permitted—if not expected—to use earthy language.

Stewart pointed away from the group and said, "It might be best if we talked privately."

The two walked twenty steps away and continued their discussion. I could not pick up any of the words from Stewart but could clearly hear the captain had additional vocabulary that included expletives for all parts of speech except for prepositions and conjunctions.

They walked back to us, and Stewart summarized the situation for her partner. "Captain Dawson here has graciously agreed to forgive the impression of our overzealous pursuit of a homicide case. In return, she'd like a free exchange of information between our two organizations. In addition, I've agreed to make the FBI forensic lab available to determine if Mrs. Skinner's untimely demise was of natural causes."

"Can you tell me how she passed?" I asked. "I hope she didn't suffer. Edith was a close friend." As I said it, I wondered if this could be considered lying to the FBI. Maybe there was a loophole here in that I was really lying to a police captain while I also happened to be in the presence of the FBI.

Up to that point, the captain had not included me in the conversation. Her face softened, and I imagined she might have realized I was a constituent and not a competitor. "Since you'll be with your friends here for a while, I might as well tell you. For some reason, Mrs. Skinner went out into her garden in her nightdress last night. She apparently tripped and fell on sharp objects. She died due to loss of blood. Based on the amount of blood on the ground, she didn't suffer long."

"I've investigated hundreds of injuries from falls and never seen one where the victim bled out."

"It's unusual, but the poor old woman must have forgotten how to place the garden stakes for her tomatoes and other climbing plants. Each stake was planted with the flat end in the ground and the point up."

I shook my head vigorously. "Still, one puncture that size could not have resulted in rapid blood loss."

"We found deep puncture wounds in seven places, including one through her heart and three that pierced major arteries."

"OK. Yeah. That would do it then."

I didn't want anyone to think me coldhearted, but I'm only human. If Edith had been insured by GFI, her death could have really cut into my office's Q2 profits. They would calculate our results in a few months, and I was counting on a nice check. If it was large enough, I planned on getting an eighty-five inch flatscreen for the family room. One with an 8K, mini-LED, OLED display. My neighbor, Tony, bought a seventy inch last Christmas. Since then, when he was at my house, he would always pretend to squint when he looked at anything on my TV. Tony was my best friend in the neighborhood. Tony and I are not a pairing you would expect to work, but then again, I didn't have many candidates worth considering for the best buddy position.

While Tony is average in almost every respect, I tend to be somewhat analytical. For example, I once identified twelve attributes commonly associated with analytical personalities, asked fifteen coworkers to give me a numerical value between zero and ten for each attribute and made a radar chart to visualize the result. The sample size was admittedly small, but the results were very consistent in showing I tended to be analytical. "To the point approaching insanity" according to one individual's comments. I think he was exaggerating for comic effect.

My Meyers-Briggs personality test results indicated that I was an INTJ based on my scores in Introversion (I), Intuition (N), Thinking (T), and Judging (J). I had asked Tony if he knew his type. I guessed it was ESFP, but he admitted when his previous workplace offered the test, he got bored filling out the form and never finished it. Tony seemed to have two passions: sports and action movies. Both were enhanced by beer, which might have really been his primary passion. A recent transplant to the South from New Jersey, Tony felt as strongly about reruns of *The Sopranos* as I did about *NOVA* episodes. Really any PBS documentary.

The captain's voice disturbed my wandering thoughts. "You said Edith Skinner was a close friend?"

I told myself not to respond like a guilty person, but recent events had made me nervous. When nervous, I also sometimes stick my hands in my pockets like an eight-year-old caught shoplifting a piece of candy.

"I live just down the street and we are—I mean were—both members of the HOA board."

"I'd like you to talk to my detectives, in case it can help."

Special Agent Mulder—or maybe it was Scully, I'd forgotten which was which—stepped in front of the captain and said, "That might be possible *if* we decide we no longer require Mr. Hanson for *our* investigation."

Their conversation devolved into an argument where the special agent's long sentences included multiple, nested parenthetical phrases and again revealed his fondness for quoting original sources. The captain's side of the disagreement was made of shorter sentences, some of which were again almost entirely words that would provide additional funds for the swear jar.

Their exhibition had drawn a crowd of my neighbors. Based on a few of their expressions, I knew we could look forward to at least one making a motion at the next HOA board meeting. Mrs. Baxter had already tried three times to have us force the cable company to put a language filter on all streaming services. Those living next to her knew she was also unable to put a language filter on Mr. Baxter. Thankfully, she had yet to bring that before the board, but we knew it was just a matter of time.

A moment of silence brought me back to the dispute. The captain took a deep breath and said, "Fine. Y'all take Mr. Hanson to your field office for now, but my detectives want to talk to him when y'all're through."

I walked with the agents back to where their car was parked. A small crowd had formed next to the yellow tape barriers. Half the people were neighbors trying to see what the excitement was about. The other half were realtors trying to get an officer to put their business cards in the mailboxes of the recently depopulated homes.

Even with Stewart's phone and navigation app for directions, my escorts were having a tough time getting out of our neighborhood. Driving through The Estates was like traversing a circular labyrinth where one wrong turn meant you wound up in a cul-de-sac. When it happened to me, I hated the need to pull ten feet into some stranger's driveway just so I could swing back out and escape a dead end. On all sides, the faux wood blinds would part so inhabitants could see who dared to trespass on their concrete. Within minutes, the localized social media site, Folks-Next-Door.com, would be on fire with people reporting "a strange man in a foreign car prowling the neighborhood." Then others would respond with "if he trespasses on my property, he'll meet my 9mm." I did not want to hasten the decline of Western civilization by feeding that monster.

I was not sure if it was malice or incompetence that drove developers to build subdivisions like a maze designed to frustrate test subjects. My birthplace in Iowa had been built using Cartesian coordinates. The north–south avenues were numbered and east–west streets labelled alphabetically with the names of trees. Though it is not strictly speaking in the Bible, I'm convinced this is how God would prefer things. If you were on Birch Street, you immediately knew you were three blocks from Elm. You might need to use fingers and toes to figure out how far you were from Sycamore, but you could be certain which direction to go.

In The Estates, the roadmap looked like a three-year-old's fingerpainting exercise. On top of that, every street was some combination of "Chestnut" and a descriptor. Since Atlanta had taken all the rights to anything Peachtree, we had Chestnut Road, Chestnut Lane, Chestnut Court, Chestnut Circle, Chestnut Crossing, Chestnut Heights, and on and on. We had twenty-seven Chestnut-somethings in the subdivision without a single chestnut tree. Even after the availability of GPS, we were a substantial contributor to global warming as delivery vans wandered in search of the right Chestnut.

On dark nights, kids still tell the story of a driver from Big Joe's Pizza. According to the tale, this driver came into The Estates on Halloween night. He'd let his cellphone plan expire. Without a mapping app, he could not find where to deliver a large pepperoni, extra cheese, with a side of garlic grits. He never returned to Big Joe's. Some say you can still find him on moonlit nights slowly cruising through the mists of dozens of irrigation systems.

As I sat in the back of the FBI sedan, I wondered if Miss Inga, Edith, and I would figure in some future story told around backyard firepits.

Chapter Four

What followed was a boring ride from the suburbs and into Atlanta. I amused myself counting billboards for personal injury lawyers I'd encountered through GFI claims. I tried to recall which had presented the flimsiest "accident" cases but the list grew too long to keep track of without a spreadsheet. Once we arrived at the FBI's field office, I was surprised that the building could have passed as my company's regional office. Or a telemarketing organization. Walking through the cubicle aisles, it appeared to be occupied by individuals who had nothing to distinguish them as individuals. There was a strong odor of overheated toner cartridges, so I knew their printer etiquette was being ignored.

They escorted me to a room where the top half of one wall was covered by a mirror. I wondered whether there were any suspects or even persons of interest who didn't know someone was watching from the other side of that mirror.

In the bare room, I could not decide where to look. I thought looking away from the mirror might appear suspicious, but looking directly into the mirror might look defiant.

I settled on oscillating between the two and hoped the average was acceptable to my invisible judges.

Then it occurred to me that since I was not under arrest, they had left me with my phone. I was sure the room was wired for sound so I didn't want to make a call, but I could text my wife.

I was sure she would be worried about me so my first text was *I'm OK dear. Just waiting to answer a few of their questions.*

A few minutes later, she replied with, *That's nice. Don't do anything to embarrass me.* She was obviously trying to put me at ease with a little joke.

My thoughts started to jump from one bad scenario to another, and her attempt at humor wasn't making me feel less nervous. I wanted to make sure the kids didn't hear any rumors that must be flying around The Estates by now. *Not sure how long I'll be able to text. Can you let the kids know what is going on? Tell them everything is fine.*

Her reply was immediate. *Maybe later. Have to help set up for Ladies Coffee today.*

I thought it was a good sign she didn't want to worry the kids if this would be over soon. I hoped she was right.

After letting me sit and overthink for another half hour, Maloney and Stewart entered and sat across from me.

Stewart didn't waste any time. "Why did you kill Miss Oskarsdotter?"

"I didn't kill Miss Oskarsdotter. I had nothing against her. Anyway, I wouldn't kill anyone."

"You say you had nothing against her, but people saw you arguing just a month ago and say you threatened her."

"I don't know who's telling you this, but I never threatened her."

Maloney looked at a sheet of paper between them on the table and asked, "You're telling us you did not say she would, quote, *not live long enough to see it all,* end quote?"

"That's taken out of context."

Stewart leaned back and put her hands behind her head. "Then please give us some context, because it sounds like a threat to me."

"You should know Miss Inga regularly showed up to complain to the HOA board. When she did, she always made a big deal about needing to get home in time to watch *The Great English Cooking Show.* She was so insistent on it last month, I thought I'd do her a favor, and I told her she could either stream it off the internet the next day or use her cable box to record it."

"Fine. You thought you were being nice, and then it turned ugly."

"No. She just got a little upset and assured me she knew all about 'how reruns worked' and didn't need me to tell her how to watch TV. She said she'd missed episodes before and wasn't going to wait for months to see the reruns. I might have gotten a little frustrated because she wasn't understanding me. That's when I told her that she could stream as many of the past episodes as she wanted. With all of the on-demand cooking show content, I assured her she would not live long enough to see it all." I hesitated a moment and added, "Trust me, I feel no satisfaction in being right about that."

After all, I'd have to be a monster to feel good for being correct when the woman had just died. Though I secretly wished the agents would say something to acknowledge I'd been right.

The two agents stared at me. I could hear the clock on the wall ticking through the seconds. Somewhere along the way, I mused, clocks must have lost the ability to "tock." Now all you ever heard was "tick"—though digital clocks had lost even that ability.

Stewart might have been thinking the same thing because she said, "I don't have time to sit through his BS," before leaving the room.

Maloney stood to follow her, but given he was currently tasked as the good cop, he asked if I would like some coffee or a can of pop.

I said I'd like a Coke Zero and decided to demonstrate my knowledge of regional variations in soft drink nomenclature. "What part of the Midwest are you from?"

"I worked four years out of the office in West Des Moines, Iowa."

I smiled at the revelation that he was clearly not on a fast track for promotion.

Then he smiled. "Almost forgot you were an investigator yourself."

I raised my opinion of him slightly with this reminder that payback is a bitch.

When he returned with the drink, he set it on the table and said they'd be with me in a few minutes. After the "few" turned into "many" I decided to take one of my wife's pills and slid a hand into the rear pocket where she'd deposited them. When I opened my hand and looked down, I saw she'd given me three of her faux Xanax. I didn't know the recommended daily dose, but figured it was enough to last through the interrogation.

I wasn't sure I'd get another chance, so I thought, what the heck, and put them in my mouth while stifling a fake yawn and quick swallow of the soft drink. It tasted a little off for a Coke Zero, but I looked forward to the pills' calming effect. I sat there for at least a half hour and didn't feel any change in my anxiety level. I decided the website was pushing a placebo.

* * *

My nose hurt, and my forehead was on the cold metal table top. I lifted my head and saw a small red pool. My nose felt stuffy and when I wiped it, my hand came away bloody. I thought that should have bothered me, but it didn't, and the fact that it didn't bother me didn't bother me, but I was losing track of the things that didn't bother me. Swirling the red stuff between my fingers, I marveled at how it was simultaneously very slippery and yet kind of sticky. I'd read somewhere that blood had a metallic smell, but I couldn't remember ever trying to smell metal. I thought I'd see if it was possible with the table top. That might have been how I woke up again with my forehead on the table while my nose was back in the red puddle.

I was examining the table from nose height when the door swung open and a half-dozen people tumbled in. An Asian man with classic pattern baldness pointed at Maloney and yelled, "I told you to keep a handle on your partner. Did you let Stewart beat another suspect?"

As he glanced my way, I raised my head, and said, "Not specious. I'm a pershun of intrest." As I spoke, small flecks of blood scattered on the table. I decided there was more I could learn from the furniture and returned to my previous position.

The next time I woke up, I was in the rear seat of another government sedan. We were headed to the suburbs and based on the traffic, it must have been rush hour. Though in Atlanta "rush hour" could be applied to any hour when the sun was up, soon to be up, or not long gone.

I was alone in the back. I didn't recognize the two men in the front, but assumed they were both agents. At least that was my guess based on their haircuts. They looked like stunt doubles for Biff in *Back to the Future*. The FBI might have added new roles in fighting terrorists and cyber villains, but clearly some things in the Bureau never change.

The driver said, "I don't care what Maloney thinks. This guy doesn't look like a killer."

The one in the passenger seat nodded. "Might bore someone to death. Stewart says he sells insurance."

"Why'd they let him go?"

"Forensics said the bullets were too deformed to match to the weapon. Stewart and Maloney have to go back to the scene and find the two spent casings. That's their punishment. Ours is babysitting Mr. Insurance while we take him to the cop shop in his suburb."

I was glad the FBI had no reason to keep me as a person of interest. There shouldn't be a problem with talking to the local police detectives about either one of the deaths they had to investigate. Still, I was nervous and adjusted the seat belt so I could put my hands in my front pockets. You know how your tongue keeps returning to probe a sore tooth, even though it hurts every time you do it? In my right pocket, I gripped a key ring in my fist so hard it hurt. In my left pocket, I couldn't stop fidgeting with two empty .22 casings.

When we arrived at the police station, my FBI handlers dropped me on the sidewalk and drove off. I was left to walk into the station in search of the local detectives while my escorts were doubtless getting back to their job of keeping the nation safe from the threats of the previous decade.

I had never set foot in the Rhodes police station before, and I was disappointed to see it looked nothing like the movies. I'd imagined a line of petty thieves and sex workers waiting for an overweight, perpetually irritated desk sergeant to process them. But in reality, there was no desk and no sergeant in sight. For a moment, I found myself questioning the accuracy of all the cop shows and movies I'd watched.

The street entrance opened on a spacious and very empty lobby that would have worked for any medical building in the area. The flat screen on the side wall was playing HGTV, though there was no one to watch.

Although I was the only one in the room, I looked for a place where no one could come and sit beside me. I wanted to avoid being next to someone who might cough in my direction. Even worse, they might want to start a conversation.

Just as I was about to sit down, I noticed a computer kiosk off to one side under a "Check in here" sign. I walked over and saw it held a touchscreen divided into four large labeled areas. In order, they read: Report a Crime, Confess to a Crime, In Need of Assistance, and Purchase Tickets to the Police vs. Fire Charity Softball Game.

It was clear from the fingerprints on the screen the third choice was the most popular. Still, I was concerned over the number of smudges on "Confess to a Crime." I tapped the button for assistance and the screen presented a request for my country of origin. After scrolling through the list of countries and matching languages, I wondered why no one had the sense to list this country under "America, United States of." We'd be between Algeria and Andorra rather than way down between the United Kingdom and Uruguay. Considering that the station was located in America, the United States of, and therefore most people seeking help or confessing crimes were likely from here, it simply made sense from an efficiency standpoint. I'm usually a patient man, but this design flaw irked me.

The last step before I got to the actual help page was a prompt to stand before the kiosk's camera and align my head for the facial recognition system. Once it had verified my identity, the speaker said, "Thank you *Hanson comma Brad* . . . for visiting the . . . *Public Safety Building* . . . in *Rhodes, Georgia*. We see you have an outstanding traffic citation for failure to come to a complete stop. You can use any major credit card to pay your fine now."

At this point, there was no option on the screen other than "Pay Fine." I inserted a credit card, but apparently it was not major enough. After trying two other cards, I got one to work and received the next prompt to add four tickets to the charity ballgame. I declined the tickets and paid the two-hundred dollar fine. No one came to my aid after I proved I was no scofflaw, but an upstanding citizen. Unless I needed to prove I was an upstanding citizen by buying tickets to the ballgame.

On principle, I avoided the ticket button and tapped other sections of the screen. The kiosk rotated through "How may we help you? Do you want to make a confession? Are you currently under the influence of a controlled substance? Have you committed a felony since your last visit?"

Tired of this runaround, I returned to my seat. Inspiration struck, and I used my phone to dial 911.

After the line rang a dozen or more times, a woman answered. "911. Please provide your current location."

"Rhodes."

"Please be more specific. Which road are you on?"

"I don't know the street names. I'm in the police station."

"If you don't know the street you are on, I may not be able to help you. Are there any significant landmarks visible?"

"I already said I'm in the Rhodes, Georgia, police station."

"Do you require police, fire, or ambulance?"

"Uhh . . . Police. They should be right here. I mean. I'm in the station."

"What is your address?"

"I don't know. It's the Rhodes city police station."

"How do you spell that?"

"R-H-O-D-E-S"

"What is the nature of your emergency?"

"I need to talk to a detective about a death in my neighborhood."

"Are you able to perform CPR or other life-saving procedures until help arrives?"

"I can't. I'm pretty sure they took the body away by now."

"Who took the body, sir?"

"I don't know. I didn't see who did it. I'm just assuming the body is gone by now."

"I need to ask you again, sir. What is the nature of your emergency?"

"Mrs. Skinner was killed, and I was told I should talk to a detective."

"Confessing to a crime is not an emergency issue. I will connect you to the public service office."

A click on the line was followed by five minutes of hold music, starting with Glenn Miller's "In the Mood." I wasn't aware big bands were still a thing, but I guess you use what you have when the budget was burned on check-in kiosks, and you've only got one cassette tape.

A man's voice came over the line. "City of Rhodes. How can I hep y'all?"

"I need to talk to someone about a death."

"Emergencies go to 911. Hang on."

Before I could object, there was another click on the line followed by ten minutes of hold music. I didn't recognize every tune but it was a string orchestra playing a medley of 90s rap songs. I guess they had two cassettes. The woman from my original call came on the line.

"911. Please provide your current location."

"I'm still in Rhodes, still in the police station, and I still need to talk to someone."

"Sir, I must inform you that 'It is a crime for any person to willfully use the 911 system for any purpose other than reporting an emergency.'"

Since I have a job that frequently involves quoting policy manuals, I can always tell when someone is using that Jedi mind trick on me.

"I'm certain you're a nice person and just doing your job, but I've had a really crappy day. I'm pretty sure I missed lunch, and they gave me a regular Coke so my blood sugar is out of whack. On top of that, the FBI thinks I killed one neighbor and your captain wants me to talk to detectives about a second death."

"Please stay on the line and remain calm. Help is on the way."

The positive was, I received a quick response. The negative was being surrounded by uniformed and plainclothes officers with guns drawn. I'd never understood the descriptions of people losing control of their bowels when scared, but I came painfully close to a complete realization. Lying face down with a gun pressed to your head while handcuffs are applied behind your back doesn't help one's sphincter control.

They took me to an interrogation room and left me while they checked my story. It was similar to the room in the FBI's building other than they used pastels rather than the federal government's preferred institutional gray paint scheme. Eventually Captain Dawson apparently assured them she had asked me to come in. The handcuffs were removed, but I'm convinced they had thoroughly enjoyed the opportunity to use them.

Their interrogation room appeared unused. A layer of dust covered the table and chairs. The investigators also seemed out of practice as they stood in the observation room and discussed what to do with me. They'd left the lights on their side of the two-way mirror, and their microphones were live as well. In other words, I could see and hear everything. That should have given me a tactical advantage in the interrogation to come, but it just made me more nervous.

"Does anyone remember who handled the last homicide?" said one of the officers. "I had a list on my desk but someone spilled coffee, and I can't read it."

After two minutes of everyone giving their excuses for not knowing, one of the female detectives solved the problem. "Let's do it the way they taught us at the academy. Rock, paper, scissors until someone gets stuck with it."

Finally, the door to the interrogation room opened and two men walked in. The heavyset white guy with thinning gray hair introduced himself as Detective Jackson and the lean Black male thirtysomething as Detective Williams. Hoping to establish rapport, I cleared my throat and asked the older detective, "I happen to know Jackson is a common surname in my hometown in Iowa. Any chance your family connections go back there?"

His wire-frame glasses were at the tip of his nose as he looked at me over the lenses. "My name is Thomas Jonathan Jackson."

When I did not provide the proper response, he added, "As in Stonewall Jackson."

The younger detective snorted as he tried and failed to suppress a laugh. I was batting .500 as I'd made points with him and lost the game with his older partner. I wasn't sure if it was good or bad for me, but when I glanced over, the onlookers from the observation room seemed to be enjoying the exchange.

Detective Jackson took a chair opposite me and opened a file of papers. He started with the usual questions.

"Where were you at 10:40 yesterday evening?"

"At home, in the basement working on my home office. That should have been about the time I was measuring and cutting the drywall."

"How did you know Mrs. Skinner?"

"Just as a neighbor and fellow member of the HOA board. We didn't really socialize."

"Do you know anyone who would want to harm her?"

"No. She didn't have the warmest personality, but I can't believe anyone would hurt her." I almost said I couldn't believe anyone would *want* to hurt her but realized that wouldn't be accurate, and they might have one of those voice stress analyzers in the observation room.

Then it got interesting.

"Do you know if Mrs. Skinner had health issues that might have affected her balance?"

"She never mentioned it."

"Do you know if Mrs. Skinner had fallen recently and hit the back of her head?"

"No. What makes you think she had fallen?"

"The back of her head had an unusual pattern of bruising," said Detective Williams.

His partner scowled at him. "Nothing unusual about old folks falling. Happens all the time. Sooner or later, they take one fall too many."

I decided it would be smart to get back on Detective Jackson's good side. "The CDC agrees with you," I said. "According to a recent report, falls are the leading cause of injury-related death among adults age 65 and older." Hanging around with insurance actuaries might not help dinner party conversations, but I thought this fun fact would work here.

I was wrong. It was my turn to get a scowl from Detective Jackson. He slapped the folder closed and said, "I don't need some federal eggheads to tell me that old farts fall down and kick the bucket." He got up and walked out. From the hallway, I heard him say, "Williams, give him your card in case he remembers something, and then escort him out of the building. See that he doesn't call 911 to find his way home."

As I stood, I heard a conversation from the still-live mics in the observation room.

"He's free to go? I thought he was the number one suspect in the shooting."

"Yeah, but the feds have that one. We're supposed to sit back and watch while they take months to grind him through the system. In the end, he goes to prison for life and the cable channels have a week of high ratings. Everybody wins."

"Except that poor sap."

I walked away from their laughter and decided I needed to have a plan, or this situation was going to get the better of me. The next day would be time enough to begin my investigation into the possible murders of Edith Skinner and Miss Oskarsdotter. In the meantime, I would prepare by binge-watching old episodes of *Law & Order.* To paraphrase Supertramp, it wasn't much of a plan, but it was the only one I got.

Chapter Five

When you work in the insurance industry, realize you fall into one of two buckets. In bucket number one you are bored. Really bored. All the time. You are bored with your job, your coworkers, and—by extension—your life. This is because normal people do not find their joy in fine print, multipart forms, and stamping "denied" on every virtual piece of paper that comes across their computer screen.

In bucket number two, you realize you do not find your insurance job dull because it is you who are dull. Even if you were in some sense normal at the start, a few years working in an insurance company will bury your bliss. Extended contact with actuarial tables changes your perception of the world. When you see someone riding a motorcycle, you will only think how much safer they would be in an automobile with seat belts and air bags. Better yet, traveling on light rail. Even better, sitting at home in front of the TV. Assuming the TV is a new flat screen that produces negligible levels of radiation and there is a safety strap firmly bolted to the wall to prevent a crushing injury. You become the person who would take their unread issues of *Consumer Reports* on vacation for a fun beach read. Except that person would never go to the beach because of the statistically significant dangers of sunburn, stinging jellyfish, and rogue tsunamis.

In my youth, I was not boring. I rode a motorcycle across the country on an epic quest for something—although I couldn't tell you today what that something was, or if I found it. After years working alongside actuaries, I considered any motorcycle to be a guillotine without a safety lock. Over time, I could feel myself steadily sliding from being bored to being boring. I'd been going through the motions in a job that required little motion. Even worse, I'd allowed that general drowsiness to migrate into my personal life. A few neighbors kept themselves busy by having affairs, but I was happily married. Not to mention, I didn't have the money or the energy to pursue that route. I needed a hobby. One I could be passionate about. Fred a few streets over was an ardent fan of conspiracy theories, but I was not willing to have a lobotomy just to join his club.

I needed something with a challenge and somewhat out of the ordinary, and here was my chance: helping the police unravel the mystery of Miss Inga's .22 caliber killing and Edith Skinner's death by garden. It would get me out from under the cloud of suspicion, and I was sure they'd thank me when I solved each case.

And that is why—for the first time in years—I felt excited to get up in the morning. It was the day after my trip to the Bureau's field office and the local police station, and I was going to start my investigation into the second murder. I considered starting with Miss Inga's murder since it was the first where I became a suspect. However, I preferred the method that had long served me well—working alphabetically. I'd already labeled two manila folders, and "Edith Skinner" came before "Inga Oskarsdotter." I debated whether I should have used "last name, first name," but after weighing the pros and cons, neither approach had a clear advantage, so I stuck with my original choice.

The local news had not yet declared Edith Skinner's death to be a murder, but it had to be. For one thing, her death by inverted garden stakes was too weird and too precise to be anything other than a homicide. For another, I desperately wanted it to be a murder. If it was an accident, then looking into it would just be a slightly bloodier version of my day job.

While I finished my breakfast of a bagel, two egg whites, and Greek yogurt, I scanned the web on my iPad. There were several stories about Inga's murder but little on Edith's passing. The headline on the paper's site referred to "a fatal garden accident." Several local TV stations parroted that line. The only outlier was the Fox affiliate that led with "Crime Wave Update: Death Stalks the Suburbs." They accompanied this with a graphic of bloody corn stalks, which I guessed they thought were tomato plants.

I hoped police and reporters would focus on Inga's home and leave an opening for me to check out Edith's garden unobserved. I found a flashlight, pen, and Hello Kitty notepad in the kitchen junk drawer. A pair of rubber dishwashing gloves under the sink completed my investigator's tool kit. Once outside, I saw Tony coming across his yard to intercept me. He might have been my best friend in the neighborhood, but that didn't mean I liked him. He just ranked higher on a scale that didn't extend far from negative territory.

Tony easily caught up with me since he cut diagonally across my yard while I kept to the sidewalk.

"Hey, Bradley. Where're you headed so early?"

"Uh. HOA duties. You know, the work of the neighborhood never stops."

"What's with the pink gloves?"

I stuffed them deeper into my back pocket and smiled. "I thought I might need them if I see dog poop. Don't want to give Mr. Price any ammunition for his trebuchet."

"His what?"

"His catapult."

Tony nodded. "What about the bump on the nose? The feds slap you around a little?"

When I didn't immediately respond, he followed up.

"I saw them drive you away yesterday. I know it's supposed to be an 'unmarked car' but who else would drive a brown sedan with hubcaps? I mean, I didn't know car companies still made hubcaps."

"The FBI had questions about the neighborhood after Miss Oskarsdotter's death."

"You helping them?"

"I was providing answers to their questions. Sort of as a consultant."

"Makes sense. You with all your insurance investigations experience." He halted and put out a hand to keep me in place. In a low voice, he asked, "A consulting detective? That's like Sherlock Holmes, right?"

I shook my head. "Not really."

"Can I be Watson?"

"That's not how it works. And all I did was answer a few of their questions."

Tony stepped in front of me and looked around. Apparently satisfied, he asked, "Did Watson get paid? In the one movie I saw, they never made that clear. I mean, I'd want it to come from the FBI directly. Wouldn't want to make you give me a cut of your pay."

"I'm not getting paid. It was a courtesy visit."

"I know I'm not a doctor like the real Watson."

"You do know there was no *real* Watson?"

"But I do have some policing know-how. I'm on the Neighborhood Watch committee."

I stepped around him and continued on my way. "How did that work out last Halloween when dozens of houses were egged and TPed?" I realized pushing back was a mistake. His voice got louder and louder as he explained the logistical nightmare of patrolling over two hundred homes with a handful of volunteers who weren't allowed to carry firearms because of the "damn libs." I tried to interject it might be dangerous to have armed neighbors out when kids were only flinging eggs and stringing toilet paper. He went into a lecture based on "that's where it starts" and "that's why our cities are all in ruins today."

As we got to the sidewalk in front of Edith's house, I shushed him and said he could assist me on an unpaid and uncredited basis. He wasn't happy but agreed to the arrangement "for our first case."

The police had taped off the front porch of Edith's house. A half dozen realtor's business cards were stuck in the door jamb. Fortunately, there was nothing to stop us from opening the side fence and walking into the backyard. Once in her garden, I could see right away where her body had fallen. The ground had absorbed most of the blood, but some was still visible on the points of the wooden garden stakes. A pile of tangled tape sat off to the side, alongside twisted strips of tape where the crime scene technicians had tried to trace the position of the body. The outline they had created didn't look much like a person as much as it did a gerrymandered voting district that included portions of six counties.

"Guess it's hard to put tape on loose dirt and mulch," said Tony.

I realized I could look forward to more such keen observations from my new assistant.

I knelt a few feet from the outline hoping this angle would give me new insights, or at least silence my helper as he saw me trying to concentrate. In my new pose, the pen, notebook and flashlight dug into my hip, so I placed them on the ground behind me.

Tony grabbed the flashlight and waved it around as he walked through the yard. He held it in his fist like he was Norman Bates, and it was a kitchen knife. It was not the first disturbing image I'd had when Tony was around.

"You realize we're outside on a sunny day, and you're using a flashlight? I only brought that in case we need to examine something inside the house or after it gets dark."

"It's how they do it on TV. Pretty sure it helps them focus on key bits of evidence."

I shook my head and then leaned forward with my hands out. The goal was to get my head closer to the surface of the garden where I could see anything unusual, though I had no idea what would look unusual in this backyard garden. I did detect a strong odor from the mulch and remembered that was one of the many reasons I avoided gardening.

After a couple of minutes of this, there was a hacking cough behind me. I looked back over my shoulder. A large man with a prominent beer belly stood behind me wearing one example from his collection of Vietnam Vet caps. It was another of our neighbors, Walter Harrison. His wife, Sally, stood next to him. Her hair was past natural gray to the point of synthetic silver with blue highlights. To be fair, she had hair while Walter had hats.

In a deep voice, Walter asked, "What's the dummy doing?"

"He thinks the flashlight will help him spot something," I said.

"I was asking Tony." Walter followed this with another hacking cough though it might have been a laugh. Either way, it went on for a full minute. Once his coughs subsided, he squinted at the garden stakes. "If you're looking into what happened, I can help. These bloody stakes remind me of punji sticks in Nam. The VC put 'em in traps."

Sally reached up to knock the cap off his head. "You boys ignore this old coot. He was a glorified plumber on an aircraft carrier in '72. They were so far offshore, he saw Vietnam on the TV same as me."

Walter leaned forward to pick up his cap, which was now somewhere on the ground. It was hidden from him by the hemisphere of golf shirt above his belt. He thought better of the effort and waited for Sally to retrieve the cap for him. While that was going on, Tony picked up the pen and Hello Kitty notebook I'd left on the ground. He flipped the notebook open.

Turning to Mr. Harrison, Tony clicked the pen several times. "What was your relationship with the deceased?"

Sally glanced at the rear of Mrs. Skinner's house. Her chin quivered slightly as she said, "Edith was our neighbor, and she was a dear lady—"

"My question was for your husband. I'll get to you in a moment."

Sally's chin was now set in stone as she turned to her husband. "Dear, you can answer how you please, but I won't stand here if he's going to be rude." With that, she turned and walked away. Her husband watched her leave, turned back to Tony, and shrugged.

"Now see what you've done. Made her run off with my cap."

"Again, and for the record, Mr. Harrison, what was your relationship with the deceased?"

"I'm no relation of hers. I don't even know where her people come from. Not sure, but I think up north."

He said the last bit as if it was a diagnosis of leprosy.

Tony wrote for a minute and then flipped to a fresh page. "Where were you last evening between 10 and 11 PM?"

"Same as always. In the La-Z-Boy watching TV."

"Were you alone?"

"A La-Z-Boy is big, but it ain't big enough for more'n one."

"So, you don't have an alibi?"

"Why in hell would I need one?"

Up to that point, I'd been entertained, but it seemed like it was time to intervene.

"Tony, could I speak to you a moment?"

He closed the notebook, clicked the pen, and followed me over to stand near the side fence.

"Do you remember which of us is Holmes and which is Watson?"

He frowned. "You're telling me I can't ask questions?"

"That's exactly what I'm telling you. Holmes was the detective. Watson's role was to assist as needed and write things down so people in the future could read about each case."

"That's lame. I'm the kinda guy that makes things happen. I'm not here to just write down what happens."

"Trust me. Writing is more fun than you think. You've heard the pen is mightier than the sword? That's because a writer can use a pen to get back at anyone who has ever irritated them."

He looked puzzled, although it was difficult to tell when he was puzzled and when he was just being Tony.

I continued, "As a writer, you can make up characters based on people you know. All you need to do is change the person's name and a few superficial details. Then you can make fun of them and say what you've always wanted to say about them in real life."

"Won't they catch on and sue you when you make them out to be jerks?"

"Jerks never think they're being jerks. They'll never see themselves in what you write."

Tony was silent for a moment. "I'd rather have a sword."

Until that point, I hadn't considered writing about this case. But something clicked beside the pen, and I started thinking of a different name for Tony's character. Something like Larry, so there'd be no identifiable ethnicity. If I put Larry's house across the street instead of next door, it should fool Tony. Heck, if I said his house had red brick instead of gray, he'd think it wasn't his. I asked for my notebook and pen and started a page for Larry's character outline.

Walter had waited while Tony and I talked, but then coughed and said, "I don't know if this is fun for you two, but I'm tired of standing here. Do you junior G-men have any other questions I can't answer?"

I stepped forward and used the official voice I usually reserved for my day job. "Mr. Harrison, do you know anyone who might have had a reason to dislike Mrs. Skinner?"

He laughed. "I know lots of 'em. You should too, being on the board with her. She was always saying 'no' anytime anyone wanted to spend money. She protected the HOA reserve fund like it was her personal bag of gold coins. Wouldn't spend a dime to fix anything unless it was in the damn dog park. The clubhouse and tennis courts are crumbling, but she'd approve anything that made her mutt happy."

"You think someone might've been annoyed to the point where they'd want to see her dead?"

"No one gets killed just for being a pain in the ass." He gave Tony a long look and shook his head. "If it worked that way, I expect Tony'd been taken care of long time ago."

Chapter Six

After Walter had left, Tony and I sat in Edith's aluminum lawn chairs. The first one Tony picked had well-worn mesh fabric, and it split the moment he put his weight on it.

He shoved off the armrests and turned to face the chair while yelling, "You piece of crap!" To complete its punishment, he kicked it aside with a clatter and took more time settling in another. I'd seen this side of Tony before—where he felt an inanimate object had done him wrong and needed discipline.

"I'm curious, Larry," I said as he leaned back in his new chair. "Why did you ask Walter where he was between ten and eleven? I hadn't heard anyone say anything about a precise time of death."

"Who's Larry?"

"Sorry. That's a guy at work who looks like you. I'm always calling him Tony."

I went back to the page with the character outline, crossed off "Larry," and wrote "Neighbor #1—to be named."

Tony seemed to accept my explanation and looked over his shoulder at the back door to Edith's house.

"You think they left her place open? It's getting warm. I could use a cold beer."

"It's not even 10 AM."

"But it's Saturday. Weekend rules apply."

"It doesn't matter anyway. Edith didn't drink. That was why she didn't think we needed to maintain the clubhouse. In her words, "People just use it for alcohol-fueled bacchanalias."

"Back-a-whats?"

"Drunken parties."

"You say it like that's a bad thing."

"I was quoting her. Back to the time of death. Who told you it was between ten and eleven?"

"No one told me that."

I was confused, so I said, "I'm confused. Why did you ask him about that specific hour?"

"I wanted to see if I could catch him in a lie. You're the investigator. You should know how that works."

"But since you don't know the time of death, how would you know if he was lying about anything? What was your next question going to be?"

He paused before saying, "It doesn't matter. He's not my top suspect. His wife did it."

I was again confused. This happened frequently when I talked with Tony. On a normal day, it was a kind of fun exercise in absurdity. In a murder investigation, it was also absurd, but not the amusing kind of absurdity.

"What makes you think Sally Harrison is the killer?"

"It's obvious. She got nervous and left as soon as I got too close to the truth."

"She left after your first question when you were rude and blew her off."

"It's an old interrogation technique. Get the suspect angry, and they make mistakes."

I wondered whether it was too late to get a new Watson. Did Holmes ever consider getting rid of Watson? I don't mean "getting rid of" the way some might imagine. That would be unthinkable. I mean, did Holmes ever consider firing Watson and finding a new assistant? Although that process would be difficult, and Watson/Tony would not go easily. It would be perfectly understandable if Holmes did think about the unthinkable once or twice. As a mental exercise and nothing more.

Absorbed in not thinking the unthinkable, it took me a moment to realize Tony was once again walking around Edith's backyard with my flashlight. As he was pacing, I noticed a rhythmic pattern of thwack-thump-pop. It was coming from the yard directly behind Edith's. The picket fence was about four feet high, but the source of the noise was a ten-by-ten wooden wall attached to the middle. It vibrated each time there was a thump.

"What's that?"

Tony put a finger to his lips and gave me a look as if I'd just passed gas in church. Knowing Tony, I assumed he'd been on the receiving end of that look more than once. He crouched slightly and tiptoed to the fence as if sneaking up on an enemy outpost. While he was carefully placing each foot to avoid stepping on twigs or dry leaves, I walked over to the left side of the picket fence so I could see around the solid section. The thwack-thump-pop ended abruptly as Vanessa Hershey caught a tennis ball in her left hand and let her racket down to her side. Although my wife assured me Mrs. Hershey had to be a few years older than us, Vanessa's face was perfectly smooth. Her hair—blonde this month—was pulled back, leaving a few loose strands to waver in the gentle breeze. Her tanned arms and legs glistened slightly and were accentuated by her short tennis skirt. I found it difficult to breathe, swallow, and think.

She smiled and asked, "May I help you?"

By this point, Tony had finished creeping to the fence and inserted himself next to me. He got straight to the point. "How well did you know the victim?"

As if this was a common inquiry for a Saturday morning, Mrs. Hershey recited, "Edith and I were very close. I think she loved me as if I were her granddaughter, and I have nothing but respect for those of her generation. I was so sorry to hear what happened."

"Do you know if she had any enemies?"

"Enemies? Of course not. We were like family. If you lived here, you would know everyone in this neighborhood is very close."

"I do live here. One street over."

"Well, forgive my poor manners. As chair of the social committee, I try to meet each new neighbor. One of the ladies on my team must have failed to bring you to my attention."

"I've been here almost a year. But . . . several families did move in that month. Maybe that's why you missed me."

"I am so sorry I didn't recognize you. It must be the poor lighting. I asked Edith several times to have these overgrown bushes trimmed, but she preferred to let them run wild. Now that I see your face in the sunlight, of course I know you, dear."

Even though it was my job as Holmes to ask questions, I had been content to let Tony stumble through until the point she called him "dear." It triggered a memory of the night she had once called me "dear." She had come before the HOA board to insist we resurface the community tennis courts.

Most petitioners before the board came prepared with a plan and supporting data when they wanted us to spend thousands of dollars. Mrs. Hershey's approach was to say we were her "dear friends" and then tell us what we were going to do. She said the tennis courts were in desperate need of updating since surrounding neighborhoods had switched from traditional green color schemes to Royal Blue on Forest Green to match the US Open courts. While we were at it, she wanted the lights replaced, because the current illumination was "much too harsh." It was difficult, she explained, to find attire that looked good both in daytime and evening games.

As treasurer, it fell on Edith to tell Vanessa that our discretionary funds for the next two years had already been committed to improving the dog park and adding pickleball courts. Vanessa spoke through clenched teeth and attempted to illuminate what it would mean to our current eighth-place standing in *Southern Spaces*' Best-Places-for-Cordial-Living list. When that failed, she threatened to move out if we installed pickleball courts "for old people who should have the decency to move into assisted living or hospice when it's their time."

Edith had smiled. "While the board recognizes you have your well-manicured tentacles in every corner of the neighborhood, we will not reallocate funds that have already been committed to other projects. Should you choose to leave, please know that you will be missed."

I remember thinking at the time *if looks could kill, there'd be two dead people here.*

* * *

Most nights, I fall asleep a couple minutes after my head hits the pillow. That was just one of the little things that annoyed the crap out of Rhonda. It took her an hour or more. Even when I was not snoring, she claimed my peaceful breathing was an irritant. It reminded her she was still awake while I had the nerve to get rest. She didn't say it exactly like that, but that was her meaning. That particular night, our roles were reversed as I lay wide awake and she started purring immediately.

Early in our marriage, she had assured me that women in her family did not snore. They were incapable of making such sounds. Likewise, they did not snort or wheeze through the night. When I naively asked how to explain the noises she produced, she would only admit to "purring" as her mother and grandmother had done. As I said, this was early in our marriage, and I had yet to learn how to hold a straight face. After a few unfortunate incidents, I learned to better control my expressions.

The reason I could not sleep on that specific night had nothing to do with my wife's purring. A normal person in my situation would have been kept awake worrying about the FBI considering him the prime suspect in a murder. Years earlier I had come to accept that I am not a normal person in some respects. What kept me awake that night was trying to work through the details of a mystery story based on Edith Skinner's unusual demise.

When I can't sleep, the best thing to do is get out of bed and work on something until I get tired enough to go back to bed. I slipped out of bed and put on slippers before walking through the darkened house and heading down to the basement. That sounds kind of ominous but in fact I've dedicated my life to avoiding ominous.

Unless your home was built on a steeply sloping lot, basements weren't common in The Estates. I was lucky that the original owner of my house had been a transplant from Nebraska. His experiences in Tornado Alley had left a lasting impression, and he insisted on putting a basement under his house as a refuge from twisters and the possibility of an apocalypse sending rampaging hordes from "the big city."

Our basement had sat empty for years other than a few boxes of Christmas decorations and the various pieces of furniture we'd inherited from my parents. There was a paisley-covered sofa with huge armrests that were too low for comfortable use when seated and too hard to use as a pillow if you had to lie down. The living room chairs were a mix of plaid and flower print that should not have been saved even if they'd matched. Finally, there were heavy Mediterranean end tables and a coffee table that must have encouraged subsequent generations to sprint to IKEA. The only commonality between the pieces, besides their ugliness, was the sticky layer of nicotine that seemed to generate a stronger stench with each decade.

Rhonda had no intention of ever using any of these items in our house. In fact, the unspoken understanding was that we'd donate all the pieces to charity at some point in the future. The exact timing was never discussed, but it was understood it would only occur when my parents' days of visiting were past.

Also understood was that, when this future donation time arrived, we would drop the furniture off in the dead of night to avoid hearing that the charity wouldn't take them, due to an already more-than-sufficient supply of firewood.

A few weeks before, I'd put some of the basement's open space to use. I covered the pile of old furniture with plastic sheets after tossing in a set of air fresheners like they were hand grenades. After letting the combination of chemicals fight it out for a while, I started building my home office in one corner. I hadn't reached the point of putting drywall on the framing, but obviously this was to become the war room for my investigation.

That night, on one of the vertical studs, I temporarily hung a seventy-two by forty-eight inch combination erasable whiteboard and magnetic surface. Then, using small magnets, I placed photos of the victims, along with the possible suspects, on the board. The pictures weren't perfect driver's license head shots, but they were the best I could scrape off social media and broad internet searches.

I first tried stretching bits of string between the pictures and the few clues I'd gathered. It quickly looked like what every movie serial killer kept in a secret room, so I pivoted to using dry erase markers to make interconnecting lines and print short lists of relevant facts. I was pretty pleased with how it had all come together.

I'd decided the perfect title for Edith Skinner's case would be *A Garden Variety Murder*, so I placed that title at the top though it was more for dramatic effect than accuracy. Now that I had the fundamental pieces in place, I needed to refine my list of suspects—each with motive, means, and opportunity.

As far as I knew, anyone in our neighborhood had opportunity if the murder occurred in the middle of the night as indicated by Mrs. Skinner's nightdress. And every neighbor had means. The plant stakes had been all over her garden and just needed to be strategically placed for the kill.

That left motive. Who would benefit most from her death? In many cases, the wise approach is to follow the money. I had directed Edith to one of GFI's local agents for life insurance and financial planning. Ignoring any thought of confidentiality, he told me "The old bat named three charities as beneficiaries." That ruled out one obvious motive unless the United Way wanted to speed up bequests and had started hiring contract killers.

Moving back to the neighborhood, I went down a list of names.

Marge Peterson, our HOA president herself. This seemed unlikely. Marge always let Edith handle contentious money issues for the HOA and watched from the sidelines. She would not want to lose Edith as she might not find another person to take the heat for her.

Herb Peterson, the HOA VP. He was also an improbable suspect. Edith's death had required careful planning in the clever placement of the stakes, and an act of passion to execute the deed of pushing her onto said stakes. Herb dozed through most HOA meetings. I had never witnessed any sign that he was capable of cleverness or passion.

Sally Harrison. When she was being sweet, she was much too nice to hurt anyone. When she was not being sweet, the only person she'd take it out on would be Walter. If she were to turn to violence, she'd limit herself to watching him blunder onto a couple of stakes. Then she could spend the next year telling him how clumsy he was.

Walter Harrison. Never. Though he pretended to be tough, he was more afraid of what Sally would do to him than he was of the police. He was wise in that.

Vanessa Hershey. Doubtful. Yes, she had a reason to dislike Edith for blocking the tennis court renovations. Edith's position on dipping into the HOA's reserve fund was well known. "You'll get money from the reserve over my dead body," was one of her favorite expressions. Vanessa might have wanted to take her at her word, but I was certain Vanessa would never commit an act that might result in getting blood stains on one of her outfits.

Mr. Price of the trebuchet. Now this was an interesting possibility. While more ornery than vicious, one could see how he might slide from one to the other if provoked. He also had a fundamental understanding of physics as demonstrated through his trebuchet. He could have engineered things so Edith would fall precisely on the stakes. While it didn't speak to his guilt or innocence, I could certainly get a number of neighbors to agree he was capable of such a crime.

Tony. Nope. I had never seen a case where the sidekick was the killer. It didn't happen in fiction or in real life. The sidekick is there so the hero has a confidant. It would break too many conventions for the sidekick to be the guilty one. Although I shouldn't rule out the possibility of a sidekick with a split personality. That might be an interesting twist.

Rhonda Hanson. Nah. I added my wife just to be comprehensive, but she would have no reason to injure Edith. If she ever found the list, I'd know who she'd have a reason to injure.

Brad Hanson. Not a chance. Unfortunately, there were already those who thought I killed Miss Inga—notably, the FBI. Perhaps they'd imagine if I killed once, I could have killed twice. But they'd be wrong.

Chapter Seven

I eventually went back to bed and dreamt of a neighborhood full of suspects. Unfortunately, the suspects in my dream all came in the form of Heffalumps and Woozles. I had regularly fast-forwarded through that section when my kids were little, but apparently Pooh Bear had left me with scars.

The next morning, I tore through my breakfast of a bagel, two eggs—including the yolks this time, cholesterol be damned—and Greek yogurt while making some notes on a yellow legal pad. I didn't want Rhonda to come into the kitchen and ask what I was doing, so after breakfast I took my work to the patio. I retrieved the cushions from the storage box and sat at our five-piece outdoor dining set. The metal bits were showing rust and the paint was flaking off the faux wicker material, but the set would be all ours after four more convenient payments.

I placed the pad of paper before me intending to move the notes to the whiteboard later. Starting with a blank sheet, I wrote out my list of questions:

- Who had a motive?
- Was the bruising on the back of Edith's head significant?
- Were the two killings related?
- Was it possible to refuse an assigned cellmate?
- If not, could I at least request a white-collar criminal?

I had filled two pages with questions and no answers when Prince started barking from the kitchen. He was very brave when walls and a door separated him from a possible intruder. Tony stepped from his yard into mine by pushing through a section of his broken fence. He was wearing shorts that seemed much more comfortable than the khaki slacks I'd chosen for the day, and he'd topped his outfit off with a T-shirt that proclaimed, "I'm not yelling. I'm from Jersey." He was known for subtlety.

He stepped past me into the screened-in porch, grabbed a set of cushions from storage and placed them on a second chair that he dragged over next to our dormant firepit. It was a small thing, but it occurred to me I would never enter someone's screened-in porch without an invitation. There were a few moments when I admired his alpha male behavior. Most of the time, he just annoyed the crap out of me.

"What's up, Bradley? You're out awfully early. Hoping to surveil Vanessa as a suspect or just trying to see how she avoids tan lines?"

Over the last year, I had spent hours trimming the azaleas along the rear property line, albeit innocently. However, I resented that Tony was projecting his behaviors on to me. And what action movie made him think "surveil" was a good verb? I know it's in the dictionary, but it sounds wrong. Like at work when someone throws around "incentivize."

"Be honest, Tony. Are you sure you didn't come over because your yard doesn't have a direct view? You're the one who's always going on about how divorced women are hot."

"I *used* to think divorced women were hot—"

"Before that it was nurses, flight attendants, secretaries, dental assistants—"

"What's your point, Bradley?"

"Nothing. Just, some people might say your behavior makes you a pig."

He smiled. "Never claimed anything else."

I had to admit he was right. His collection of T-shirts even included one that said, "Pig and proud of it."

He continued, "Anyway, I'm not interested in divorcees. There's a reason their husbands left 'em. I've switched to married women who are looking for a little on the side."

"So, you admit to being 'little?'"

It was my turn to smile. It wasn't often I got a zinger in on Tony. I felt good to have the upper hand for once. Knowing his current marriage was his third, I decided to give him another gentle jab. "What about divorced men? Wouldn't there be a reason their wives divorced them?"

He looked at me as if just noticing I was there. He smiled again, but this time, I could not help but imagine an alligator smiling at someone who had just fallen out of a boat. I froze my expression in place. Throughout my school years, I had perfected remaining immobile and blending into the environment so as not to attract the attention of bullies.

It occurred to me for the first time that there might be more to Tony than just acting as the neighborhood clown. As a result, I might have overlooked some of his potential as a useful ally. From what he'd told me of his youth, he had been something of a tough guy, if not a bully. Though he rationalized his actions as just what it took to survive in his neighborhood. While I had no reason to think the killer would target me, it could not hurt to have a little muscle on my side.

While I was thinking through how Tony could prove useful, his short attention span came to the rescue. He jumped to talking about the game he would watch that afternoon before spending the evening rewatching his Blu-ray of *Rambo: First Blood Part II.* He was the only person I knew that still purchased physical media. In this case, he claimed he had no choice because this movie was special. I didn't understand his need for a physical movie collection, but in the past I had assumed it was similar to my habit of buying hardbound copies of every book written by my favorite authors. I mentioned this to Tony once, and he corrected me immediately. His issue wasn't the same as paper books versus e-books. He couldn't understand why I would buy books in any format when I could watch movies—they took less time to finish and the sex scenes were better.

However, for the time being, Tony was still my Watson, so I started to discuss the two "cases" with him. The biggest problem for the authorities seemed to be the lack of witnesses. Without anyone to point fingers at other suspects, I was the only one in their sights. Even without a ballistics match, the .22 pistol smelling of cat piss provided a literal smoking gun.

Tony told me he'd checked with the other Neighborhood Watch guys and none of them reported anything suspicious. Although, they had pulled over a white van that was slowly and silently cruising through the neighborhood. It turned out to be an ice cream truck with a broken sound system.

"It's possible someone saw something, but they're afraid to talk to the cops," he said.

"Why would—"

"Everyone knows the cartels and the Eastern European gangs are paying off the cops."

"Everyone knows?"

He lowered his voice. "You can't tell me you haven't noticed all the people around here with funny accents."

I had to let that sit for a while. I wanted to see if he would perhaps amend his statement on further reflection. Finally, I said, "To most of our neighbors, you have a funny accent."

His chin went up and his eyebrows dropped to try and meet in the middle. "Whatta ya talkin' about?"

I hesitated because it wasn't clear if he was trying to be funny or if something I said had triggered his native tongue. After a moment, I decided to pretend that part of the conversation hadn't happened and hope his short-term memory would paper over the gap. I reminded myself I wanted to keep him around, and even get his help in my search for suspects. It was time to take him into my confidence and share what I had worked on in the basement.

I had Tony follow me down to the basement where we each grabbed a folding chair from the stack under the steps and placed them in the center of my "office." Though the walls were not finished, the large whiteboard was covered with headshots, "fact lists," and lines connecting the items.

Tony was silent for a moment. Then he made a grunting sound. "You think this is something normal people do?"

"Normal people aren't suspects in multiple murders. Anyway, don't act like I'm the only person in the neighborhood with a whiteboard for brainstorming."

"It's just when you said you were building a 'home office' down here, I thought that was your secret code for making a killer man cave."

I winced. "Don't say 'killer.'"

He chuckled. "Yeah. I can see why you'd be touchy on that. Still, if you're going to all this work, why not make a decent man cave? You know, a space for a pool table, huge TV, and a bar in the corner?"

I nodded. "I'm planning on that next. I figured I'd make my mistakes on this small space before tackling that project."

Tony put his hand over his mouth and coughed while calling it out as BS under his breath. Some skills learned in the eighth grade follow you for life.

"Anyway," I said, "I thought since I had this started, I would use the space to sort through what I know about the murders and what I need to find out."

"Just don't draw red x's over the victims' headshots. That's a sure sign you're a serial killer." He laughed. "Then again, that could make you the star of a true crime docudrama."

"Thanks, but this room is going to help me avoid that future." I walked over to stand before the board. "This is laid out so I can work through the possibilities. The notations are color coded. Things I consider documented facts are in black marker. Unsubstantiated statements are in blue. Pure speculation in green. Open questions in red."

After I covered the meaning of the other eight colors I used, Tony raised his hand.

"Yes?" I said.

"How do you remember which meaning goes with which color?"

Happy to show off the thought I'd put into my display, I pointed to the small legend in the lower right corner where I'd placed the colors and their matching explanations.

He grinned. "I got an idea where you can place the brown marker."

His meaning wasn't clear to me, but knowing Tony had a twelve-year-old's fascination with potty humor, I chose not to respond. Instead, I shifted my focus to the top center of the board, where I had placed the pictures of Edith and Miss Oskarsdotter. The pictures weren't the most flattering, but I wasn't sure if flattering pictures of these two existed. The next row had pictures and a list of column headings for each suspect, followed by a couple of placeholders for as yet undiscovered suspects, uncategorized facts, and a final column for "Open Questions." The suspects included:

Sally Harrison
Walter Harrison
Vanessa Hershey
Marge Peterson
Herb Peterson
Mr. Price
Unknown neighbor
Unknown outsider
Brad Hanson

"You put yourself on the list of suspects?" Tony burst out. "Are you seriously going to try to prove you're the murderer? Wouldn't a confession take less work?"

I gave Tony a look that would have chastised any other person, but he failed to notice.

"I'm sure the police and FBI each have a chart like this somewhere in their offices. I want to reverse engineer theirs so I can see how close they might be to pinning everything on me."

"When they show up at your door with a SWAT team, that'll be a pretty big hint."

As if in response to Tony's comment, I heard Prince barking upstairs followed by the sound of first the doorbell and then the door knocker. Tony must have noticed the blood drain out of my face. He said, "Don't worry, Bradley. If that was SWAT, we would'a heard them bust open the door by now."

As I bolted up the stairs, he called after me. "Want me to shred anything before they get down here?"

Once I made it to the foyer, I grabbed Prince and ran back to shut him in our bedroom. The door bell and knocker cadence had ended, replaced by sounds of a scuffle. If it had been a SWAT team, I would have expected something more dramatic, possibly explosive. Still, I approached the front of the house with caution,

As I turned the doorknob, the door flew into me and a blonde woman stumbled backward into the house. I caught her just in time to prevent a fall—though not without taking a stiletto heel to the top of my left foot. On the porch, her red-faced assailant gasped for air—though, judging by her lethal footwear, he might have been her victim.

As she regained her balance and he recovered his breath, both began talking at once, thrusting business cards at me like they were offering priceless treasures. That's when I noticed their matching forest green blazers, embroidered with the logo of Real Dixie Real Estate. Eventually, I gathered that my subdivision was part of her territory within RDRE's sales team. He claimed his right to my business since he was responsible for distressed properties.

He said, "Given your current delicate circumstance, I am certain you would like a quick sale to cover unexpected expenses and preclude a government seizure."

She grabbed my shoulder to get my attention. "I'm afraid my colleague is trying to scare you with something that won't happen. Don't sell out of desperation. I'll make sure your house brings top dollar now that you're a cause célèbre."

I didn't have time to convince them I didn't want to sell my house. Pointing past them, I said, "Is that another realtor putting a 'for sale' sign in my yard?"

When they were halfway down porch steps, I slammed the door and locked it. I hadn't even made it to prison, and I'd picked up an attitude.

Chapter Eight

When I returned to my office, Tony was standing before the whiteboard. He'd taken the green marker and scribbled his name at the bottom of the list. "If a desk jockey like you made the list of suspects, might as well add my name too. A guy like me's got street smarts and wouldn't sweat getting nabbed by the local yokels."

I stepped to the board, erased what he'd scrawled, and used another marker to print his name. "You've got a point. From law enforcement's point of view, your name might be on this list. It would be unsubstantiated speculation, however. That needs to be in blue."

"It's too bad the detectives aren't here now to see how you're playing with crayons. They'd take you off their list in a second."

"You might think this is funny, but you're not the one they're trying to build a case against. If you want to be my Watson, help me out here."

Tony shrugged and dropped into one of the folding chairs. "Sure thing, Sherlock. I'll be your guy to bounce stuff off. Fire away with whatever you gotta ask."

"First off, I want to know why you suddenly sound like you're from the cast of *Goodfellas*?"

He made a noise that was somewhere between a snort and a laugh. "Maybe all this talk of cops and killers takes me back to the old days. You know, when I hung out with the other yutes?"

I was more comfortable with that film reference than the one I'd thought of and decided to focus on the whiteboard.

"Let's start with the top row. What did Edith and Miss Oskarsdotter have in common?"

"You mean besides the fact they were both mean old bitches?"

"Didn't anyone ever tell you not to speak ill of the dead?"

"I know you're not supposed to say what you think about 'em at the funeral. Maybe you can whisper it at the cemetery. After that, I was taught 'The evil people do lives on long after they're gone. The good is left with their bones.'"

I turned from the board to look at him. "Someone taught you to quote Shakespeare—or at least paraphrase him?"

He waved me back. "That didn't come from any fancy Brit. That came from the guy I'm named for—a fellow goombah named Anthony."

As particular as I am about accuracy, there are some things that aren't worth correcting.

"With that established, can we get to the point of this exercise?" I said. "Let's start by asking who would have the most to gain if Edith and Miss Inga were murdered. As far as we know, they didn't have any living relatives, so let's assume they weren't killed for their inheritance. Of course, that doesn't mean someone didn't have something to gain if they both died."

Tony moved to the front edge of his seat. "This is my favorite part. Show me the money."

I thought for a moment. "The bad news is, we don't know if there is any money or how someone would stand to gain from the death of these two individuals. The question we have to ask is what the two old b—ladies had in common?"

Tony raised his hand. "They lived on the same street. Just one house between the two of them—that big POC the Shumakers built."

This, I thought, *is why a Sherlock needs a Watson.*

I grabbed a marker without even checking on the color and started writing in the first empty suspect column. At the top, I wrote "Shumakers." The marker was yellow, and the print wasn't readable. I wondered if the marker companies had ever tested this color on whiteboards or if they just included it to round out the set.

I started over with a black marker to capture notes on what I knew about the Shumakers. A year before, they'd purchased the only "contemporary" house in the neighborhood. The previous owners had failed to keep up with restaining the wood siding, and it had become an eyesore. It even prompted a change to the HOA bylaws to prevent anyone from inflicting this on the neighborhood in the future. The Shumakers' first step was to have the house torn down. Everyone rejoiced.

Their next step was to build a three-story McMansion that filled the lot from side to side and covered much of what had been the front and back yards. The neighborhood was united in hatred of the new home. Not only was this monstrosity significantly out of place in The Estates, it made all the other houses look inadequate by comparison. Everyone who was related to a lawyer called them to find out how they could force the Shumakers to build a respectable Georgian "five four and a door" consistent with the rest of the community. Not only had the Shumakers built a monument that flaunted their wealth before the world, they were doing a significantly better job of flaunting than anyone else in The Estates.

With all that in my head, I jotted down a few bullets to summarize the Shumakers' impact on the neighborhood in a couple of bullets.

- McMansion—ostentatious and therefore universally hated
- McMansion—located between two crime scenes

When I finished printing, I stepped back so Tony could see the list. I had not heard anyone make a raspberry since my kids were toddlers but he made a good rendition of one, followed by, "What's that word in the first one?"

"Ostentatious? It's a word to describe someone who makes a show of how much money they have."

"And that's a bad thing?"

"Well, it can be. It makes other people jealous, and they think the rich people are snobs."

"Sounds like that's the other people's problem."

He had a point and that irritated me. I was supposed to be the one to make points.

"The trouble with this," I mused while surveying my notes, "is I don't see why the Shumakers would have a reason to kill anyone. Only why others in the neighborhood might want to harm them."

"Maybe they were having trouble with their closest neighbors, and they snapped first."

Watson scores again.

"Yes!" I rubbed my hands together. "I remember Edith complaining that the McMansion blotted out the sun, and she was having a tough time raising anything in her garden as a result. I don't know of any problem from Miss Inga's side, but I know I'd hate having my view blocked by that castle. Maybe they were both getting to be a pain, and the Shumakers couldn't take it anymore."

I wrote furiously in the Shumaker column and drew arrows back to the two names on top to provide emphasis. I didn't even notice Tony had grabbed a marker and made his own addition. He'd written "Who killed Roger Rabbit?"

I should have been satisfied that my Watson had made two worthwhile contributions to the investigation that day. Still, it bothered me that he'd used the wrong marker and then placed his contribution under the heading of uncategorized facts when it should have been on the list of open questions.

I walked to the whiteboard and used my capped pen to tap on the aerial photo of the Shumakers' house and the immediately surrounding homes. A neighborhood kid said he had taken a set of these images with his drone. He'd sold copies for $20 a piece until it got out these pictures were available for free from a realtor's website. When you figure in the cost for ink, I wasn't sure he was clearing much selling 8.5 by 11-inch glossies. Either way, I was amazed at the quality of the photo and thankful this shot covered the three houses at the center of the investigation. It might provide some bit of critical information to help solve the crimes.

If not, at least it really added to the high-tech vibe of my war room. I continued to tap the image while thinking what

I really needed was a large flat screen on the wall. I could use one of those to expand images like this one. Then I could rotate them in real-time while applying filters to make it look like I had infrared capabilities. As soon as this whole murder suspect thing was behind me, I was going to get back to setting up my version of the Batcave.

"This is boring," Tony whined from behind me. "I'm gonna grab another beer and go back to the firepit."

The fact he considered that firepit more fun than my war room/secret lair said everything about Tony that I already knew about the difference between the two of us.

He was three-quarters of the way up the stairs when I thought to say, "Now I know why Bruce Wayne never invited people over." He might not have heard me, since I got no reaction.

As I was reluctant to give up on discussing the overhead shot, I moved the magnets holding it on the whiteboard and took the picture with me before following Tony upstairs. Once we were both seated outside, I held up the drone image and directed Tony's attention to it.

"Perhaps I'm jumping to conclusions, but the McMansion sitting in the middle of the two crime scenes is a potential factor to help us understand what happened. It is literally too big to ignore."

I paused to see if Tony shared my view on its importance. I took his silence as acceptance and continued.

"Let's step back and look at the Shumakers' residence and consider what role the house itself might play in all this. How did it come to sit where it did in The Estates? Why did such a carefully crafted neighborhood allow an obvious aberration like this to be built?"

Tony was studying the label on his beer as though it contained the secrets of the universe. I continued talking as if he was listening while I worked through my list of fundamental questions.

I spent a few minutes discussing the Shumakers' motivations for building their monstrosity. There were too many unknowns in this, since there was no way I could put myself inside their heads. It was easier for me to imagine what might drive the killer's actions than it was to grasp why someone would want to live in a house that screamed "Look at me!" while the closed captioning read, "I'm overcompensating, but can't help myself."

It was simpler for me to return to my comfort zone and talk about how insufficient thought had gone into the neighborhood's regulations. As you would expect, the original bylaws covered acceptable exterior materials and colors, fence construction, the crucial handling of garbage containers, including how such containers would be stored, and the time constraints on placement at the street. Per our covenants: "Containers for trash and recycling can be placed at the curb only from sunset on the evening before pickup and must be returned to a position not visible from the street before sunset on the day of pickup."

Not satisfied to stop at defining the "thou shalt" and "thou shalt not" conditionals in the bylaws, our first board exercised their creativity on a scale rarely seen unless one includes the Chinese Communist Party.

The Estate's founding mothers and fathers were either extremely conscientious protectors of our property values or closeted fascists. Your view on that depended on how far their fondness for regulations infringed on your personal space.

They wielded a double-edged paper cutter and sooner or later everyone got sliced.

At times, their zeal was applied in the wrong direction. As when they used three pages to describe the acceptable types, sizes, and number of allowed holiday decorations. You'd think after detailing how big Santa could be on your lawn, they could spare a paragraph for the maximum allowable height for houses. They eventually corrected that oversight, but only after the Shumakers had completed their architectural middle finger to the neighborhood and achieved grandfathered-in status.

It was probably wishful thinking on my part to hope Tony would provide another helpful comment. I returned to a comment he'd made earlier but put it in different words to make a dramatic moment out of it. Something that make a good sound bite if this story ever made it into a true crime podcast.

"The McMansion itself might be a motive for murder," I said.

That seemed both significant and profound to me. A potential turning point in the case. I let the comment hang there to sink in.

"You think that big house is haunted?"

The moment passed, and nothing had sunk in.

"The house isn't haunted. This is real life, Tony. Not a Stephen King novel. I'm saying that disputes over properties have been known to bring people to violence."

"I got it. You think the two old broads were planning to off the Shumakers because they put their castle in the middle of the neighborhood? The Shumakers must've gotten wind of the plot and so they moved fast and wasted the old hags."

"I would not have worded it that way, but it's one plausible scenario."

He nodded, said, "Totally. I can see that," and returned to examining his beer. He used one thumbnail to carefully peel down strips of the label.

"We need something other than our own speculation. We need a witness," I said. "Just one person to step forward and say they saw something."

"Too bad we don't have traffic cameras."

I slapped the table in surprise. Once again, Tony had shown he could be useful.

"I should have thought of that. Half the neighborhood must have video security systems of some kind. I wonder if the police or FBI thought to check with Miss Inga's and Edith's neighbors to see if they have anything recorded."

"You mean the doorbell things that catch kids stealing packages off porches?"

I pointed up to the small weatherproofed cameras I'd mounted under my eaves. "And some of us have these installed as part of our alarm systems."

He looked up and waved at the lens. "Yeah, fancy. But I've got a system doesn't cost me a cent. I just 'borrowed' a couple of security company yard signs from one street over and now the bad guys assume I've got a live system." He chuckled. "All the protection and no monthly fee."

I missed the next part of his conversation as I wondered if deceiving a would-be thief is a sin. On one hand, Tony was stealing when he "borrowed" the signs and lying to everyone to make them believe he possessed an active alarm system. That was bad. On the other hand, he could be preventing someone from breaking into his house and starting or continuing a life of crime. That was good. Was this a case where the ends justified the means? I wondered.

"You with me buddy, or are you Sherlocking out the details of the crimes?"

I nodded. "Running through the possibilities. I think it's time to examine the houses near the crime scenes—particularly the Shumakers'—to see if there are any cameras pointed in the right direction. Are you up for some fieldwork?"

"Sure, why not."

I smiled. "The game is afoot, Watson."

"What game is a foot? What's that mean?"

I told Tony it didn't mean anything. It was just an expression.

It did make me rethink our partnership for the tenth time that day. For every surprising and useful suggestion, he offered dozens of reminders that he could hardly be considered quality company. My neck was sore from all the head shaking I'd done in the last two days.

As he got up from his chair, he stretched out his back. "Some fieldwork will be good. That'll show the doubters."

"Doubters?" I said. "I don't follow you."

"Yeah. Don't worry. I told them you're the real deal, you got me?" He slapped me on the back. "Not the wannabe investigator everyone's saying."

Chapter Nine

While I was eager to get going, I was increasingly bothered by the fact that I didn't know what information the police had gathered about the two murders. I had speculated on my whiteboard and tried to match their thinking, but that wasn't good enough. How could I go about finding out? Certainly, learning where they were on each case would save my time and help me avoid pursuing dead ends. Not to mention, it would be nice to know how the police and FBI were proceeding with their cases against me. I couldn't make any progress if they brought me in and decided to keep me next time.

However, before I could start on the next phase of my investigation, I had to tackle the "Honey Do" list my wife placed under a refrigerator magnet. Her husband might be under suspicion of murder, but to Rhonda, it was crucial that no one see our house and yard in anything but pristine condition. This may not have been her dream home, but she was determined to do the best with what she had. Every time I came up for a promotion at work, she reminded me of her desires for a larger home placed on at least an acre. Her preference was to live in a community built around a golf course. If we ever acquired such a home, she insisted the game could not be too difficult to learn, and she had several golf outfits hanging in our closet for that day.

I checked off the items on her list one by one to ensure we remained in compliance with the HOA guidelines and in the running for Yard-of-the-Month. Six hours later, the lawn was cut and clippings bagged, bushes trimmed, both cars washed, and gutters cleaned. I again regretted my choice of long pants that morning, but I was sensitive to Rhonda's comments about my pale, skinny legs, so I suffered in silence and took my second shower of the day. Refreshed, I told Rhonda I had some HOA work to take care of and would be back in a couple of hours. I wasn't keeping my investigation a secret because I didn't trust her. I was keeping it from her because I didn't want a lecture on why an independent investigation wasn't necessary and if it was necessary, I wasn't the right person for the task.

If she'd asked for details that morning, my prepared story was that I needed to touch base with the Architectural Control Committee Head over some violations. One neighbor had installed a swing set that was 2.5 inches higher than the covenants allowed. The homeowners adjacent to that backyard were convinced that neighbor's fourteen-year-old son was climbing to the top to get a better view into their windows. I had gotten to the point of saying "Architectural Control" when she left the room with a "That's nice" tossed over her shoulder.

Rhonda often complained that I would end a conversation by "zoning out" when my mind went elsewhere. Her tactic was simply to leave the room. I followed her through the house, so I could ask again about talking to the kids.

"Honey, don't you think it is time we bring the kids up to speed on what I'm going through?"

She spun around, and I almost collided with her. "What are you going through?"

I blinked then spoke with as much control as I could manage. "Oh, you know. The whole thing about being a murder suspect."

"Oh, that." She shrugged. "I talked with them already and assured them everything was going to work out."

"And you didn't think I would want to be part of those conversations?"

"You know how difficult it can be to arrange to get everyone on a call. And anyway, I told them not to bother you because you had a lot on your mind." She turned and went up the stairs to the second floor. "You should thank me for taking care of it so you don't have to."

As much as I wanted to talk to Kate and Luke, Rhonda might be right that I shouldn't burden them with what I hoped was going to be a very temporary situation.

And it was important for me to concentrate on the next steps in the investigation. I texted Tony to meet me outside while I grabbed some cold beers.

When I met him on the sidewalk, he pointed at the two six packs, "You sure this is enough? There's a lot of daylight left."

"We're going to see Robert Clark. I checked with him, and he's waiting in his backyard."

"Three of us and two six-packs? Where'd you learn math?"

"This is just to prime the pump."

Robert Clark was the only neighbor I knew who was actually in law enforcement. As the city's forensic scientist, he could be a valuable resource if I handled things right. My opening was knowing he detested the detectives he worked with. They looked down on him because he was a civilian employee and not permitted to carry a gun on duty. Though it was not one of his responsibilities, they also made it clear that at his weight, he'd never be able to chase down a perp that someone hadn't shot in the leg first.

"They call me 'Bobby' even though I keep telling them that's not my name," he said twenty or more times when I spoke with him at the last neighborhood BBQ. I'd made the mistake of asking "How're things at work?" He'd had a few beers by that point, and I hoped to get him in the same shape during today's visit.

Tony and I walked two streets over to Robert's house. It struck me again how one could see a clear hierarchy through our neighborhood based on the economy at the time the developer built each phase. Brick houses were the most desirable. Then came stucco—though Rhonda considered it an acquired taste. One she was proud to have never acquired. Hardie Plank followed that and finally—and almost to be pitied—vinyl siding. Our home was a compromise. The front facing the street was brick. The other three sides were covered with vinyl. Years before, we'd planted evergreens on the front corners. That way, from the street no one could see we didn't have brick on all sides. The trees had finally grown to cover most of the shame Rhonda felt each time she drove up to her home.

Since Robert's house was on a corner lot, we could get to the backyard without risking the ire of his neighbor. I forgot that guy's name, but he'd kept "no trespassing" signs around his property until the HOA's lawyer contacted him the third time. He'd taken down those signs and replaced them with hidden motion detectors that set off an amplified recording of a pump shotgun being racked.

Robert was sitting in the shade of an awning and had already started managing the heat with an ice-cold beer. Tony hated to see someone drinking alone and ran to grab a chair. He sat and popped open his first can in one seamless motion. I took a third chair and a cold one as well.

It was difficult to read Robert with his dark glasses hiding his eyes, so I started slow.

"Thanks for giving us some of your time, Robert."

"I treasure the few hours of rest I get on the weekends, but I'm happy to share a brew with good friends."

Apparently, a conversation at a cookout was all it took to be good friends.

"Things hectic at work?"

He nodded while taking a swallow from his can. A small stream of foam flowed down his chins and on to his Hawaiian shirt.

"We get a lot of drug cases. I've tested for more controlled substances in the last few years than any of the nearby counties."

"Like *Breaking Bad*?" said Tony, leaning forward in his chair.

"Nah. Around here we get cocaine, opioids, and designer drugs. Not that cheap-ass meth the rednecks use in the sticks."

I made a note to share this with Rhonda. One more distinction she could hold over her sisters was our city's prominence in illegal drugs compared to their small towns.

I let the can in my hand get warm as I watched Robert and Tony go toe to toe, downing beer after beer. Thankfully, they didn't seem to notice I wasn't drinking. Tony was doing a great job of stroking Robert's ego by feeding him questions about the day-to-day tasks of a forensic scientist. Hearing what he did at work made me feel better about my job as an insurance investigator. Things really warmed up when Robert got to his favorite topic of "I get no respect." Rodney Dangerfield had been my dad's favorite old comic, and Robert seemed to channel him more and more as the afternoon wore on.

"The pricks even put a sign on the door of my lab that said, 'CSI Lite.'"

It was time to get to the purpose of our visit before he fell asleep in his chair.

"You must be extra busy now that there are two suspicious deaths to handle," I said.

"Of course, with y'all being a person of interest and such, I can't talk to you about any of the details," he said as he looked around as if to convey he was about to do just that. He then slurred in a loud whisper, "Les' just say my work has gotten more interesting of late. Not that I get any credit or help. They 'spect me to test for drugs one minute and run ballistics tests the next."

"It's a shame they don't appreciate your skills," I said.

"Damn straight. Those idiots didn't even bring in copies of the security camera videos from the crime scenes. I asked them about it and they said, 'Cool your jets, Dr. Von Braun. We'll go get the recordings on Monday. No reason to spoil the neighborhood's weekend along with ours.' The arrogant jerks. They've got no gun match, not so much as a fingerprint at either scene, and they're sitting on the one chance we have of getting some useful evidence."

Tony was nodding at Robert while I jotted down notes underneath the table.

Pointing at me, Robert continued, "They still think you're their prime suspect despite zero evidence. If I thought there was a chance you were guilty, I wouldn't tell you this, but I know you weren't involved. I told the detectives it would take real balls to kill someone."

Tony slapped his beer down and drops flew across the table at me. "That's right. Brad's too scared to step up to the mic on karaoke night. Do you think old nerves of rubber here could whack two people?"

Robert nodded and looked in my direction, but he didn't seem to be focusing. "And then sit here clueless while we talk about it?" It was Robert's turn to slam down his beer and give us all a brief shower. "Tha's good. The detectives are clueless. Brad's clueless. Everybody's clueless."

I felt I should defend myself and convince them I had both the balls and smarts to murder two people, but decided this might be a time to take advantage of my reputation rather than fight it. They finished their beers while I sat in silence. I had poured mine into the grass ten minutes before.

Robert stumbled into his house with one more comment. "I like you, but I hope you understan' I can't tell you anything of substans' about an ongoing investigation—even if that ongoing investigation has crap to go on." That seemed to strike him as funny, and we heard his laughter fade as he disappeared into his house.

When Tony and I were back on our street, I asked him, "What do you think about what he said?"

"What he said? You mean about the Braves going all the way this year? He's full of sh—"

"No. About the police coming back on Monday to see if there are any recordings. I think we should go over to both houses right now. We can see if there are any cameras placed where they could help prove my innocence."

He staggered a bit. "You do what you want. I'm too relaxed to go in search of recordings tonight. We have another day. Let's do it tomorrow. We'll wait 'til after dark when no one will see us."

"Why? It will be harder for us to spot cameras after dark."

"But the dark will hide us if we need to break in and grab the recordings."

"I'm already a suspect, and you want me to risk breaking and entering? You're crazy if you think I'm going to go along with that."

Tony smiled. "I'm not crazy, but I grew up in a rough part of Jersey." He paused and lowered his voice. "What I do have is a very particular set of skills."

"The line is 'what I do have *are* a very particular set of skills.'"

"That's good. We both have skills—though I bet mine are better. We can put them to work tomorrow night."

He walked off, and the flat sidewalk beneath my feet began to feel like a slippery slope.

* * *

A few years earlier, my wife decided we had to have a corgi. She'd expressed no interest in dogs before that but watched an episode of *The Crown* and saw Queen Elizabeth owned corgis. I think Rhonda liked the implied connection between our home and royalty. And when it came to our corgi, I was in fact personally convinced he was part of a long royal bloodline. There were signs pointing to years of inbreeding.

The first sign was when it took several years to housetrain Prince. He was slow to pick up the concept and had no interest in doing his business out among the common dogs of the neighborhood. When he finally deigned to go outdoors, he insisted on leaving his royal waste within five feet of the front door.

I tried to get Prince to go on walks with me, but the only exercise that appealed to him was humping the leg of every person who walked through the front door. This did not fit the noble image Rhonda wanted to convey. As a result, she placed pictures of our corgi in the living room and then locked the actual dog in another room any time we had guests.

On the day following our meeting with Robert, I decided I was finally going to get some return on the years I'd paid for "organic dog food made from free-range chickens who had lived a good life and expired from natural causes before being respectfully processed by caring workers who received a just salary and health benefits." That might sound like I'm being sarcastic, but despite the cost, I was happy to pay a bit more to purchase dog food that aligned with my values. The downside was it made it that much harder to save for Rhonda's planned kitchen renovation.

I wanted to check out the houses on either side of the two crime scenes. Walking a dog—even a reluctant dog—was a perfect cover for my reconnaissance run. First, I put on the "bucket" cap I wore for sun protection. Rhonda hated it because she said it made me look like Gilligan. I'd given up trying to convince her of the dangers of melanoma, so I only wore it when leaving the house on my own. Then, I put a leash on Prince and grabbed some plastic poop recovery bags. The poop bags weren't really necessary since nature never called

Prince once we left the boundaries of our yard. Still, they added to my cover, and I did not want to become the next target for Mr. Price's trebuchet.

I knew from studying YouTube videos on surveillance techniques that I should stop periodically and check behind me by using the reflections in store windows to spot a tail. Unfortunately, our subdivision included no commercial zoning, and the homes were set far from the sidewalks, so I could not use that tactic. In its place, I decided I could bend down roughly every twenty paces to pet Prince and surreptitiously glance behind me. To avoid being predictable, I used an app on my phone to randomly vary my paces from seventeen to twenty-three. After several minutes of this, my back hurt from stooping down to pet the dog. As for Prince, he seemed confused by the unusual amount of affection and attention. It would seem I had one more thing to feel guilty about.

I made a mental note to get a taller dog when Prince crossed the rainbow bridge. That started me thinking about how dogs have it much better than us. Dogs meet their end peacefully—from natural causes or when they are "put to sleep." If the movie was to be believed, all dogs go to heaven. I'm pretty sure the rest of us are expected to work our way in. I like dogs, but that doesn't seem fair. Our pastor insisted heaven was a matter of grace and not good works, but I suspected there might be a catch.

My toe caught on some broken concrete on the sidewalk. This was an insurance claim waiting to happen, and I hoped the homeowner did not have a policy with my company. I looked around and realized I had walked many houses past the crime scenes. On the bright side, I realized by going past those houses and then reversing course, I had possibly thrown off any tails. Unless they had a camera drone. I looked up into the bright sky, but just because I didn't see a drone right away didn't mean it was not there.

Why hadn't I considered that before? Even a cheap hobby drone would be good enough to follow one person and a dog as they ambled down a sidewalk. On top of that, the police and FBI combined certainly had enough people to run multiple tails. I reversed course and resumed my periodic bending down and glancing back routine. Now I added a quick glance up while wishing the developer had put in more trees to provide cover from above.

When I got close to Miss Inga's house, I stopped, knelt, and pretended to adjust Prince's collar. While examining the house from multiple angles, I could see down the sides of her home and the neighbor's home on the right. There were no cameras. I performed a similar stop on the other side of her place and saw two cameras placed on the Shumakers' house on the left. The Shumakers had aimed the cameras at their yard, but I guessed they would also cover Miss Inga's. I did not know them well, but since their McMansion sat between crime scene number one and crime scene number two, like it or not—and I imagined it would be "not"—they were now a part of this investigation. Checking the other side of their house, I spotted another set of cameras that looked like they would also capture most of Edith's property.

Finally, something was going my way. The Shumakers had cameras covering both of the houses that were the scenes of the murders. Even better, there was a free newspaper sitting in their driveway. It was the same newspaper that got dropped on every driveway of the neighborhood, every Saturday. Most people tossed them without reading. Here, it was a sign the

Shumakers were out of town. With their place empty, and the empty crime scene houses on either side, I could use Tony to sneak in after dark. He could find out if the camera recordings were sent to some service in the cloud. It was also possible they were like me and hated those monthly subscriptions. My cameras' video was kept on a digital video recorder in the basement. Either way, we needed to see what the Shumakers' cameras had picked up. It was risky, but Tony had assured me he could get into any house in under three minutes, and I didn't want to leave my fate to the detectives or Mulder and Scully. The recordings could prove my innocence or at least point the investigation in some other direction. It might not leave the cops with an unbroken chain of custody. But no matter what, I wanted to see what was there.

"Excuse me. Can we help you?"

I spun around while still kneeling next to Prince and fell back on my butt. Looking down at me was a young couple in athletic wear. The woman was pushing a carbon fiber jogging stroller with a Porsche Design logo. I thought, *so this is what gentrification must feel like.*

I struggled to get up off the sidewalk with my usual grace.

"No, thanks," I said. "I'm fine."

"Are you sure? Your family must be worried about you. We have cell phones and can call to let them know where you are."

The way the man slowed down his speech and increased his volume was concerning—to my ego.

"No, thank you. I'm really fine."

While the husband pointed to the phone in his hand to demonstrate he had one, his wife was using hers to capture the interaction on video. Ah. Perhaps they were influencers of some sort, and I was going to be their soon-to-go-viral good deed?

"It's no trouble, sir," said the woman. "We helped another gentleman last week with a hat just like yours. He managed to walk here all the way from the Memory Lane at Rhodes Home. His daughter and the staff were so worried about him. Won't you let us help you?"

She stifled a scream at that point because Prince started to hump her leg. Her husband pulled the dog away and Prince transferred his affection to him without missing a beat.

"Where'd you find the dog?" he asked as he attempted to shake Prince off his leg. "I didn't think residents could have pets in Memory Lane."

"I'm not from any assisted living place. I live in this neighborhood. I was just out for a stroll."

They looked at each other and nodded in unison.

The husband said, "I understand. Can you tell me what month it is?"

"Why? Don't you know?"

"Of course, I do. It's June. I was asking to see if you knew."

"You're correct. It's June."

He seemed content with my performance.

I said, "For your next question, the answer is 'person, woman, man, camera, TV.'"

He scrunched his eyebrows, but before he could respond, his wife touched his shoulder.

"Dear, it will be time for Cayden's snack and nap in . . . twelve minutes." She looked at her Apple Watch. "We need to complete our run now or we won't make our activity goals for the day." With that, she took off with the stroller. The husband looked at me one more time, shrugged, and followed his wife. I wasn't sure if I'd passed his test or if he'd decided to abandon a potentially misplaced senior for the sake of his activity goals.

For a moment, I was pleased with myself. There are days when you need to take what victories you can. Then, the concept of this pass-fail test reminded me of a pearly gate examination, which reminded me of the importance of my current mission. After all, Georgia was one of the states that still had the death penalty.

That possibility didn't align with my future plans. Sort of like those free-range chickens, I planned on meeting my end only after I'd lived a good life and expired from natural causes before being respectfully processed by caring workers who received a just salary and health benefits. The crucial part for me was expiring from natural causes after a good life. The respectful processing was not required but would be nice to have.

Chapter Ten

Although every part of me screamed it was the wrong thing to do, I waited on Sunday evening for Tony to show up with his particular skills. He had confidence in his plan, and I didn't have a better one. The single adjustment I'd made to his scheme was that there was no way I was going to enter the Shumakers' house. It was his idea and his particular skills. I planned to use *my* particular skills to hide in the bushes nearby. I hoped that would give me plausible deniability if things went south.

The appointed hour arrived and then passed. Twenty minutes later, Tony appeared next to me wearing a gray hoodie and carrying a bag with grease stains. The hoodie had to be uncomfortable considering the lingering heat of the day. I realized I hadn't done anything to disguise myself, so I flipped up the collar of my shirt and tried to pull my head closer to my shoulders.

Tony grinned. "Nice look, Elvis."

"What's in the bag?"

"An old blanket and a towel I picked up at a thrift shop today, a fresh roll of duct tape, and some gloves. Don't worry. I went to the next county to get the stuff."

I had to reconsider Tony's skills.

"I'll put on the gloves first, then put a layer of duct tape over a window at the back of the house," he said, as casually as if this was a typical outing for a Sunday night. "The duct tape keeps the glass from flying all over and making noise once it breaks. I throw the blanket on the ground below the window to catch any loose pieces that do fall."

"You're going to break the window just wearing gloves?"

"No, dummy. The gloves are so I don't leave prints. I'll pick up a rock from their yard and wrap the towel around it so I can break the window with as little noise as possible. Once that's done, I get inside. If they use a digital recorder, I'll grab it. If not. I'll grab their computer so we can check their cloud files. Either way, it'll look like a simple robbery. On the way out, I quietly scatter some broken glass and leave the rock. The cops will assume some kids did it."

"I'm impressed. You came well prepared."

"Not my first rodeo. And you owe me $24.87 for the supplies."

It occurred to me that I had underestimated Tony. While I was pretty sure he'd never seen a cowboy roping a steer, this wasn't his first time breaking and entering. I wondered if he'd be willing to make a speech to the next local meeting of the American Association of Insurance Investigators. We'd have to wait a while to make sure no one made a connection to the break-in at the Shumakers', but I thought his stories would be more interesting than yet another presentation on the creative billing practices used by medical offices.

We walked in silence and followed a roundabout path to approach the Shumaker's house from the opposite direction. Tony checked his watch several times along the way, and it seemed to me he slowed slightly after each check. Under the full moon, I could see sweat on his face and dark stains forming on the gray hoodie. He was certainly committed to the mission.

He pointed to a spot under the next streetlight and told me I could watch everything from there and keep an eye out for a random police car or neighborhood watch on patrol.

"Doesn't that make it easy for people to see me? Won't they get suspicious?"

"A person hiding in the bushes in the dark is suspicious. A person under a light is just out for a walk. Plus, you have that great disguise."

"But I'll be standing, not walking."

"Then bend down and retie your shoelaces. Do I have to think of everything?"

I walked to the location he'd selected and tried to avoid looking suspicious as I hunched over my shoes. That was when I remembered I was wearing slip-on loafers. Committed to the charade, I tied and retied invisible laces while I prayed no one would jog by as I carried out my improv routine.

My mind enumerated the risks I was taking as an accomplice to Tony's burgling. That thought and my bent-over pose made me think of all the bad jokes about making friends in prison. The other prisoners were always guys that'd been thrown out of professional wrestling for excessive use of force. And they had lots of gold teeth, or missing teeth, or just bad teeth. It was always the unusual teeth that made their smiles even more menacing. In my uncomfortable position, what seemed like a bad idea the day before seemed like an incredibly bad idea at that moment.

A pair of tennis shoes came into sight and stopped before me. I looked up and saw Vanessa Hershey, who appeared to be just as startled as I was. Though, to be honest, she looked much better than I did while being startled. She was standing with her right arm bent and that hand on her hip as if she was posing on the red carpet.

"Mr. Hanson, what are you doing?"

Thinking fast, I said, "I'm tying my shoes."

"Oh. Alright. Never mind."

As she walked off, I was left to wonder what she was doing out, where she was headed, and whether she owned anything other than tennis outfits.

Tony had disappeared, and I assumed he was taking another circular and nonobvious path to the back of the Shumakers' house. Before that evening, I didn't recall ever taking a circular and nonobvious path in my life. Then again, before that evening, I'd never mimed tying my shoes under a streetlight. It was a night for new adventures.

In the middle of this road-not-taken revery, I heard a whump. It was a very distinctive sound—not really an explosion, but something with more concussive power than a simple thump. Whatever it was, it was not the sound of a rock wrapped in a towel hitting a duct-taped window. Tony had not provided instructions on what to do if I heard a whump, so I remained at my post under the streetlight and watched the Shumakers' home. A minute passed, and I wondered if I should get back to my invisible shoelaces. Then an unsteady light illuminated the trees and houses surrounding the Shumakers' backyard. The light was accompanied by the sound of bacon sizzling in a pan and the smell of burning pine. I wondered if Tony had set off some kind of alarm as more lights came on from neighboring houses.

Arson was not one of my specialties, but over the years I'd visited the scenes of a number of fires. Most of them had a smell that quickly powered through any fabric mask. It would take several showers to clean off the stench and a box of tissues until blowing my nose didn't leave a black spot in the center of each one. The smell that night also started as burning pine, which wasn't too unpleasant. I guessed that was the Shumakers' back deck. Soon, the pine was overpowered by the stench of burning plastic. It appeared mine wasn't the only home in the neighborhood with brick in the front and vinyl in back.

It was fascinating to watch the fire grow. I forgot all about my lace-free untied shoes. My phone began to vibrate, and when I pulled it out to check, my notifications showed that word was quickly spreading through the neighborhood and beyond via group texts and social media posts. That was the moment I realized I'd been the victim of target fixation. While my focus for the evening had been on finding any video footage surrounding the murders, I'd ended up standing where I could be seen by people up and down the street and even caught on their doorbell cameras. Head down, I crossed the street to stand under a tree in relative darkness.

I moved just in time as a few brave souls came out of their homes and took selfies in front of the spreading flames. After documenting the fire, each returned home—no doubt to make edits before posting. It's difficult to get the contrast right when you're backlit by a burning building. Eventually, one of those posts must have gotten the attention of the city emergency services, and I heard sirens approaching. It was the usual mix of whee-ohhh-whee-ohhh and whoop-whoop-whoop from police cars. Then came the air horns of fire trucks, and I knew that a few civilian drivers had tried to make a last-second dash through an intersection in front of the emergency vehicles. I'd interviewed a driver last year who'd been T-boned by a firetruck. He acknowledged the firetruck might have been responding to a life-threatening situation. Still, he didn't accept any wrong on his part but kept repeating his defense that "the light was green." I wondered if he was on the road that evening, and if he'd manage to make it through the intersection this time.

It occurred to me that the police and firefighters would be there any moment. I didn't want to hang around as a possible witness, and certainly not as a suspect in yet another crime. I headed for home. Tony, with his particular set of skills, would surely make a successful getaway. I had no thought of taking a circular or nonobvious path, so I walked straight to my house as fast as I could without seeming to run from the scene. Several emergency vehicles raced past me and stopped in front of the Shumakers'.

Once safe in my house, I turned on the TV and resumed watching *Double Indemnity*. I know it's a bit dated, but it's an insurance-caper classic. Most civilians don't give it enough respect. I watched it on repeat for hours—expecting a knock on the door at any time. Somewhere along the way, I fell asleep.

The knock at the door finally came just as the sun was rising. The noise from the entrance, paired with the light filtering through the windows, worked together to drag me from sleep. Despite their insistence, I fought to stay in my dream. I was in a courtroom, laying out the details of the murders. Rhonda smiled at me from the front row, and the judge led the audience in a slow clap that quickly gained momentum.

When I realized it was the real world knocking that was speeding up, I stumbled to my feet and made my way to the front door. Standing there were two detectives from the group I'd seen at the station earlier in the week. After introductions, they got straight to it.

"A home in your neighborhood burned to the ground last evening. We were wondering if you might know anything about how the fire started?"

"No sir, I've been in my house all night."

"And you didn't hear the sirens?"

I tried to appear sheepish as I confessed, "My wife doesn't like the noise from the action movies I watch." I held out my Bluetooth earbuds. "I wear these. It keeps the missus happy and does a good job of blocking out noise for me too."

"You sure you didn't leave the house all evening?"

"No, sir."

"Meaning you're not sure if you left the house?"

"No. I mean, 'no, I didn't leave the house all evening.'"

"Then how do you explain the neighbors who saw you standing under the street light across from the house that burned down? A few even showed us images from their door cameras. The guy in the videos even had his shirt collar popped just like you do now."

I tried hard to remember any of the lines people had used on me as I investigated them for insurance fraud. Some of those attempts had been almost believable, but I could not recall any of them now.

"I . . . uh . . . don't know."

"Then perhaps you could explain why your clothing smells like burnt vinyl siding?"

* * *

The officers took me down to the station and parked me in the interrogation room I'd been in days before. I suspected the force only had one such room and felt honored they'd reserved it for me twice within a week. At least this time, the lights were off on the other side of the two-way mirror. And they'd cleaned up the small spots of blood I'd left on their table. In fact, I could tell by the scent that the cleaning crew had used Lysol. It reassured me they'd killed 99.9% of the bacteria, even if it was my own bacteria.

The first cop to sit down asked, "Where were you on October fourth of the year before last?"

"What?"

"It's a simple question. Where were you on October fourth of the year before last?"

"I have no idea. That was a long time ago."

"Where were you on October seventh of that same year?"

I shook my head.

The second cop pointed to the microphone in the center of the table.

"We need a verbal response. Where were you on October fourth, seventh, sixteenth, and twenty-fourth two years ago?"

"I can't tell you, because I can't remember anything about specific dates that far in the past. If you let me use my iPhone, I can check my calendar."

Then it occurred to me I'd have to unlock my phone to check the date. That might be their real objective—to have access to my private data.

I said, "On second thought, I ran out of space and remember erasing all the calendar entries for previous years, so it won't do me any good. Why do you want to know about where I was on those days?"

"October fourth was the day someone set the first in a series of fires. Arson occurred on and off for weeks and then stopped," said the one I'd tagged as the Good Cop.

"Until last night," said the Bad Cop as he slapped the table.

Not wanting to disappoint him, I jumped in response. My reaction must have pleased him because he smiled and looked at his partner as if to say he was nailing the "bad cop" routine.

Good Cop said, "It's not your fault you're a pyromaniac. It's a disease like any other addiction. Just tell me about the fires, and I can get you the help you need."

"You call that a *disease*?" Bad Cop exploded. "That's a snowflake excuse. He lights fires because he likes to see things burn. Not that I don't enjoy a good flare up once in a while. Last Thanksgiving, the idiot next door to me dropped a frozen turkey into a container of hot oil. It was just like the YouTube videos, but I could feel the heat on my face." He paused and stared at me. "Is that why you do it? To see the flames and feel the heat?"

"Wait a minute. You think I'm an arsonist now? Just last week, the other detectives were sure I was a murderer."

Bad Cop backhanded Good Cop on the shoulder. "I told you he looked hinky. He's the one Jackson and Williams were trying to nail for killing the old bag."

"Which old bag? The one who bled out or the other one?"

Bad Cop said, "I think the one that took two in the back of the skull." Then he looked back at me. "Is that the one you did?"

"I didn't shoot Miss Oskarsdotter."

Good Cop flipped open a folder and asked, "OK. So now you're saying you stabbed the other one with a bunch of wooden stakes? Who do you think you are—some kind of vampire killer?"

Bad Cop slapped the table again. “I saw that. He’s like the Von Hellson guy with a crossbow.”

“You’re thinking of the fictional character,” I said. “Van Helsing.”

Bad Cop looked confused. “You’re playacting as this Van Halen then? Did you kill her with wooden stakes or with a crossbow?”

“I didn’t use anything to kill anyone. I told the two detectives last week, I didn’t do it. They must have believed me, because they let me go.”

The door opened as if on cue, and Detectives Jackson and Williams walked in.

Jackson turned to his partner. “He *thinks* we believed him. Either our acting has gotten better, or he’s dumber than he looks.”

I sat still and tried to project an image of innocence. It didn’t seem to work because Williams said, “Partner, your momma is the only one ever said you could act, and she lied. This perp is as dumb as they come.”

Jackson and Williams then got a quick rundown on the reasons Good Cop and Bad Cop had brought me in for questioning. When they finished their summation, Williams asked for the address of the fire.

“Now that is interesting,” said Jackson. “The house that burned down sat right between the scenes of two murders. Who here believes in coincidence?”

Never good at recognizing a rhetorical question, I raised my hand and said, “‘From a statistical perspective, coincidences are inevitable and often less remarkable than they may appear intuitively.’”

The four cops stared at me as if annoyed, which I guessed they were.

I shrugged. "I've used that sentence from Wikipedia so frequently in reports, I've memorized it."

Having delivered countless presentations to my managers at GFI, I could tell the detectives were teetering between puzzled and irritated. It was time to take a different approach. I'd attended several courses on speaking to groups, and it was time to lighten the mood with the lesson from the "Win 'em over with humor" lesson.

"I'm sure you know a few insurance policies include an 'Act of God' clause. I bet you don't know what we call it in the office."

"No, but I bet you're going to tell us," Detective Williams said, with a scowl.

"We call it the 'Shit Happens' clause."

Bad Cop was the only one to smile. "We have jokes too. We get pissed when a suspect jerks us around, so we put them in a cell with a lifer who has nothing to lose. When the suspect asks why, we say 'Shit happens.'"

They all chuckled as if it was the first time they'd heard it.

It was time to ignore the lessons in my 'Everyone Is in Sales' folder and start using some of the other expertise I had gained over the years.

"I assume you have all seen *Law & Order* at some point?"

Bad Cop said, "What the—" but didn't finish.

Detective Williams held out a hand and said, "No. I want to hear this."

I stood and began to walk back and forth as taught to make sure their attention was on me. It must have made Bad

Cop nervous because he slid his chair back and began to rub his meaty paws together.

I resumed. "Of course, there are several spinoffs of the original classic, but every *Law & Order* shares the same basic structure. I think you will agree with me it applies in this case."

Detective Jackson took a seat, and I knew I had them.

"In every episode, the police 'who investigate crime' focus in on one suspect. The detectives and the audience see that everything points to the one with blood on their hands, often literally. Then the district attorneys 'who prosecute the offenders' work to prove the suspect's guilt beyond a reasonable doubt."

Bad Cop sneered, though I wasn't sure if he disagreed with the cop/lawyer workload balance or wasn't a fan of the shows.

"This takes forty-five minutes, though I suspect it requires more time in real life. Anyway, at this point, new evidence is revealed and the prosecution has to swivel in the final act to convict the person they now think did it."

Their blank stares reminded me of the last time I tried to ask my manager for a raise.

"You see? I'm your first suspect. The one who is always a red herring. Obviously, in time you'll discover new clues that will lead you to the real killer or killers."

I closed with my best impression of the *L&O* signature "Dun. Dun."

Williams dropped into a chair at the table and rubbed his forehead.

"Since we are still in Act One," he said, "let's go through the motions, shall we?"

"Certainly. I'll help in any way I can."

He took the folder from Good Cop and looked at the top page.

"Why were you outside the Shumakers' house last night? By chance, were you trying to destroy evidence we'd missed at one or both of the murder scenes?"

What he did not know was that I'd crossed my fingers while saying I'd help "in any way I can."

"I had to take my dog for a walk. He's very particular about where he'll do his business. He has to sniff every yard until he finds the right one."

"My dog does the same thing," said Good Cop, which earned him a scowl from Jackson and Bad Cop.

"Before I knew it, I was in front of the house everyone calls a McMansion. Prince, that's my dog, was taking his time so I was still there when the emergency vehicles pulled up. I didn't want to get in the way of the professionals, so Prince and I walked home."

Williams closed the folder and sat looking at me.

"Are you charging me with anything, or can I go? My wife must be worried about me."

There was a lot of chin rubbing and staring at each other until Jackson snarled, "You are free to go. For now. Just stay where we can find you."

Williams checked his phone as I was getting up to leave. Holding up the screen, he said, "This is interesting. We thought someone might have destroyed the house to get rid of any evidence from the Shumakers' surveillance cameras. Turns out we're in the twenty-first century and their system streamed video directly to the cloud. We just need to get their signed permission when they get back in town so we can download the files and examine them."

Bad Cop opened the door and smirked. "Have a nice day. And I mean that. If I were you, I'd enjoy the next twenty-four hours."

Jackson and Williams then went back and forth with, "We should tell him. He deserves to know," alternating with "Nah. We shouldn't tell him."

"Whatever it is," I cut in, "just go ahead and tell me."

Jackson nodded at Williams. Williams cleared his throat.

"We've verified the alibi of our *first* suspect. *You* had been our second suspect, and that means we're ready for Act Two."

Bad Cop added, "Dun. Dun."

Chapter Eleven

I used a rideshare app to get home. One trip per day in the backseat of a cop car that smelled of vomit and illegal substances was enough. At least the rideshare only smelled of an overpowering lilac air freshener that almost hid the odor of illegal substances. That was the same smell that permeated my grandmother's house when my cousin was living in her basement. His nickname was Space Cowboy. He told Grandma it was because he'd applied to NASA for astronaut training. We thought she'd bought into his deception until the day we caught them sharing a joint. It suddenly explained a lot about Grandma.

While I rode home in the back of the generic sedan, I thought it would be a good time to bring the kids up to date. They deserved to know, and I could use their moral support. Since Rhonda had not been a fan of this earlier, I wanted to get her agreement first. I texted, *I should probably talk to the kids about all this, right?*

It did not take long for her reply. *Why would you stress the children with this?*

I typed in and erased several messages. I wanted Rhonda to see I needed the support of Kate and Luke. Also, while still in college, they were adults and deserved to be involved in something this big. Whatever the outcome for me, it would impact their lives as well. In the end, I deleted the texts and waited until I could talk to Rhonda. Whether she realized it or not, this was more than I could handle on my own. I scanned my contacts for Jill Richards. She was an attractive defense lawyer who lived a few streets over. It was becoming clear I needed a defense lawyer, although I don't know why I always added "attractive" any time I thought of her.

I'd worked with Jill when the homeowner's association got sued over what the local press tagged "Goose-gate." It could have just as easily been "Duck-gate" but the NBC affiliate station had available B-roll video of geese, so they went with that. The lawsuit was formally known as "Kastner v. The Estates of Chestnut Lake Homeowners Association."

Like a lot of neighborhoods around us, our subdivision had a pond in the middle. Some might have been fooled into thinking it was a lake given our neighborhood's full name, but it was only a retention pond for stormwater runoff. Though it didn't impact the lawsuit, I was also fairly sure there were no chestnut trees in our subdivision, just scraggly pines along with a few dogwoods and Japanese Maples. As for estates, the lot sizes ranged from one quarter to one third of an acre at most. Not properties one would associate with an estate, particularly this far outside the Perimeter, where a square foot of red clay was still considered relatively cheap by the folks up north.

Most people in the neighborhood called it "The Estates" since it was easier, but still implied a certain cachet. No one referred to the retention pond as a lake, but it was ours. It was the foundation of the surrounding "Nature Trail" as featured in real estate listings. The trail was an oval dirt path around the pond. The nature was provided by the creatures that thrived there, primarily mosquitos. Though for several weeks in the spring and again in the fall, we'd see a handful of ducks and geese. To some, the birds were essential to the natural landscape. To others, they were a nuisance and a source of the droppings that covered cars, lawn furniture, and occasionally unlucky residents out for a walk.

Goose-gate started when Mr. Kastner slipped on a pile of bird poo, damaging the cartilage in both his knees. There were no witnesses, but he claimed it had to be from the birds since the location was well outside the range of Mr. Price's trebuchet.

Price's lawyer was Donnie Gamble. His advertising tagline was "Never Gamble with Your Case." Apparently, his clients were not good at parsing syntax. We knew him at GFI, as he was on our list of lawyers who give personal injury lawyers a bad name—which is an accomplishment of sorts. As expected, he sued the HOA the following day seeking one point five million dollars. In an amazing coincidence that matched the liability coverage the HOA had purchased from GFI.

The only good part of the trial was I was able to work with Jill. As a happily married man, it was stupid of me to have a crush on her, but then it had been stupid for me to have a crush on the head cheerleader during my freshman year in high school. In both cases, I knew it would come to nothing, but the heart wants what the heart wants. I viewed it as a harmless infatuation since I was, after all, a happily married man.

Mr. Kastner's claim rested on the assertion that his injuries directly resulted from the HOA's failure to stop some residents from feeding the water fowl. According to his attorney, Mr. Kastner was the "victim of an unthinking and unfeeling bureaucracy that, through incompetence or malice, caused my client great pain and suffering." I could grant the unthinking and unfeeling parts, but claiming we were a bureaucracy gave us credit for far more organization than we possessed.

The trial did not last long. Under Jill's *Perry Mason/Matlock/My Cousin Vinny* cross examination, Kastner broke down on the stand and revealed he was annoyed with the HOA, but his target was GFI. Their medical insurance plan would not cover his age-related knee replacements. The judge sympathized with his plight and noted it was not unusual for a person to detest their medical insurance company. Everyone does.

From my point of view, I was happy the HOA was victorious and GFI was saved from a large payout, but my connection to Jill came to an end far too soon. For the following two years, I would only catch glimpses of her as she traveled through the neighborhood.

The rideshare driver dropped me off at home, and I used the app to tip him and provide a positive review. I learned later he left a lukewarm rider review for me and commented I looked guiltier than most he picked outside the police station. I climbed the front steps and sat on one of the Adirondack chairs that decorated our porch. They were rarely used and, sliding back into one, I remembered why.

After I tapped on Jill's work number, her clear alto let me know my call was important to her and she would get back to me. I left a message but was not satisfied with my clumsy wording and the number of crutch words I used. A quick tap of "*" gave me another shot at a clean recording, but after five tries, I decided I should write out my message so I could deliver it in one clean, confident take.

A moment after I hung up, my phone rang and the caller-id displayed "J Richards."

My "hello" was more tenuous than I wanted.

"I saw you in my call log, but there was no message. What can I do for you?"

"I don't know if you remember me. This is Brad Hanson."

"Of course I remember you. We worked together on Goose-gate."

That made me feel good until she continued.

"I've only heard bits and pieces about what's happened, but you should have contacted me days ago. Please tell me you haven't talked to the police without a lawyer present."

I let Jill's question hang there for a moment.

She sighed. "I was afraid of that. Have they charged you with anything?"

"Not yet."

"It's just a matter of time based on what I'm seeing online. I'm in my office for the rest of the day. Come and see me if you want to discuss representation."

I agreed to meet her in an hour.

Rhonda was never good at accepting bad news, but the timing wasn't going to get any better. I walked to the back of the house and found her in the kitchen watching reality TV.

Rhonda did not look up when I entered the room.

"I took a rideshare home from the police station. Didn't want to bother you."

"Um, huh. Well, you're bothering me now. It's just getting to the good part."

She'd seen this episode at least a half dozen times while I was around, so who knows how many times total. The bride was from southern California and hoped to be cast for *90 Day Fiancé* so she could then qualify for a spot on a reboot of *Real Housewives of Orange County*. The groom was from "a remote section of Idaho"—which seemed redundant. He had thought he signed up for *Naked and Afraid* and was disappointed to find the show he landed was not only filmed in a big city, but he and his partner would be clothed. The couple discovered they would be in a show for those deemed incompatible from the start—*Married at First Slight*. It was based on the premise that most married people start out believing they have found their perfect mate and eventually learn things about their partner that really annoy them. *MaFS*'s storyline started at the point of annoyance and worked backward from there in the hope the couple would eventually fall in love. If they didn't, that was OK. The creators knew viewers would prefer to watch people in conflict over contentment any day of the week.

I waited ten minutes for a commercial break and then recalled the show was part of our streaming package. Desperate times call for desperate measures. Knowing I might soon go on trial for a charge of murder, bold action was required. I reached over and hit the pause button.

"What are you doing? I told you it was just getting to the good part."

"You already know what happens. They decide to ignore their many differences and move across country together to get on *Real Housewives of Des Moines*. They live in unscripted but preordained conflict for the next three seasons."

"You know I don't allow sarcasm in this house."

Whenever she said this, I couldn't think of anything clever that wouldn't violate her ban.

"I'm going to clean up and go see if Ms. Richards will act as my lawyer in case the police press charges."

"That's ridiculous. You don't need a lawyer, and anyway, we don't have the money to afford a lawyer and the kitchen upgrade you promised me."

"Honey, the police—and maybe the FBI—think I had something to do with the deaths. I need a lawyer before this goes any further."

"Fine. Then why don't you use one of those public defenders? They're free, which would save us money, and they must be good lawyers with all the practice they get."

"I think overworked is not the same as well-practiced."

"Then what about that nice Mr. Gamble? I hear his ads on talk radio all the time."

I bit my tongue. I knew it was cliché, but it often kept me out of trouble.

She opened a drawer and pulled out a flyer. "Look here. He has a coupon for a free consultation and 10% off his hourly rate if we call before the end of the week."

"I realize you like the weekly coupons flyer, but might I gently remind you of the duct cleaning bait-and-switch?"

"And when the TV news covered Goose-gate," she continued, "Mr. Gamble looked very professional."

"But he lost."

"So? I'm sure Ms. Richards has lost a few cases over the years. And they have been hard years from the looks of her. You can see her roots. Who wants a lawyer that doesn't take care of herself? I support women in most professions, but I don't see why you'd take her over an accomplished lawyer like Mr. Gamble."

"He specializes in personal injury cases. Ms. Richards is a defense attorney."

"That's another reason to pick him. You go in there with a defense attorney, and they're going to assume you're guilty."

I remembered the sarcasm ban and humbly promised to consider all my options. Once I hit the play button, our conversation was over.

After a quick shower and shave, I was feeling better about everything except my wardrobe for the meeting with Jill. I could not remember which shirt I'd worn the last time I worked with Jill on Goose-gate. It had been two years, but I wanted to avoid a repeat. My work shirts were all long-sleeve button downs and too corporate. My golf shirts were too casual and all of them had a GFI logo over the left breast. I'd once looked good in a colored t-shirt and blazer, but the *Miami Vice* ensemble was now reserved for Halloween and too many people didn't get it then. I compromised with a blue Oxford button-down, but with the sleeves rolled up.

Chapter Twelve

Ms. Richards's office was in a small complex of two-story Georgian buildings similar to those surrounding the GFI office park. Most residents of the Peach State believed the architecture was named after the state of Georgia, but the red brick building style came from the days of King George, one through four, inclusive. I hoped the topic would come up in a future trivia contest at our local pub. My team had zero knowledge of baseball stats, and less regarding rap lyrics, so we never came close to winning. Our strategy was to collect obscure factoids like why this style of building was named Georgian. To date, our factoid gathering plan hadn't helped, but we kept collecting nonetheless.

I entered the small lobby and noted that the building's occupants included a podiatrist, a financial planner, a dentist, and two insurance agents. There was a smell from a recent cleaning and the muffled sound of screaming. I circled the lobby but could not determine if the screaming was from the dentist's office or the financial planner's.

I opened the door labelled "J. Richards, Attorney." The furnishings had not changed since my last visit. The current occupant of the receptionist's desk was a young man of roughly college age. I remembered Jill's previous receptionist was a paralegal in training, and assumed this was his stepping stone as well.

He looked up from his mobile phone game and told me Ms. Richards was expecting me and to go right in. I opened the door, but she did not notice me. She had her legs up on a low credenza and was looking out the window while talking to someone on the phone. I tried not to pay attention to her shapely limbs but was not successful.

"Mr. Adams, I understand you believe your son is innocent and you do not like the idea of a guilty plea, but they arrested him after a fifteen-minute high-speed chase in a stolen vehicle . . ." She used her free hand to rub her forehead. ". . . and the police have body cam recordings showing him in possession of the drugs."

She switched to running her hand through her hair—a habit I recalled from our previous association.

"I realize that, but the police consider two pounds excessive for 'personal use.' And they have his signed confession." She pulled on her hair. "I can see why you might like them to consider it a foolish high school prank, but he's thirty-two years old. I would not even attempt to get his case transferred to juvenile court."

Her hand returned to her forehead.

"I am sorry you feel that is necessary, but it is your prerogative. I will send the bill for my hours worked to this point, along with the case file for your new lawyer. I wish you the best of luck."

She tapped her phone to hang up, turned, looked at me, and yelled through the open door.

"Damn it, Jason. I told you to keep visitors out there when I'm on the phone."

Then, in a quieter voice, she said, "I apologize. You should not have been privy to that conversation—particularly how it ended. I try to not to lie to my clients, but I don't wish him luck. I hope he gets his ass handed to him, and that goes for his next lawyer too."

"No need to apologize," I said. "In my job, I have to deal with irrational clients all the time."

"It's the price we pay for working with the public."

I nodded. "But I feel sorry for that man. I've never had to deal with anything like that with my kids. A couple of speeding tickets and they took responsibility for them and paid off the fines working summer jobs."

"I remember you talking about your kids when I worked on that case for The Estates."

"Kate did have that biting incident in preschool but I still think she was provoked."

"I'm sure the statute of limitations has passed on that in any case." She smiled.

I pulled out my phone. "I've got some recent pictures if you'd like to see."

Jill gave a smaller smile. "Perhaps some other time. Right now, I think we should concentrate on why you're here." The smile vanished as she looked at her watch, then grabbed a legal pad and a pen.

"Mr. Hanson, based on what I've read, I think I know the basic outline of your troubles. The police are investigating the deaths of two women in The Estates. You are a suspect in at least one of those deaths. Do I have that right?"

I nodded.

"Do you wish to engage my services as your defense lawyer?"

"I guess. I mean, that's why I'm here."

"When you're on the stand, try to deliver responses with more confidence. At any rate, as I am now representing you, this discussion is under attorney–client privilege. Did you do it?"

"What?"

"As your lawyer, I will defend you to the best of my ability, but I will do a better job if I understand the facts of the case. Did you directly or indirectly cause the death of Miss Inga Oskarsdotter?"

"No. Definitely no."

"Same question regarding Mrs. Skinner."

"Again, no."

"That's better. I might even believe that response if you deliver it that way in court. Before we get started, do you have questions for me?"

"Uh. A few. How many murder cases have you handled?"

"I assisted in one case when I had just started working at a firm in the city. Since I went on my own here in the 'burbs, I haven't seen another one. That said, you are not likely to find anyone else in the area with more experience. Homicides have not been a common occurrence in Rhodes over the last few years—though it seems they're getting more popular."

"How much is this going to cost?"

"Good question. Murder cases are time-consuming. I promise not to pad my bill, but accounting for my hours and that of my paralegal, you are going to be looking at a substantial amount—possibly well into six figures. On top of that, there could be costs for expert witnesses and a private investigator if we need one. Then—unless you want to bunk in the county jail—there will be bail, and I don't know how high the judge will go on that."

While I was considering how much I could pull from savings without incurring penalties for early withdrawal, I got a text message from my wife.

Your boss tried to reach you. Said you should take a leave without pay for now. They can't have you working cases while under suspicion.

A moment later, a second text came through.

Will this delay my new kitchen?

Jill tapped a pen against her desk pad. "You are paying for my time by the hour now, so you might want to play games on your phone after you leave."

"Sorry. I wasn't playing. I got some urgent texts."

"While you are working on your defense with me, there isn't anything else that's urgent. Can we agree on that?"

I nodded. Apparently, a murder case brought Jill to a whole new level of intensity. It had to be more of a challenge than defending yet another shoplifter—though I am sure those have a charm all their own.

"Now, you said you had a few questions. What are the rest?"

One question had been nagging at me since the start of our conversation. "You said you had some knowledge of my case based on what you've read. What have you learned?"

"I learned your neighbors are about split on whether you're guilty or not, and many are scared—concerned there might be more murders until the police find the killer or killers."

"I've tried to keep up with the local news stories, and I haven't heard any of that."

"You wouldn't get it from the local news. I rely on what I pick up from a 'wretched hive of scum and villainy.'"

Her knowledge of *Star Wars* trivia impressed me, but I didn't catch her meaning here.

"You hang out in seedy bars full of illegal aliens?"

"Do not use the phrase 'illegal aliens' in my office. Some of my clients are undocumented immigrants, but I can see you've missed my point. I vicariously experience the worst of Rhodes by reading posts on Folks-Next-Door.com"

I nodded. "Where one person will ask for help finding a lost cat and soon another person blames it on the Libs?"

"That's the one, but you've apparently just dipped your toe in the swamp. Spend some time there and you'll find out that your neighbors are not only under the spell of conspiracy theories but are spinning their own."

She rotated her computer monitor so I could see the windows mirrored from her laptop.

"It masquerades as friendly social media, but lets you yell 'Get off my lawn' without getting off your couch." She flipped through a few pages.

"I ignore the political disputes," I said, "and try to focus on the harmless funny stuff. I don't mean to be condescending, but it looks as if they gave a voice to People of Walmart."

"I'm curious. What are you like when you *do* intend to be condescending?"

I was not making a positive impression and needed to get on a better track with her. I read a few more. "This one is scary. Says he's going to grab a gun if another teen trespasses on his driveway."

"Let me jot down the name. I hope he doesn't follow through, but people like him are steady business for me."

After scrolling a bit more, she pointed at a picture of me from my evening outing.

"You'll find a lot of images from doorbell cameras on here. Nice casual pose under the streetlight, by the way. As your lawyer, I'm suggesting you don't do that again. People love to put out warnings when they see a 'suspicious character.'"

"What makes someone a suspicious character?"

A voice behind me said, "It can be almost anything, but usually a suspicious character is someone who looks like me."

I turned in my chair. A tall Black woman with a shaved head, wearing jeans and a black leather jacket, had entered the room.

"Meet Cassandra Dixon," said Jill. "She handles investigations for me."

The woman held out her hand to shake. "You can call me Dix." She must have noticed my expression and continued, "The irony is intentional."

As she pulled her hand back, I stared at the heavy rings adorning every finger.

"Those are very distinctive," I said.

"They're not for decoration. They put dents in people that make me mad." With that, she nodded, said, "Nice to meet you," walked out of the office and closed the door.

"I can see I don't want to make her mad."

"I'd advise against getting on her wrong side. Rest assured she is a talented investigator. We've worked together for years."

"Didn't I see her on the reboot of *Cops*?"

Jill could produce a stare that let me know I'd just stepped on a landmine.

"I've accepted you as a client, but we haven't gone before a judge yet, so that's easy to change."

"I apologize. I just thought—"

"You didn't think. You jumped to the wrong conclusion based on your prejudice."

"But the getup—"

"Cassandra has a flair for the dramatic and uses many personas in her work as an investigator. I met her when I needed an expert witness for a case involving art forgeries. She has one master's degree in art history and a second in theater. Despite the impression she makes with today's attire, she is extremely intelligent, just lousy at picking majors that could lead to a 401(k)." Jill took a breath and continued, "She works part-time selling shoes at the mall when she isn't working for me. She's dressed like she is today because she's auditioning for a role in *The Last of Us—The Musical*."

There was a tap on the door, and I was saved from further embarrassment. The receptionist/paralegal-in-training stuck his head in.

"Sorry to interrupt, Jill, but you wanted to know when I heard anything from my friend in the police department."

"And what 'anything' did you hear?"

"First, they've estimated the time of death for Miss Oskarsdotter as approximately 10:20 PM and Miss Skinner's death as 10:40. Next, the ballistics lab was not able to make a solid match between the bullets they recovered and the gun they found in Mr. Hanson's garage. My guy also said someone had tried to wipe it down, but they did match some of the fingerprints on the gun to your client."

"Jason, you work for me. That means he is 'our client.'"

"Yeah. OK. Anyway, as for the Shumaker couple, they've been waiting for them to come back from their trip so they could get access to the surveillance video on the cloud account. According to my contact, their plane landed a couple hours ago."

"So, the police have the video?"

"No. The Shumakers never showed up at the police station."

"Well, where are they?"

"No one knows. Their car was found behind the Chili's restaurant, but there's no trace of the couple."

After he closed the door, Jill looked at me and raised an eyebrow.

"Please tell me you don't have any potential prosecution witnesses in the trunk of your car."

"No. Definitely no."

She smiled. "Excellent. I want you to retain that certainty if we go to court."

"My VW Golf is a small hatchback. There is no way I could get two bodies in the back."

"Before we go to court, I also want you to learn when to shut up."

Chapter Thirteen

I left Jill's office and walked back to my car. I know I'd just said two bodies could not fit in the rear of my hatchback, but I peeked just in case. The thought occurred to me that someone might plant a couple of corpses on me. It had turned into that kind of week, and I think I had every reason to be a little paranoid.

Once inside my car, I realized I didn't know where to go or what to do next. I felt somewhat better since I had an attorney I trusted, but not that much better, since I imagined there were cork boards in the police and FBI offices with my picture prominently displayed. They probably got a headshot by grabbing a selfie off one of my social media posts. Despite upgrading my phone every two years to get a better camera, I'd never mastered the art of smiling without looking like I was sitting on something uncomfortable. Even if the evidence was insufficient to convict me, looking at one of my self-made mug shots wouldn't make anyone eager to exonerate me.

I decided my best option at that moment was to go talk to Tony again. That was a reminder of how few options I had.

I had no expectation of great insights from Tony, but he could be a good listening post as I worked through the possibilities. But before talking to him, I had to go home and reassure Rhonda that I had an attorney and things were looking up.

After years in The Estates, I still used a mapping app to find my house while silently cursing the unknown street designer. The layout wasn't the only problem, but it made things worse. With each house in Phase III based on one of five model homes and painted in one of six approved paint schemes, it was even money you'd find your home's twin one or two streets away.

Rhonda hated my reliance on my phone's directions. More than once, I'd followed her wishes and, as a result, pulled up to a house that looked like mine, only to find the garage door opener did not work. Those instances no doubt prompted another post or two on Folks-Next-Door.

This time I had faithfully listened to SIRI's directions and pulled on to the correct street. Though the HOA encouraged residents to put their vehicles inside their garages to improve the overall look of The Estates, I could see Tony's Lincoln Town Car sitting in his driveway, as usual. As a 2011 model, it was more streamlined than the earlier versions, but still reminded me of the worst in '80s and '90s automotive design. Tony said it was a classic and had a special status with his crowd back in Jersey. I'd ask if that made it worth driving at twelve miles per gallon while missing out on modern safety features. His response was always that climate change was a fraud, and he was not worried about what would happen if "an electric toy car bounced off his bumper."

As much as I considered Tony a Neanderthal, I admired his confidence and ability to flout conventions. That day, I took my own stand against conformity. I left my car sitting in the driveway. I made a note to put the car in the garage before evening. But for the moment, I savored the taste of rebellion.

Since Rhonda usually kept the door locked, it was unusual when my key easily turned and the door swung open. Laughter was coming from the back of the house—it seemed we had company.

As I walked through the kitchen, I saw my wife sitting with Tony at the table in the screened-in porch. She was sipping from a tall ice-filled glass. Tony was drinking a craft beer. I recognized the bottle as one I'd been saving for a special event. Rhonda must have forgotten that, or just wanted to be the perfect hostess for our guest.

Using one foot to keep Prince from getting out, I opened the sliding glass door, and they both swung their heads toward me.

"That was a quick visit," said Rhonda. "I assume she turned down your case?"

Tony took another swig of his drink. "How is the lawyer with the legs? Getting better with age or just older?"

"I'm happy to say Ms. Richards agreed to represent me."

Rhonda grimaced. "Fine. I just hope she doesn't wear that navy pantsuit that she had on practically every time we saw her during the incident with that awful Mr. Casten."

I said, "His name is Kastner, and I'm sure she will wear whatever she deems appropriate for court, should it come to that."

Tony finished his bottle and leaned toward me as Rhonda went to get him another of my premium beers. "Tell you what, I hated that pantsuit too. Never could figure why she'd want to hide those legs."

"What the hell happened last night at the Shumakers'?" I exploded, surprising even myself. I wasn't one to casually swear or shout. But looking at Tony casually downing beers on my screened-in porch, he didn't seem at all upset by the fact that he had burned down an entire house the night before. Not to mention, I didn't appreciate his unsavory comment about Jill. "I thought you were going to use your 'particular skills' and make a stealthy entry to find their security videos. The next thing I know, the house is burning down."

"I think what you mean is the house was burning up." He must have registered my frown, because he pulled an innocent face and flung up his hands. "Hey! You're the one's always fussing over correct words."

"Fine. Burning up then. What happened and where did you go?"

When Rhonda came out of the house, I finally noticed she was wearing the sleeveless sundress she'd bought last year for our trip to the shore. A smile came to my face as I remembered that trip and saw again how great she looked in that dress.

She returned my smile with a quizzical look, set the fresh bottle before Tony, and turned to go back into the house. "It looks like you two are plotting again, so I'll leave you to it. I'm better off not knowing."

When she was gone, he leaned toward me and said, "Well, I snuck around back of the house like we'd planned, but the

Shumakers must be really paranoid. I tried to bust through the glass like I told you, but it wouldn't break."

"I should have thought of that. They might have installed laminated security glass after that group of kids were stealing things off back decks last year."

"Yeah. Whatever. Anyway, once I saw I couldn't get inside, I thought the next best thing was to keep their videos from the cops."

"You burned down their house on purpose?"

"Burned up, alright? And yes, I did that for you, and you don't sound very appreciative."

"Up or down, you intentionally set fire to their house?"

He sat back with a smug look and said, "Asked and answered, your honor. You're not the only one who watches gangster movies."

"*Law & Order* is not a gangster movie. It's a combination police procedural and legal drama."

"Fine. I'm a better person now I know that."

I took a deep breath and considered for a moment if I might benefit from hyperventilating. My mother had engaged in the practice from time to time, and it seemed to help her get through episodes of extreme stress.

For the moment, I left it with a deep breath. "Why did you burn *up* their house?"

For a man who spent a lot of time grinning, Tony gave me one of his biggest.

"I took a personality test on Facebook last year. It said I was 'results oriented.'"

"You produced results alright. After you told me to stand under the streetlight, the police know I was present at the scene that night. Now they think I'm a murderer *and* an arsonist."

He looked at his watch before he said, "Yeah, that sucks, but you'll figure out something. I have faith in you."

With that, he finished my beer and walked through my backyard to go to his house.

Rather than working through possibilities with Tony, I was left more confused than before. The confidence I had felt leaving Jill's office had dissipated. Even the thrill of minor rebellion was gone, so I walked to the front to move my car into the garage in accordance with the dictates of "good order" and the wishes of my peers.

As I opened the door to my VW, I looked over at the four-wheeled ocean liner Town Car in Tony's driveway. I could not remember the details, but I'd once seen a Myers-Briggs analysis of a psychopath. It made me wonder about Tony's personality. How far he would take his "results orientation"?

* * *

Rather than just move my car into the garage, I took a drive around the neighborhood. One thing I liked about my job—back when I could say it was my job—was the opportunity to leave the office and drive somewhere in the course of an investigation. Since I started at GFI, I was a company man all the way, but still appreciated the opportunity to get out of the office when I could. In this century, forward-thinking corporations allowed people to work at home when possible. At the other end of the spectrum, GFI's executives looked at their investments in office space and decided they needed butts in seats to justify the millions they'd poured into brick and steel. The top-level managers preferred tall buildings where their corner offices had a dramatic view of the city. Not to mention a covered parking spot with free charging for their Teslas.

The brick and steel didn't matter much to me, but I could think better in my car than I could sitting in an open office listening to forty people having simultaneous phone conversations. My coworkers didn't seem to understand the concept of an inside voice.

Besides having a contemplative car ride, there was a second benefit to a work-related road trip. GFI's mileage rate for use of a personal car meant—on top of gas and maintenance costs—I was making at least a nickel for every mile I drove on company business. A nickel might not sound like much, but over time, it added up. When I used my car to get to the site of a suspicious fire or industrial accident, I could clear fifty dollars for every thousand miles I drove. It wasn't a large amount, but it all went into the savings account for Rhonda's aspirational kitchen. She had decided to swap out the granite countertops for marble and that was going to require a lot of business travel once I got back to work.

I had just turned from Chestnut Way onto Chestnut Trace—or it might have been the other way around—when I spotted Vanessas Hershey backing out of her driveway in her pink Miata. At first, I thought there was a child in the passenger seat, but then saw it was just a large pink tennis bag. She didn't look in my direction as she reversed into the street. A quick tap on my brakes avoided a collision that would have clearly been Ms. Hershey's fault, at least according to Georgia Code 40-6-144. I embarrassed Rhonda every time I quoted an entry from the Uniform Rules of the Road, but here in my car, alone, I was free to cite what I wanted.

Watching the Miata speed away, I guessed she hit at least forty-five miles per hour before she got to the intersection. Even without posted limits, the maximum legal speed in a residential area was thirty miles per hour. I knew that was according to 40-6-181 in the same Georgia Code, but I could not recall the specific penalties. I'd have to read up on them when I had time.

When investigating insurance fraud, I had learned to look at small moral failings as an indication that someone might be capable of larger malfeasance. Someone who will lie about the origin of a minor dent might fabricate an elaborate scam to get an entirely new vehicle, financed by their GFI policy. Was it possible that someone who ignored the rules governing "Emerging from Alley, Driveway, or Building" might also ignore the law when it came to ending someone's life? Had Ms. Hershey tumbled down that slippery slope because Edith hadn't gone along with her request to upgrade the tennis courts? Were shades of Royal Blue or Forest Green worth a human life? And what on God's earth would convince someone to have their Miata painted pink? That alone might be evidence of a twisted mind.

I knew I should have ignored Edith's case and put my energies into finding out who might have a reason to kill Miss Inga. The police and FBI suspected me of killing Miss Inga, given that stupid .22 pistol of Dad's they'd found in my garage. They only had conjecture to tie me to Edith's death. The problem was, I didn't know where to turn with Inga's investigation. I'd tried to appear calm, but my insides were churning.

My uncle had spent years as a tank commander in the army. He'd told me they trained him to "make your mistakes on the move." I planned to follow his advice and get moving and make some mistakes. I had no illusions about ever being a tank commander. I just hoped taking some action would produce results and calm my stomach. Maybe, in due course, I could pin Edith's "accident" on someone. Then I might get lucky and find I could tie the same person to Miss Inga's death.

Jill had the contacts and an investigator to help me. They'd only had a couple hours to work on it but I wanted to check on their progress. Grabbing a couple of TUMS from the stash I kept in my car, I headed straight to her office to make sure they were also on the move. When I say "I headed straight" within The Estates, I mean I wandered through various cul-de-sacs every time I lost focus and failed to heed my mapping app's insistent verbal directions.

When I entered Jill's outer office, I saw her para-receptionist was again on his mobile phone. He glanced up and said, "Hang loose while I find out if she's free."

I expected him to use an intercom to buzz my attorney, because that's what happened in the old movies, but he continued to tap the screen of his phone. Eventually, without looking up from his screen, he said, "Go ahead."

Jill sat at her desk and held her phone away from her ear as if it might contain an alien parasite. Her investigator, Dix, was lounging on the office's small leather couch. Earlier in the day when I'd seen Dix, she had a shaved head and sported a leather look. This time she had flowing auburn locks and looked like she'd walked out of an Old Navy store. Two subtle gold bands had replaced the brace of metal rings.

She seemed amused, and I learned why as Jill continued her phone call.

"I am sorry you could not find another attorney willing to take your son's case, Mr. Adams."

I took a chair between them when Jill gestured with her free hand.

"I'm not surprised they recommended he take a plea—"

She made a pounding motion on her desk without actually making contact.

"I understand there's an additional charge of attempting to bribe a guard—"

She switched to pretend-pounding her forehead.

"The fact that you stopped his allowance does not change—"

She closed her eyes.

"My advice to you is to hire the cheapest attorney you can find . . . Why? Because I don't think there's a lawyer in the county who can pull your son's dumb ass out of the hole he's made for himself. And if you love your son, don't let his lawyer call you as a character witness."

She looked at me as she placed her phone on the desk.

"My apologies, Mr. Hanson. That was unprofessional."

"You don't know how many times I've wanted to say something like that to a policyholder."

Dix grinned. "I think you've been a corrupting influence on me, Ms. Richards. What would happen if I were to emulate your language while having brunch with friends at Applebee's?"

I thought a reaction was expected, so I stifled a laugh. Jill gave a small grunt and reached for two file folders.

"Thanks to a contact at the coroner's office, we got early copies of the reports on both of the deceased. Along with pictures. Would you like to see them?"

"Not unless there is something you think can help get me off the list of suspects."

Dix walked over to the desk and opened the "Skinner, E." folder. "The shots of her front aren't pretty, but they're what you expect when big holes get made in a small body. This one isn't as gross and does have some interesting details. Might be worth a look."

She pulled one picture out of the back of the folder and placed it in front of me. The label said it was a photo of "Skinner, Edith—occipital region."

Before I could ask, Dix said, "Occipital region. Back of the skull."

There were metric rulers on two sides of the image, so I could tell I was looking at a fifteen-centimeter square. Inside the square, the skin was very white and sparsely covered in wisps of gray hair. It looked as though someone had taken a pink pen and drawn two sets of parallel lines at ninety degrees to each other. The grid was perfect in the middle, but the lines warped a bit the further they got from the center.

I asked what I thought was the obvious question. "Why did they draw this grid on her head?"

"No one drew that grid," said Dix. "It looks like someone took a swing with a tennis racquet and used Miss Skinner's head as the ball."

"The coroner thinks there would have been significant bruising," said Jill, "but she lost a great deal of blood after she fell on the garden stakes. There are a few spots where the grid shows bits of blood, but if her hair wasn't so thin, they might have missed this entirely."

"What do the police think?"

"Colonel Mustard," said Dix drily. "With the candlestick, in the conservatory."

Jill gave her a quick look before she turned back to me and said, "From what I hear, they're ignoring it. They don't know what caused it, and there's no reason to think she died from a bop on the head—with a tennis racquet or with a candlestick. They're certain her death was due to the pointy objects on the ground, and they're focused on how those pointy objects got there."

"But you don't agree."

"The trick with the garden stakes is unusual in itself. I'm not prepared to rule out this pink grid as a coincidence quite yet."

Dix's smirk vanished, and she pointed to the not-quite square rectangles in the pattern. "I scanned this picture and sent it to the professor of sports medicine who also happens to be the head tennis coach at the university. He thinks it came from a custom-built racquet. A typical racquet is designed so the strings form perfect squares. The vertical spacing in this pattern is slightly larger than the horizontal, meaning the grid is made up of rectangles. His guess is whoever made this racquet used an unusual string pattern, possibly fourteen by twenty-one."

"Is that supposed to tell me something?"

"It tells you there are fourteen vertical strings and twenty-one horizontals. Not many racquets have that pattern. It's only used by players who like to put a lot of spin on the ball."

"So, you want me to find a neighbor who likes to put their own spin on things?"

Dix looked at Jill. "You're right. He is too damn literal for his own good." Then she looked back at me.

"No, we don't want you looking for a type of person. We want you to look around your neighborhood and see if any tennis players might have a racquet with this string pattern."

"I can dig out my old racquet and hang around the men's matches in the neighborhood. That will work for mixed doubles as well, but don't you think you should be the one to cover the women's games?"

Dix shook her head. "I'm willing to take reasonable risks on behalf of Jill's clients, but I'd rather walk into a redneck biker bar than sip white wine with a women's tennis team. Some of them have perfected a whole new level of bitch."

Chapter Fourteen

Although my wife literally wasn't in the same league as Vanessa, she did play tennis and might have known if someone in the neighborhood had a racquet with the unique string configuration. I drove home from my lawyer's office, wondering how I could question Rhonda without annoying her. I didn't consider her a hostile witness exactly, but lately she had seemed very touchy when I broached one of a list of wrong subjects.

Part of the problem was that I did not have any idea how many items were on that list. I had learned that I shouldn't mention anything that had to do with our household budget, jokes I found funny, or the difference between the DC and Marvel universes. As I encountered more taboos, I added them to a "topics to avoid" file on my laptop. The spreadsheet now had one 173 entries. Some covered broad topics—like a discussion about my parents or anyone from my side of the family. Others were more specific—like the difference between mean, median, and average.

I found Rhonda watching TV in the kitchen. It was an episode I hadn't seen. It took a few minutes of quiet observation to learn this new season of *Marriage: Fast & Furious* would follow the same pattern as the previous. A twenty-something ski instructor with an indeterminate European accent and possible Mediterranean heritage was discussing his desire for children with a sixty-something woman from Oklahoma. He was convinced a child would cement their love and his green card. Somehow, he'd gotten the impression a hysterectomy and twenty-plus years could be reversed.

This one wasn't part of a streaming service, and every time the show came back from a commercial break, the voiceover recapped the situation in full. I did not understand how the producers could stretch a relationship train wreck over eighteen episodes when I could see the inevitable conclusion after a few minutes.

I wisely waited until the second major commercial break and tried to greet my wife with a smile. I didn't want her to worry about my growing legal problems when I was more than capable of worrying for both of us. She had not been requesting regular updates, so I guessed she was happy with the arrangement.

"I'm curious. Do you ladies ever compare your tennis equipment?"

She looked at me as if I'd touched on something that should not be discussed in polite company. It seemed as if I'd hit another topic to add to my spreadsheet.

"What do you mean?"

"Do you ever discuss which tennis shoes work the best, or where to find the little decorated towels to dry the swea—uh, condensation from your brow?"

I'd never gone to a parochial school, but I imagine her expression would have matched a nun's when a student asked a question about puberty. I tried to distance myself from my last question in the hope she would ignore my clumsy implication that she might actually be capable of perspiring.

"While I'm thinking about it, are tennis bracelets still a thing?"

I'd given her three as gifts over the years. Each one was more expensive than the last, and none of them ever came close to an actual tennis court.

"Yes, the nice ones are still 'a thing.' However, my birthday is months away and anyway, I update my gift list every week. If you're worried about what to get me, you can look there. Or better yet, just let me buy what I want, and I'll hand it to you to wrap and surprise me with."

I nodded. That had been my practice for the last few years. I balanced the expense of her more extravagant choices against the time I saved. When she bought her own presents, I didn't have to drive all over town shopping and then retrace my steps when she asked me to return the items I'd spent hours selecting.

"That's fine," I said. "I wasn't thinking of shopping this early. I was listening to a program on NPR about some new research into the science of tennis."

She wrinkled her nose as if the very mention of NPR brought a strong scent into the room. "That's a good example of why I refuse to allow that station to play when I'm in the car. Please tell me you're not going to mention your fascinating insights to anyone we know."

I assured her I would not mention it outside the house and then listened to her lecture on why she refused to listen to news about countries she could not find on a map—which to her meant they couldn't be that important. That somehow became a launching pad into her skepticism of a news source that implied there was any truth to "climate change," since there was no such thing, and they were trying to scare us so they could raise our taxes to allow more so-called experts to live off government grants.

When she ran out of air, I jumped in.

"I'm sure the 'research' was faked on this too, but I thought all tennis racquets were the same. Turns out they can be very unique. Do you know if anyone around here plays with an atypical arrangement of strings?"

"Brad, like I tell every company's 'customer support' people from those foreign call centers, we speak English in this house. What in hell are you asking?"

"Do you know if anyone has a racquet with a fourteen-by-twenty-one string pattern?"

For the first time in this conversation, she looked me in the eye. "That's a strange question. Why do you ask?"

I wasn't sure how far I wanted to take Rhonda along on my Sherlock Holmes fantasy. She had a way of raining on my parade, and this investigation was important if I wanted to hang onto any hope of clearing my name.

"Like I said, I was listening to this NPR program, and they mentioned how rare this particular pattern was. I was curious if anyone here used it."

"I wouldn't know. I don't count strings, and it seems stupid to think I would."

She proceeded to give me a lecture on how I'd never really supported her love of the game, and that was no doubt the reason she had never been promoted from the Estate's B-level to the A-level team. I was unsure how my support or lack of support had anything to do with her weak serve and inability to play the net, but she seemed convinced. I assumed I had demonstrated my support when I purchased her latest set of racquets, which—based on the price tags—must have been constructed from rare-earth metals. I'd made a joke at the time that I guessed they were made with a combination of Beskar and Valyrian steel. She didn't laugh.

One thing that helped me in my insurance investigations and hurt me in my interpersonal relationships was my persistent search for answers, particularly when I wasn't sure of the right questions.

"Have you ever noticed what kind of racquet Vanessa Hershey plays with?"

"How would I know? She plays in the A-level league, and we're not on the courts at the same time. Is this a subtle way to rub my face in my ranking?"

Another lecture followed on the string of victories she'd had from high school, through college, and into her twenties. It was my desire to have children that had put an end to her dreams of continued dominance on the courts. That, and my refusal to move to the next county and the more exclusive Kensington Boroughs subdivision.

Rhonda longed to live in that gated community. She admired the secure brick wall that surrounded the community, though a middle school kid would have no trouble climbing over it. She liked the fact that each home sat on an acre or more. She could see herself enjoying a Long Island Iced Tea served by the staff at the country club. The beverage would be part of her celebration after yet another tennis win. She would be sure of many such victories. The Kensington Boroughs had several advantages for her. First, The Boroughs' tennis players had taken themselves out of ALTA—the

Atlanta Lawn Tennis Association—years earlier. When playing "away games," they did not appreciate the amenities supplied by lesser neighborhoods. Not to mention the snacks that were often still sitting in the Styrofoam containers with the supermarket price tags affixed. Their home games were no better. While their hospitality was beyond reproach, the ladies of The Boroughs did not appreciate the small hoard of domestic SUVs that would descend on their club. It wasn't any specific behavior, but the guest team members did not fit in with The Boroughs.

I suspected an additional motivation for Rhonda was that in the Boroughs she would be one of the few young players, where "young" meant less than sixty. She would be certain to dominate the inter-Boroughs matches. Unfortunately for her dream, there was no way my salary would ever support the purchase of one of their homes nor the lifestyle we'd be expected to adhere to. Neither of us had any wealthy relatives, so there would be no windfall inheritance, and I was not likely to win the lottery since I never purchased a ticket. As you'd expect from my occupation, I believed in statistical probabilities and not luck. Even if I had believed in luck, I wouldn't buy a lottery ticket if my past performance was any indication of future results.

Since it didn't look like Rhonda would be of any assistance in looking into the "tennis racquet as murder weapon" theory, I decided to see if talking to my Watson could get me anywhere.

There was no response when I knocked on Tony's front door. I didn't bother with the doorbell since it had stopped working months ago and Tony saw no reason to bother fixing it. I walked around the side of the house. Soon, I could hear a game in progress. I was not surprised when I found Tony on his deck, beer in hand, listening to a small speaker.

"How are the Braves doing?"

Tony turned toward me.

"How should I know, and why would I care? I'm listening to the Yankees game. They're playing the Red Sux."

"Boston?"

"Don't use that word in my house."

"Technically, I'm not *in* your house."

"Don't be such a bozo. I can see why your wife thinks you're too damn picky."

A loud cheer from the speaker and rapid babbling from the announcers saved me from hearing more about how my preference for exact language was a fault and not an asset. Tony reached over to switch off the speaker before closing an app on his smart phone. A stream of expletives followed. I waited until he slowed down and took a breath.

"Sorry for whatever just happened, but I came over to see if Watson was in."

"Who the hell is Watson?" Then the lightbulb came on. "Oh, yeah. He's here, I mean, I'm here. You got any new clues?"

"More of a potential lead that might turn into a clue."

"What does that mean?"

"There were marks on the back of Edith Skinner's head that might have come from a custom tennis racquet."

At that, Tony looked deep in thought, although I wondered how deep the depth went.

"Whose racquet?"

"I don't know, but the most likely suspect is Vanessa Hershey. She takes her racquets with her everywhere and she had that disagreement with Edith over the court renovations."

He smiled. "Want me to talk to her?"

Even though I had reason to think Vanessa might be involved in Edith's death, and that unsolved crime was one threat to my freedom, I could not consider subjecting her to whatever Tony's version of "interrogation" might involve.

After surviving the toddler years with two children, I knew it was best to encourage healthy behavior rather than focus on the bad—which wasn't really bad if one understood it from the perspective of the child. Unfortunately, with Tony it was difficult to pin down the correct meaning of "age appropriate."

In the end, I decided I would be direct. I told him in what I considered very clear language that I had no intention of letting him waterboard Vanessa. Tony looked me in the eye and got a smile like a demonic Cat in the Hat. I cut him off before he could say whatever had given him that look.

"I just want to check her racquets to see if they match a particular pattern."

He stopped looking directly at me and dropped his head as if he felt the need to examine his shoelaces. I was fairly sure it was in disappointment at the lost opportunity.

"No problem," he said as he looked up. "I'll just boost her bag and bring it to you."

"If you steal her tennis bag, any evidence would be worthless."

"You think I've never snatched a bag before today? This one's bigger but—"

"I'm sure you grabbed your share of purses as a kid and possibly as an adult. The problem isn't the size of the bag. The problem is that any evidence from her bag would get tossed out immediately. It wouldn't matter if one of her racquets was silver and gray with Edith Skinner's hair. The problem is with the chain of custody, so—"

"Custody? Who got locked up?"

To this point, Tony's attitude had been one of amusement. The word "custody" seemed to snap him into a more serious frame of mind.

"As far as I know, no one got locked up," I said. "I'd be the first to know since I'm at the head of the queue. The problem with stealing the bag is that Vanessa's lawyer would point out there was no paper trail to prove the evidence hadn't been tampered with. No 'chain of custody.'"

"Oh, yeah. That's what helped this guy—Zachary—in my old neighborhood. The cops could never prove the gun was his, even though the dummy had 'Zack' engraved on the handgrip. Lucky for him, it was a popular name back then. The neighborhood had so many guys named Zachary, the jury couldn't convict."

"And he got away with it?"

"For a while. After the trial was over, the idiot asked the cops for his gun back. They couldn't do anything cause of that jeopardy thing, but the vic's cousin knew for sure that Zack was the shooter and carried out his own sentencing."

He ended the story with a laugh. Before this, I'd always chuckled along at his ruminations about the old neighborhood and its petty hoodlums. This time, I wondered if I should take them more seriously. All of his other stories seemed to be stolen scenes from an action movie. I hadn't seen every such film, but I'd never heard of one with a twist like this.

Tony was still laughing and shaking his head as he walked away.

"Don't you worry, Sherlock. I won't mess up any chain, but I'll get you something that'll prove something."

It had been many years since I read Arthur Conan Doyle's books, but I did not recall his Watson using the specificity of "something that'll prove something." I was also pretty sure the original Watson didn't do anything that could get his Holmes arrested.

During our conversation, the iPhone in my pocket had been vibrating and nagging like a four-year-old begging for attention. I retrieved it from my pocket and saw via several glaring icons that I'd missed a stream of social media notifications, text alerts, emails, and voice calls. After years of indoctrination by the tech giants, I felt guilty I hadn't immediately responded to each notification bubble.

Out of habit, I started with the text messages, since those senders had the least patience and often the briefest attention spans. Between reminders to get my oil changed, return the overdue library books, and schedule an HVAC checkup, there were also a dozen texts from neighbors urging me to read the email from the HOA. Another dozen told me not to worry about what people were saying about me on social media. There is nothing better at prompting worry than a dozen people telling you not to worry. Though I had to admit I was at the same time excited that someone was finally saying anything about me on social media.

My posts rarely got more than a couple of likes and almost never prompted any comments. I felt that was unfair. Others seemed to generate a score of likes and comments every time they posted a picture of their farm-to-table meal or seasonal porch decor.

Every day, I saw at least one picture of a friend toasting with margaritas while on a vacation I could not afford and still hope to pay for Rhonda's new kitchen. Perhaps I needed to add more alcohol to my selfies and try to smile without looking like I had just been threatened. I'd never actually been threatened during a photo shoot, though I feared them all the same. In my childhood, I'd been admonished each year "not to ruin the family Christmas picture again."

Email was next. Earlier that morning, I had reached "Inbox Zero" as I did at the start of every day. Now, a small flood awaited. The first was from The Estates HOA, followed by over twenty copies others had forwarded to me to make sure I saw the original. The board—which I thought included me—had sent out an email to everyone in The Estates to announce a special meeting at 7:00 PM that evening in the clubhouse. I had been present when the board decided to only have "special" meetings, in addition to the required annual meeting. I had once made the mistake of titling a meeting as "ad hoc." The result was a flurry of questions inundating our email server and calls to the president wanting to know just what we were pulling with an "ad hoc" meeting and why it hadn't been scheduled in advance. My subsequent secretary reports and emails to the community took into account the fact that many of our neighbors did not own a dictionary or know how to search one on the internet.

The text of the first email announced the general topic was "recent events and the safety concerns of our community." Several members of law enforcement would be present to provide an update on their investigations and answer questions from the residents. As the secretary of the board, I should have been the one to send any email, but apparently being a person of interest would place a sour smell on even an electronic communication. The person who had sent it was obviously a rookie with our email service because they had placed the entire neighborhood distribution list in the TO field as opposed to using BCC.

The result was the email went to everyone in The Estates with something to say but without a clear understanding of the workings of "reply all." I scrolled through their responses. Everyone was eager to weigh in on the possible suspects. I was at the top of the list, followed by "unknown individual but probably an immigrant." This speculation was exceeded only by the number of people who responded with "please take me off this list" and "me too." The most surprising was the number of my neighbors that still had email addresses ending in aol.com.

I plowed through each response, but every time I got back to the happy equilibrium of Inbox Zero, another reply-all would pop in. I gave up on that front and switched to the Facebook app and the private group for The Estates. After tapping and scrolling for thirty minutes, I tired of seeing how many "liked" each post where someone claimed they had seen me in handcuffs.

I should have known better, but once I'd dipped my toes in the rest of the digital pools, I couldn't help pulling up Folks-Next-Door.com. With greater geographic coverage than our neighborhood's private Facebook group, the comments ran on for pages. The first few posts contained the basic facts as related by the local news. The comments exposed the wide chasm between a poster's politics, faith in government institutions, and understanding of "innocent until proven guilty."

The comments also revealed a huge gap in vocabulary and spelling abilities weighted heavily toward the lower end of the normal distribution. I'm generally in favor of anything that will lower taxes but was alarmed at the number of gun owners willing to "take care of it for free."

I'd never practiced doom-scrolling through the news of the day and avoided social media when it got contentious, but I kept reading through the comments, hoping I'd find someone was defending me. Or even better, proposing an alternative scenario to explain the deaths. Instead, the consensus was that I was guilty of both deaths in our neighborhood, the McMansion arson, and the missing Shumakers. Not to mention any number of unsolved cases across the region. While no one used the word "waterboarding," several alluded to the value of "enhanced interrogation."

When I finally tired of searching for a hint of compassion, I saw it was almost time for the special meeting. It was stupid to expect anything different there, but I hoped someone in the neighborhood would stand up at the meeting and defend my good name. Without the protective distance provided by the internet, perhaps my neighbors would be more compassionate and willing to give me the benefit of the doubt. While that was my hope, I thought it would be wise to seek some protection in anonymity. Since few had seen me dressed in anything but some degree of business casual, I grabbed a hat and jean jacket from my son's closet. The jacket was worn ragged, and with the hat pulled low, I thought I had a chance of lurking in the back to observe the proceedings while remaining unnoticed.

With this as my goal, I intentionally took a meandering route through the neighborhood. I probably wasn't being watched, but didn't want to take the direct route from my house in any case. I began walking at a brisk pace but slowed as I approached the clubhouse. My stomach was churning as if I'd just dined at the nearby hole-in-the-wall café that shared space with a gas station. Trendy diners praised its "authenticity" but that did not make up for its failing score from the county health inspector.

I stopped a half block from the clubhouse and pulled out my phone to use the meditation app to lead me through a few cleansing breaths. The deep breathing was helping a little when I heard heavy footsteps behind me. I didn't have the chance to turn and see who it was before someone grabbed my arm.

Chapter Fifteen

Whoever had a grip on me pulled me off the sidewalk and away from the door.

"You couldn't find anything that fit at Banana Republic?"

I turned as Dix let go of my arm, though it took a moment to recognize her. She had a different wig this time, pulled into a tight bun, and was wearing a navy business suit with heels.

"I didn't want people to recognize me," I said.

"I get it. In my line, I have to change my look to blend in." She sighed. "What you don't understand is when you're already under suspicion, you should avoid doing anything that looks suspicious. Like playing dress up and sneaking into the back of the room."

"It isn't like I'm in disguise or anything."

"You regularly wear a raggedy-ass jacket and a boy band baseball cap?"

"Sometimes."

She sighed. "Courtroom behavior is in Jill's corner, not mine, but if you're going to lie, you got to make it work. Don't look at the ground like a twelve-year-old trying to sell Mom that you don't know how the pictures landed on your laptop."

I shrugged off the jacket and bent the cap to tuck it into one sleeve, before folding the jacket to carry it.

"Better?" I asked.

"Yes. Now, I advise against you attending this meeting, but if you insist, I suggest you keep your mouth shut. You get a direct question, don't say, 'no comment.' Everyone who says that is guilty. And don't say, 'my lawyer has instructed me' or any crap like that. It also makes you sound guilty."

"What can I say?"

"Say you don't know, you got no idea, or something like that. In other words, act dumb. Based on what I've seen, that should come easy."

"You fill me with confidence."

"Not my job to fill you with confidence. I'm here to listen to what is said tonight in the hope I can learn something to help you. I doubt it'll happen, but I was already dressed like a local branch bank VP, so I figured I'd stop in. Lucky I did so I could keep you from doing too much damage."

Despite her sarcasm, I felt better knowing she was working any angle she could. While I had my years investigating insurance fraud, Watson and I were not getting very far. I had to admit her experience was probably more relevant. And I doubted she would burn down anyone's home.

As we walked back toward the entrance, I asked her if we should stand together or not.

"Most of your neighbors are as pale as you are, so stand near me and they won't pay attention to either of us," she said. "I've found that some white people aren't comfortable looking me in the eye, so they'll make an effort not to glance our way."

As we walked, I noticed she was dead on. No one was making eye contact.

Once we made it inside the clubhouse, I was astounded at the size of the crowd. I suppose it proved what powerful drugs fear and curiosity could be. All the armchairs up front were occupied by the fifty-five-plus members of the neighborhood. They had no doubt wanted comfortable seats up close and had arrived early to grab them. Behind them were rows of folding chairs pulled from the storage room. Dust covered those chairs, as the neighborhood get-togethers didn't draw the numbers they had in the past. In the first few years of the development, everyone had seemed eager to get to know their neighbors. After getting to know a few of those neighbors, the enthusiasm for meeting the rest had dropped off.

Behind the rows of seated individuals, it was standing room only. I guessed there were at least a hundred people inside the clubhouse. Through the gaps in the crowd, I could see some enterprising souls had claimed the chairs on the back porch, giving them a clear view through the open windows. Someone out there had lit up a cigar and the breeze brought the smoke and stench into the room where the ceiling fans distributed it. On the positive side, perhaps that would shorten the meeting.

The board—without me—sat behind one of the six-foot folding banquet tables in front of the gas fireplace. No one had used the fireplace after last Christmas when the social committee went overboard with decorations. They'd placed a papier-mâché Santa too close to the grate and it caught fire. The committee had to cancel the party scheduled for that night. On the positive side, word was two of the recently divorced ladies managed to get phone numbers from the single firefighters.

Marge and Herb shared the table with two new board members. The impressively named "Constitution and Bylaws of The Estates of Chestnut Lake Homeowners Association" called for regular election of board members for two-year terms and the election of two alternates. The alternates were there so that—like the Miss America runner-up—they could step in if one of the elected members was "unable to complete their duties." For beauty contests, the release of risqué pictures from one's past would mean the winner was no longer able to reign. For our HOA board, it seemed a little thing like suspicion of homicide was enough to boot me from my spot. Innocent until proven guilty was apparently not to be found in our bylaws. On the other hand, I could understand the need to replace Edith after she fell victim to a bespoke tennis racquet and improperly installed garden stakes.

Chelsea Daniels was now the secretary according to the handwritten nameplate in front of her. Tad Carroll was Edith's replacement as treasurer. They both beamed as if they'd been named homecoming king and queen. Chelsea and Tad had been the also-ran alternates for the last several elections as they continued in their attempts to add a bit of community involvement to their resumes. They had been so determined in their quest to get promoted to full membership on the board, I wondered if one or both had resorted to murder to finally attain their HOA leadership dreams. I whispered this theory to Dix, and she gave me a look I took as disapproval.

Even with Dix's lack of enthusiasm, I could not completely dismiss the "position envy" theory, but another thought came to me. I didn't know Tad's middle name, but it had to be pretty awful for him to not choose it over being a "Tad" for the rest of his life. How he survived middle school with that name was beyond me. It could be that living with that moniker had slowly turned Tad from a bullied youth to an adult serial killer. I'd had a fairly benign middle school experience with my name. It wasn't until high school that some kids discovered the cult of *The Rocky Horror Picture Show* and started saying "Dammit Janet" every time I passed in the hall. It was annoying at first but eventually gave me a plausible excuse for my retro wardrobe.

I considered raising a point of order as the meeting started. As far as I knew, there wasn't a specific clause in the bylaws that required removal of a board member just because they *might* be a murderer. It could have been in there, but you'd think that would be something that I would notice. However, over the years, the bylaws had expanded to over 100 pages, and I didn't know anyone other than me who had read the entire thing. There were entries to cover the maximum—but not minimum—length of a dog leash, prohibit visible spider webs on the front of a home other than between October 24 and November 1, and ban any Halloween costume that displayed too much cleavage. That last one had gone through several revisions prior to settling on three inches. To be fair, it applied to all genders.

Given the import of this meeting, Marge had acquired an actual gavel and used it to attempt to get everyone's attention. Her initial taps did nothing, so she raised the gavel higher. Still, the crowd didn't seem to notice. They finally silenced after the lights flickered off and on a few times. Behind me, I noticed Dix at the switches.

She leaned toward me and said, "Not my meeting, but I got plans tonight. I don't want to be late because these people want to chat. We might as well get straight to Act III."

"Act III?"

"Sorry. In college I played Reverend Joan Hale in a color- and gender-blind casting of *The Crucible*. But then every theater nerd was in *The Crucible* at some point. Act III is set in a courtroom and the stuff hits the fan. Don't be surprised if you get accused of witchcraft."

The board faced the now-silent crowd. Marge shuffled papers, looking like a substitute teacher in search of the lesson plan. Herb didn't have any papers and seemed uncertain of where to look while a thin trickle of sweat ran from under his comb-over. Chelsea had a pen ready to take notes like the good board secretary she had yearned to be for so long. Tad was also sweating, but I guessed it was not so much from nerves as from the suit and tie he chose for his first time at the big persons' table. Except for Chelsea—who looked like a mid-forty version of a pony-tailed teen—the board appeared to be a group of corporate functionaries. They could have been there to explain how their company lost money while they received bonuses.

Marge called the special meeting to order and announced that the board had called the meeting under the provision of bylaw 17.3.4b as a response to the general concerns of the community. I was fairly sure the "general concerns" had reached Marge through multiple texts and phone calls. As part of opening the meeting, she clarified that pursuant to bylaw 43.2.1a, the board would only entertain questions on this single topic. Before she could move on to more details, Cliff Cantrell in the front row raised one of his near-skeletal hands.

"We're not here to be entertained!"

Cliff's wife, Norma, pulled his arm down and yelled in his ear. "Hush up. That's not what she said."

Half the crowd seemed amused by his interruption while the rest turned to each other and asked, "What did he say?"

After the murmurs died down, Marge shared the agenda, which consisted of an update from local law enforcement, followed by a brief question and answer period.

Since the passing of Miss Inga, Mr. Price had risen to the number one status in the HOA's pain-in-the-butt rankings. He did not disappoint as he leapt to his feet and declared, "I move to amend the agenda to allow for public comments prior to the law enforcement update. The people will be heard."

His motion was followed by a smattering of applause that never quite caught on with the majority but was kept alive by a determined few. This was the vocal minority who were predisposed to go against anything proposed by Marge and the other officers. Mr. Price and his fellow true believers regularly fielded unsuccessful candidates for the board who ran on a "small government" platform. Since the HOA board comprised four individuals, no one was sure how small they expected it to go. I could pick them out of the crowd from their T-shirts that read "Defund the IRS, the HOA, and ILM."

Dix leaned over. "Industrial Light and Magic? Why don't they like George Lucas?"

"They're convinced the special effects people that made *Star Wars* are now pumping out doctored videos for fake news."

"You're kidding."

To placate Price's group, Marge called for a vote by the people in the room to decide the order of the agenda. I started to raise my hand, but Dix grabbed my arm and pulled it to my side.

"What do you think you're doing?" she whispered through clenched teeth.

"There is nothing in Robert's Rules to allow for a vote on an ad hoc agenda."

"We are here to *observe.* Calling a point of order is not the thing to do if you want to stay inconspicuous. And you do." To make sure I understood, she did not let go of my arm.

Marge tapped her gavel again, as if that made the procedure more official. "All those who wish to reorder the agenda raise your hand and keep it raised while Tad takes a count."

The new board member made a show of counting hands voting for the "motion," and then those against. He wrote down his results and passed the paper to Marge, who announced the outcome was eleven for adjusting the agenda, ninety-seven against, and six abstentions. That should have been the end of it, but Mr. Price demanded a recount and raised an objection because they had not included the people on the porch in the count. The room waited while Tad went out to the porch and returned after completing his tally. Marge read the adjusted count of eleven votes for the motion, 122 against, and the same six abstentions.

The crowd applauded the results except for Mr. Price's cohorts. Never one to recognize the insanity of his position, he requested a second recount, which Marge turned down after verifying this with her new parliamentarian. Cheryl seemed eager to please Marge and didn't bother with any justification for her ruling. Based on the same because-I-said-so reasoning, Marge rejected Price's request for signature matching and ID verifications for the voters. Faced with no recourse, he led his group in a "Stop the Steal" chant until they realized no one was paying attention other than a few who were pointing and laughing.

I whispered to Dix that the vote was not binding because they had included votes by every individual present—including every spouse or partner—when the bylaws clearly stated there should be "one vote per household." From her glance, I could tell she didn't care.

Marge then introduced her guests. Until then, I hadn't noticed Captain Dawson standing to the side along with detectives Jackson and Williams. I assumed the detectives felt totally out of their depth facing the crowd of homeowners—some of whom looked frightened by the thought of the murders, some bemused by the thought their little corner of Georgia could generate this much excitement, some angry, and some just curious. With the skill of a born politician, Captain Dawson spent ten minutes delivering an advertisement for her department, interspersed with a few passing references to the two murders, possible arson, and disappearance of a husband and wife under suspicious circumstances. She ended by reassuring everyone they had nothing to fear while under the protection of her department. The crowd burst into appreciative applause. I was surprised no one spoke up to point out Miss Inga, Edith Skinner, and the Shumakers had also been under the protection of her department.

As the applause died down, Herb handed a paper to Marge. She glanced around the room and then announced there was a member of the press present. It took me a bit of searching, but eventually I spotted the "member of the press." Fifteen feet to my left, a twenty-something was holding up his iPhone and recording the proceedings. His T-shirt displayed the logo for the true crime vlog/podcast, "Hella Yes, He Did It!" I remembered how they had to expand their title and get a new Internet address when the third season brought more diverse criminals. The correct title was now "Hella Yes, He/She/They Did It!"

While the fifty-five-plus contingent continued to look for some sign of a reporter and camera crew, a few Gen Y through Z members pointed to the podcaster. I could see the camera lens on his iPhone as its gaze swept past me, halted, and came back to rest. Many in the crowd noticed as well and shifted their attention in my direction. In that moment, it seemed everyone in the room raised their phones to capture a shot of guilty-until-proven-innocent me. Even worse, Detective Williams nudged Jackson and pointed in my direction.

That's when I blacked out. At least I was told I blacked out. I don't remember, but that's one of the problems with blacking out, isn't it?

* * *

The next thing I remembered I was opening my eyes to see a circle of faces staring down at me. A couple I recognized, while others were strangers. Most were holding a cell phone and capturing the moment. A few were kneeling to take selfies with me as backdrop and jumped away when I opened my eyes. Based on his running dialogue, I guessed the podcaster was live-streaming the event. Once edited, my collapse would no doubt be a cliffhanger to transition from one episode to the next.

"Dr. Tom" was at my side and pronounced me sufficiently recovered from a momentary anxiety attack. "Dr. Tom" insisted everyone in the neighborhood call him that although he'd received his PhD in Hospitality and Tourism Management. His dissertation had covered an analysis of the optimal number of waffle makers needed for the free breakfast buffets across the line of EconoComfort Suites. Technically, even his degree from an online university allowed him to use the honorific of "doctor," so I supposed he was within his rights. I tend to like technicalities, but it still seemed a bit of a stretch.

Feeling a little shaky, I was just trying to wrap my head around how to deal with all the amateur paparazzi when Dix pushed her way through the crowd and bent down to grab my arms and pull me to my feet. I stumbled out of the clubhouse with her support, and she directed me toward her car. It was a short drive to my house, but I was glad for the chance to slump down in the seat where no one could point a camera in my direction. When we arrived in my driveway, Dix walked with me to the front porch. While I fumbled for my keys, Dix rang the doorbell. Rhonda came to the door but refused to let us in until I had assured her it was really me and that I wasn't being held prisoner by the woman helping to steady me.

Rhonda eventually responded to my pleading and opened the door. Dix pushed me into the house and escaped into the night. I cannot say I blame her. Rhonda insisted I sit with her in the formal living room so I could tell her "what all this fuss is about." No sooner had we placed ourselves in the furniture—that had now been used four times since our son's high school graduation party—the door swung open and Tony strutted in.

Although my explanation had just started, Rhonda headed for the kitchen to get a beer for Tony. He paced in front of me. Energy was practically radiating off him.

"Brad, I've broken the case. I have the evidence we need to get the FBI and the cops off your back." He pulled out his cell phone and showed me a blurry picture of a car interior. "See? It's right there. Bam!" He whacked his thigh. "Proof she did it."

I squinted at the image, but that did nothing to help bring the shot into focus. "What am I supposed to see?"

"Wait, that's the wrong one." He turned the screen in his direction and started swiping back and forth. After a few more flicks, he stopped and rotated the screen toward me again.

The image was much sharper. I could see a tennis bag with racquets sticking out.

"I see a tennis bag with "VH" on the side. So what?"

"This is Vanessa's. Look closer. You're supposed to be the investigator."

"This doesn't do any good. The racquet head is hidden inside the bag so I can't tell what string pattern she uses."

Tony pushed the screen closer to my face. "Just look at the bag."

The bag in the picture was the same pink one I'd seen before. It looked like once again it was sitting in the passenger seat of Vanessa's Miata. The pink color was washed out by the camera's flash, but you could see her initials at the top and the trace of something that had spilled on the side.

"You snuck over and took a picture of Vanessa's tennis bag in her car. What good does that do me?"

"You're about to lose your title, Sherlock. Look at the side of the bag. When she put the murder weapon—A.K.A. her racquet—back in the bag, some blood must have dripped onto the side. In her haste to get away from the scene of the crime, she didn't see it."

I'd like to think it was the aftereffects of my blackout that made me slow to absorb Tony's story, but the bits and pieces were finally falling together. Could this be it? The proof that exonerated me?

While Tony sent the photo to my phone, I found Detective William's business card and called his cell phone. He said they were still in the area and would come right over, though

I could hear his partner growling in the background. Hearing the police were on their way prompted Tony to grab the beer from Rhonda's hand as a "roadie" and head out the door.

"Gotta go. Can't be around when the police show up," he said with a knowing look in my direction.

"Of course," I said. He'd told me several times about teenage escapades that made him allergic to police presence. I wondered if any of those adventures had involved arson.

When the detectives arrived, I tucked my elbows into my sides so the detectives would not see the dark spots in my armpits. Detective Williams listened to me and examined the photo that Tony had messaged me. Of course, I attributed it to an anonymous source.

A conversation between the detectives followed.

"I don't see why I should get excited about a fuzzy picture of a pink bag in a pink car." Jackson said with no attempt to keep me from hearing. "Do we think Barbie's the perp?"

"That's cute," said his partner. "But failing to follow an important lead in this case could be considered misconduct."

"Who's going to file that? Ken?"

I could imagine Detective Williams counting slowly to ten before his partner gave in. "Fine. If it means that much to you, we'll go over there and check it out."

"Thank you. It might be nothing but we need to follow up on it."

"Maybe. Maybe not. But I do know you're buying dinner when we're done."

Detective Jackson turned to me. "I think this is a waste of time, but you've convinced my young partner we should look into it. But I want you to come with us when we ask this nice lady if she's a killer."

That is how I got another ride in the back seat of an unmarked car. While Mulder and Scully were not my favorite members of law enforcement, I have to say they kept a much cleaner vehicle than these two detectives. It probably had to do with the federal criminals who might lean toward white-collar misdeeds, which though morally just as egregious, were less physical than those of the local delinquents. Whatever the root cause, the air freshener swinging from the rearview mirror could not keep up with the gym locker fragrance of the detective's car.

After the short trip to Vanessa's house, we walked together to her door. As before, I was sandwiched between the detectives though I had assured them I was not going to "make a break for it." I still saw myself as one of the good guys. While I knew the detectives did not yet see me as a member of their peer group, I hoped the dramatic confrontation about to unfold would give me a boost.

Chapter Sixteen

When we got within twenty feet of Vanessa's porch, a security light came on, and we could hear the whirr as a camera rotated to aim in our direction. A taped voice said, "You are being recorded." It startled me, and I looked directly at the lens—which was probably the intent of the announcement. Pointing at the camera for the detectives, I said, "GFI provides a five percent discount on your home insurance if you have a security system." Our regional manager had drummed into the staff that in her region "everyone is in sales." Most of us took her seriously, even if we weren't very good at sales. It made her happy, which was our actual goal.

Jackson laughed and Williams said, "I'm sure it generates an eighty percent drop in the incidence of ding-dong-ditch attempts."

So much for a status boost in their eyes.

Vanessa's house was typical for The Estates—a brick five-four-and-a-door. All the blinds were drawn, but the lights were on behind them, and I could hear Michael Bolton singing "I Said I Loved You but I Lied." Detective Williams rang the doorbell, and we waited. The only thing that changed in the house was that the vocal number ended and an instrumental tune started playing.

"What the hell?" said Jackson.

"Sounds like Kenny G, 'My Heart Will Go On,'" I said.

Williams leaned toward me and whispered, "He wasn't asking about *that*. And word to the wise, he really hates that song. It was a favorite of his ex."

This time, Jackson hit the button and left his finger on it in an attempt to get someone to the door. We could not hear the doorbell when the sax had the melody, but it came through when the Irish penny whistle took the lead. Eventually, the music cut off. In its place we heard what sounded like a pack of enraged Dobermans. Spotlights blinded us from their perches on the roof corners. Cutting through the barking, the speaker above the doorbell announced, "You're being recorded by my video cameras, and I'm ready to trigger the alarm for my security company if you don't leave my property immediately."

Jackson flipped out his badge wallet and held it up toward the nearest camera.

"My partner and I are here on official police business," he boomed.

I had my wallet out as well and tried to raise my GFI ID card so it was also visible to the camera when Williams put his hand on my arm and forced it down. In a slightly louder whisper, he said, "He already wants to arrest you tonight. Don't force him to shoot you first." I nodded and put my wallet away before Jackson could see it.

The spotlights shut off, and the sound system flipped from enraged dobies back to Kenny G. Jackson winced. The door opened a crack, though a security chain stopped it from letting us enter.

"Badge," demanded Vanessa, scrunching her fingers. Jackson handed it over.

I assumed she was making sure it was authentic—as if high-quality color printers and laminating systems weren't available to the general public.

She peered at us through the crack. "It looks real, but how do I know you are who you say you are?"

Jackson slid a business card through the door and told her to call the number on the card; they would confirm his identity. It might be my line of work that makes me suspicious, but if I were on the other side of that door, I would know anyone can get business cards printed in twenty-four hours at an Office Depot. It seemed Ms. Hershey was either more trusting or more ignorant than I was. And based on the impression she gave her neighbors, she wasn't that trusting.

The chain came off, and the door opened, but just wide enough for us to slip in sideways one at a time. She closed the door after we were all inside and told SIRI to stop the music. Then she stood with her arms crossed like your mother when she expects an explanation. No one spoke for a moment. She was wearing a white terrycloth robe like the ones they want you to steal from upscale hotels so they can charge your card $250 for a $32 robe. The crucial difference was this one was far from knee-length. More like a shirt with a low neckline. It seemed to have an effect on Jackson as his face turned red. Perhaps that was also the reason for his long silence.

Since I wasn't sure how long we'd be in here, I thought it was smart to take the moment to examine the room. She did not ask us to sit down, but it wouldn't have mattered, since there were no chairs and no couch in her living room. The only piece of furniture was a seven-foot Stellar Flare tanning bed. It must have been a pro model, because it was connected to a 220-volt outlet. That explained her perpetual tan and fine wrinkle lines.

Pointing to the industrial-grade tanner, she said, "You need to keep this confidential. It's not against the law, but I don't want the jealous harpies in this neighborhood talking about it."

She gave a vicious tug to the belt on her robe. Since Jackson remained speechless, Williams jumped in. "Ma'am, we're here on official business and won't share anything with the local harp—neighbors."

"That's fine. Just be sure you don't." She took a deep breath and let it out. "I know why you're here. But I want you to know it didn't happen the way the witches think."

I doubted she noticed, but I could tell Williams switched from his just-a-visit voice to official-interrogation voice. "And how did it happen?"

"I don't know. I mean, I wasn't there to see it happen, was I? But I know Oliver had nothing to do with it."

"Oliver? Who's Oliver?"

"For detectives, you obviously haven't done your prep work. Oliver is my cat."

"Cat?"

"Of course, Oliver is a cat. He'd have to be a cat, wouldn't he? How else could he have gotten that bitch Cleo pregnant?"

"Cleo is a bitch?"

"Well, not really. I mean, I know lady dogs are bitches. I don't know what lady cats are supposed to be called, but I call Cleo a bitch, along with her owner, Mrs. Abernathy."

"You think we're here because of a pregnant cat?"

"Of course. Cleo got herself knocked up—probably by some mongrel from that trailer park that shouldn't even be allowed in this county. You're the police. Can't you do something about that? We shouldn't have a trailer park this close. It's a disgrace."

Jackson finally regained the power of speech. "Ma'am, that is an issue for the zoning board and the county commissioners and not something that falls under our department."

"So, you're not really serious about 'protect and serve' when it comes right down to it?"

"You're thinking of the LAPD. Our motto is 'To strive to improve the quality of life within the city limits by reducing the measurable impact of illegal activities and continuing to make process improvements consistent with established law enforcement best practices.'" He took a breath. "It's on the side of our cars, but I can see why you might be unfamiliar with it. The print is kinda small."

I had not realized our city government took direction from outside consultants, just like GFI. It could have been the same consultants we'd used, who specialized in adding words while removing meaning.

Williams tried to regain control. "Ma'am, can we get back to why we're here?"

"I've already told you. Oliver might have gotten out one night—or at most two—but I'm sure he has higher standards than to fool around with that bit—Cleo. Now Mrs. Abernathy wants me to fund a paternity test to prove Oliver isn't the father. I didn't even know that test was even a thing with cats. Real or not, I refused to pay. That's when she said she was going to report me to the police, and that's why you're here."

I saw an opening to get into the conversation with some of my expertise.

"One of our insured was sued by a neighbor in a similar case—although the pets in question were dogs. The ruling came down in my client's favor because the female was the one who'd dug under the fence to initiate contact." I recalled the adverse publicity that followed and wished I'd kept my mouth shut.

Williams pointed at me. "I remember that story. 'Big insurance company won't pay after no one knows who screwed the pooch.' The viral videos were hilarious."

I regretted mentioning it even more as memories of all the B-word memes flooded back. I still think the negative exposure was held against me that year when I came up for my performance review.

Vanessa seemed to realize for the first time that I was in the room. "What are *you* doing here? You're not with the police."

Jackson said, "Mr. Hanson is . . . connected to this case and here with our permission."

"Is he a witness? Did he see Cleo and Oliver doing it?"

"No, ma'am, and we are not here because of your neighbor's knocked-up cat. We are investigating the suspicious circumstances around the death of Edith Skinner."

"Skinflint Skinner? I thought the old fool just took a tumble. What would I know about it?"

Jackson took the time to explain they were at her house because it was their duty to follow a lead they'd received and wanted to examine her tennis bag. She—as expected—refused, because they didn't have a warrant. He—as expected—said they would wait with her while the city prosecutor's office got a judge to issue one. She accepted the inevitable, which she could have done five minutes before if she had watched half the police procedurals I had and knew what "as expected" meant.

She pointed behind the officers to the bag, which had been sitting next to the front door during the entire discussion. Williams put on a pair of latex gloves and placed the bag atop the Stellar Flare sarcophagus. I could feel chills as we got closer to proving my innocence. The surface of the bag we could see was spotless, so I asked Williams to spin it around. As Tony's picture had captured, a trail that could be blood was running down the side.

"Detectives, I told you," I said.

Vanessa glanced at the bag and then at me. "Just what did you tell them?"

Accusing someone of murder is much simpler when they're not in the room. I froze.

Williams broke the silence. "Any discussion we have had with Mr. Hanson is privileged."

Her voice raised itself in volume and pitch. "What is this about? Why do you want my bag? I demand an explanation!"

I was glad to stay out of the conversation as the detectives alternated between trying to comfort Vanessa one minute and falling back on intimidation the next. She played her part well and volleyed back by alternating between a helpless southern belle and an angry Cersei Lannister from *Game of Thrones*. After several minutes, with neither side able to gain a commanding lead, Vanessa left the playing field to "powder her nose." As soon as she was out of the room, I had to speak up.

"Aren't you taking her in for questioning?" It was what they'd done to me, with far less evidence.

Jackson shrugged. "We'll have to see what the lab finds."

I did not want to wait while the bag sat in the police lab's queue. I wanted to walk out of that house without the cloud of suspicion that had followed me for days. "Take out her tennis racquets," I begged. "You'll see at least one of them has strings in a fourteen-by-twenty-one pattern."

Williams removed the two racquets from her bag and laid them atop the tanning bed. Like a group of toddlers practicing our numbers, our lips moved as we each counted the pink strings.

Williams pronounced the verdict. "Both of them are sixteen by eighteen."

"She obviously got rid of the murder weapon and bought new racquets," I said.

Williams pointed at the worn tape on both grips. "These look well-used."

"She could have had these spares lying around as part of the coverup. There is still the bloodstain on the bag. Aren't you going to arrest her?"

"What?" exploded Vanessa.

Darn. She'd returned to the living room during my little speech . . . and I could only assume she'd heard it all.

Shakespeare might have thought "Hell hath no fury like a woman scorned," but he'd never seen Vanessa after she was accused of murder. She let loose with a string of expletives that took several minutes to complete. Then she turned on the detectives.

"I'm good friends with Lance Weaver. I'm sure you'll recognize the name. He's the district attorney for Rhodes, and he will see you two are walking a beat tomorrow—or whatever crap job he can find."

Jackson smiled at Vanessa. He seemed to enjoy it when people threatened him. "By District Attorney Weaver, you must mean Madeline Weaver. She's been the DA for two terms since her husband was convicted of violating his oath and took a plea. He lost his law license and has been the assistant produce manager at a Kroger while he's on probation."

Vanessa made a sharp intake of breath. "I should have known that lying SOB was still married." She followed this with another string of expletives.

I sensed this whole operation was getting off course. My hope of a quick exoneration was dead in the water, but if they'd just take her in for questioning . . .

"You have to take her in," I said. "Her and the bag. It's proof!"

Jackson held up his hand to silence me. Then he walked to the bag and bent over to examine it. Unlike his partner, he was not wearing gloves, so he surprised me when he reached out with a finger and touched the dark red trickle. He sniffed his fingers.

Williams grimaced. "Oh, man. That's gross."

Jackson turned and looked at me. "How stupid do you think we are?"

Fortunately, I realized this was a rhetorical question and didn't answer him.

He placed his red-stained finger in his mouth and licked it clean. "BBQ sauce. My guess is it's from Big Mama's, but I'm sure you want the lab to do some tests to verify that."

Vanessa pulled at the belt on her mini-robe and spun toward Detective Jackson. "That is not possible." She took her model's pose—right hand on her hip with elbow jutting out.

The movement opened the robe a bit more to the point it wouldn't be permitted as a Halloween costume in The Estates.

I swear I heard Jackson emit a small moan, but beyond that he was again incapable of speech, so Williams spoke up. "Not possible? As in, 'it's not possible that it's BBQ sauce?'"

She turned to Williams, which allowed Jackson to resume breathing. "It's not possible that it would be from Big Mama's. I rarely eat BBQ—too much fat and then there's all the sugar in the sauce. But I would never, never be caught dining at a restaurant called Big Mama's. It either condones obesity or it's body-shaming the owner. Either way, it's just gross. If that's not enough, I'm sure that place is full of rednecks. Do not get me wrong. I don't have anything against disadvantaged rural people, but I cannot stand to be around them."

"How did the BBQ sauce get on your bag, then?" I said.

Jackson wiped his moistened finger on his pants. "Not relevant. There's no blood on the bag, so there's no connection to Skinner's death."

Vanessa clasped her hands. "I am so glad there is one intelligent man here."

Jackson smiled as if she'd announced she was giving him the Nobel prize, but more important, after awarding the prize, she had invited him to a private dinner in her hotel suite to celebrate.

With Jackson lost in his thoughts, I returned to the task at hand—proving someone had killed Edith and Miss Inga, and that someone was not me.

"But what about her other racquet?" I said. "The one she used to hit Edith on the back of the head."

Seeing Vanessa's expression made me think I could have been a little more diplomatic.

Thankfully, Williams remained on task and asked, "Ma'am, do you have another racquet—other than these two?"

She blinked several times. "Why would I have more than two? I'm not one of those women who have nothing in their life but tennis."

I looked at Detective Williams meaningfully, but I don't think he got my meaning. We had not gotten her to reveal the location of a third racquet, but now this obvious lie told me she was hiding something.

Jackson was still in his fantasy world. "Vanessa—may I call you Vanessa?"

"Certainly, Detective."

"Well, Vanessa, on behalf of the City, I want to apologize. I failed to stop my overeager partner and our suspect from bothering you tonight. I can assure you I will not let them go rogue again."

"And I do appreciate that, Detective," she said as she walked us all toward the door.

"Of course, the real danger is posed by the killer—or killers—stalking this fine neighborhood." He was walking backwards to keep facing her as she continued toward the exit. "Take one of my cards. It has my cell number, and you can call me anytime—day or night—and I will be here in minutes."

Vanessa's smile gave him a glimmer of hope even as she said, "You are really so kind. I feel safer just knowing you are guarding the city." Having added Jackson to the list of men who would do anything she asked, she pulled the robe's belt tight and opened the front door. Williams and I took the hint and left. We stood outside on the sidewalk and waited for Jackson. He apparently didn't realize his chances with her were equal to the likelihood of the Falcons winning the Super Bowl that year. In fact, the Falcons had a better shot than he did.

Once he joined us, he said, "Nice try, Hanson, but I'm sure you expected us to waste more than an hour on that little goose chase. Did you really think you could make us believe that lovely woman was a killer based on some spilled BBQ sauce?"

"I swear I thought she was guilty. I'm still not sure she didn't do it. Just because the substance on her bag wasn't blood doesn't make her innocent."

"You know, you could do all of us a favor if you'd just confess. You know you're guilty. We know you're guilty. Let's cut the crap and just wrap this up tonight."

"But I'm not guilty. I'm not a murderer."

Jackson opened the back door of their sedan. He put his hand on the top of my head and pushed down harder than necessary as I ducked inside.

From the front passenger seat, Williams said, "If you haven't figured it out by now, my partner is very persistent once he gets his teeth into a case. He won't stop until he gets a confession."

Jackson got behind the wheel and nodded. "It'll go easier on you if you make this easier on us. You've got no idea how much work I have to go through to fabricate evidence."

I waited for one of them to say he was just joking, but we rode in silence.

Later, as I walked up to my house, I thought about his comment on fabricating evidence. It might have been an attempt at humor, or he could have been saying the silent part out loud. I had no way of knowing. It also made me wonder if Tony had faked the BBQ/blood drip. Assuming he had, was it an attempt to help me by getting the police to look at a different suspect or something else? I needed someone to talk to. Someone to help me straighten out all the twisted threads. I hadn't wanted to burden Rhonda with my troubles, but I couldn't talk to Tony about Tony. I decided it was time to tell Rhonda everything. By this point in the evening, she would have had at least one glass of wine, which should have improved her mood.

The downstairs was dark, but I could hear the TV was on in our bedroom. As I climbed the stairs, it sounded like yet another couples-in-conflict reality cable show. I could hear a husband complaining to his wife about the many ways her mother was interfering in their marriage. As he finished, he said, "I don't chew my cabbage twice."

Her lyrical response was "Oh my God. Like what're you tryna say?"

"Y'all know. I'd like'ta toll you once already."

"Like whatever."

I guessed he was from Appalachia, while his wife sounded SoCal.

I coughed to let Rhonda know I was home, but she waved her right hand to shush me. There was a half-full wineglass in her left hand. After a few minutes, the show cut to commercial and I saw the title was *Valley Girls Meet Mountain Boys.* When I had time, I planned to work out the permutations available to the Disclosure-Plus network. Given the number of stereotypes and clichés available, they could no doubt pump out identical variations for centuries.

I knew this network averaged four-minute commercial breaks interspersed with five minutes of what they loosely called content, so if I was going to give her an update on my troubles, I had to make my point quickly. I told her how the trip to Vanessa's didn't work out, and I thought the police might soon figure they had enough circumstantial evidence to make a case.

"Circumstantial?" she asked. "They don't have any actual evidence against you?"

"No. Nothing concrete. They just have their suspicions about how Edith died."

"What about Miss Oskarsdotter?"

"They seem to have even less to go on there."

"Then I guess we can't let them see what I found rattling around in the dryer after I washed your clothes today."

She walked over to the dresser, picked up a plastic sandwich bag, and handed it to me. I had completely forgotten the pair of .22 shell casings I'd carried in my pants pocket.

Chapter Seventeen

Given the growing number of people looking for evidence that I was guilty, it occurred to me I should have kept better track of those specific shell casings.

I took the bag and put it in my pocket. "I can explain."

"I don't want you to explain. I don't want to know—"

"Rhonda, you have nothing to worry about. There's a thing called 'spousal privilege.'"

"You think I'm 'privileged?' What does that even mean? That I haven't worked hard to be a good wife? That I did nothing to deserve it and was somehow handed this home because I'm your spouse and have some made-up privilege?"

"No. That's not it at all. Spousal privilege just means a wife cannot be compelled to give testimony against her husband."

She took a moment to think about the implications. "So, even in court, they can't make me tell what I know?"

"That's what it means."

"But what if I want to? I mean, they can't stop me, can they? Don't I have rights?"

Rhonda had never been good at telling jokes, and this was an example. I appreciated her trying to lighten my mood with a little humor, but it wasn't working. I thanked her for the attempted distraction and told her I really needed to talk to her because the police still seemed intent on pinning one or both deaths on me. As I was trying to say I thought there was a real possibility I'd be arrested soon, the off-screen announcer was back, describing the situation facing another couple—Scooter and Dakota. I wasn't sure which one was the Valley Girl, and which one was the Mountain Boy, but couldn't seem to bring myself to care enough to stick around.

It did matter to Rhonda, however, who turned back to the screen and waved a hand to dismiss me. Not wanting to wait for my next four-minute opening, I reconsidered heading over to talk to Tony. The problem with that plan was that our recent interactions seemed to just get me into deeper trouble. Not to mention, I felt I lost a few IQ points each time.

I considered reaching out to my kids. If I recalled correctly, Luke had declared criminal justice as one of his majors in his first or second year of college. But, despite her somewhat unclear reasons, Rhonda was still insistent that I keep them uninvolved. For now, it seemed more important to keep her satisfied than to lean on them for support.

After wandering the house for several minutes, I grabbed my iPad and sat on the couch with no goal in mind other than to find some mindless distraction. I should have known better, but I returned to Folks-Next-Door. There were the usual inconsequential posts asking for recommendations for a good pest exterminator, inexpensive dentist, or a tattoo shop that sterilized their instruments at least once a month. Those I ignored since I had already found the first two and had no interest in the third. I skimmed over the lost dog pictures and reflected on the fact people rarely posted about a lost cat. I knew if Rhonda ever decided to get a cat and it went missing some day, I'd keep quiet about it.

What I needed for a diversion was the good stuff, which in Folks-Next-Door territory meant the posts that were so over the top that they would provide a chuckle and reassure me that I was one of the few sane people left in the world. I longed to confirm that no matter what stupid decisions I might have made in life, there were others that made me look like a cross between the humanity of Mother Teresa and the business savvy of Warren Buffett.

To get my mind off my troubles, I needed to dip my toe in the fetid swamp water of other people's largely self-inflicted tribulations. Still, I did not want to wade in too far. There was a possibility I'd get caught in a riptide and dragged under. I'd seen it happen to others. Such as my brother-in-law—the one on my wife's side of the family. Like me, he started with lurking—watching silently in the shadows, leaving no trace of his visits. But then, the temptation got too strong. He made one brief comment on the inconsiderate people that make left turns from the right lane. That elicited thirty-two follow-on comments split between "it's my right as an American" and "why can't we all just get along?" Ignoring the "don't feed the trolls" warnings, he'd tried to explain what he meant without granting a full apology. The result was another fifty-seven replies before the moderators deleted the whole thing after two antagonists agreed to meet at dawn with pistols to settle things in a duel.

That "conversation" would have been restarted, but everyone involved got distracted by the warning about the white or beige van that was slowly cruising the streets when it wasn't parked on a cul-de-sac and might have had blacked-out windows but was definitely being driven by a scrawny white dude or perhaps a thickset twenty-to-forty something who was probably an illegal immigrant. My brother-in-law had posted on that thread after he saw that exact vehicle, except it was a black sedan. From then on, he was hooked on the combination of positive affirmations and hostile rebuttals. He fell down the slippery slope and, last I heard, he was posting multiple times a day. His particular areas of expertise covered people speeding through his neighborhood and a human trafficking ring stalking the local supermarket parking lot. Though the two topics were unrelated as far as I could tell. Extended family dinners were never the same, and even his annual Christmas letter contained multiple phrases IN ALL CAPS!!!

My goal that night was to observe Folks-Next-Door from a safe distance and tell myself again how fortunate I was to not be one of "them." The FBI and local cops might have me in their sights for two homicides, but at least I wasn't using my real name to post threats against the local school board. The Germans have a word for it and—like many of their words—schadenfreude is long and hard to pronounce. That particular night, I was not experiencing my usual pleasure at the misfortune of others. I did chuckle and then worry about the invitations for like-minded folks to meet in a private chatroom—an echo chamber that was free of any need for facts, logic, or spell checking. When the third entry stating "If they come to my door, they'll get a greeting from my 9mm" failed to spark joy, it was time to try something else.

I grabbed a pen and a legal pad before returning to sit at the kitchen table. My first manager had regularly shared his mantra of "Plan the work and then work the plan" without ever explaining how to do either one. But over the years, I had developed my own method based on his motivational-poster-inspired message. The general outline I'd been using for the present situation included step one—binge-watch *Law & Order* in all its various forms and step two—find the "real killer" aka "not me." The first I'd accomplished, but I had no measurable results for the second. It was time I put more effort into step three—talk to my lawyer.

The clock said it was almost eleven, which was too late to call. But my current boss had demonstrated over and over that it was never too late to send a text message. If you didn't get an immediate response, your late night or early morning text would put your request at the top of the recipient's queue when they did start their workday.

I typed a text message to Jill's number. *Hi Ms. Richards. The police did not find anything linking Vanessa Hershey to Edith Skinner's death. What should I do now? Brad Hanson*

Since I didn't expect an immediate reply, my iPhone was almost back in my pocket when it vibrated.

Dix is the investigator. I'm the lawyer. You're the client. Stay in your lane.

The message was direct, but not harsh. Still, I was embarrassed that she'd felt it necessary to correct me. While I continued to stare at the screen, the phone vibrated again, but this time with an incoming voice call from Jill. After the usual greetings, she got down to business.

"I'm not trying to insult you, and while I appreciate your enthusiasm, Dix is the one who should pursue leads on your behalf. There is no room here for amateurs."

"You might not remember, but my job for years has been to investigate possible criminal activity."

"Oh, I remember what you do for a living. The last I checked, your job doesn't involve dealing with homicides." She was using the same voice she used with Mr. Adams. It was time to backtrack a bit and apologize.

"I'll do better, Ms. Richards" I promised, trying to sound appropriately humble—which is not a great stretch for me even on a bad day.

"I'm glad you understand, Mr. Hanson. It really is best if you let us do the work you hired us to do."

With the message delivered, she asked if I could meet in her office at 9 AM so she and Dix could get more details about my visit to Vanessa Hershey's. It had been unauthorized, but they might as well glean what they could from it.

"Listen," she said, "I've got to go, but since we'll be working together for some time, you should just call me by my first name. With your permission, I'll do that same."

"That's fine," I said.

"Good. We'll speak tomorrow, then, Brad," she said, and disconnected.

I felt the blood rush to my cheeks, followed by an involuntary grin at this development in our relationship. I remembered the same feeling when the freshman homeroom seating chart placed me next to the cutest girl in school. Both situations meant nothing to the women involved but triggered something in my amygdala, nonetheless.

The smile fell from my face as Rhonda entered the room. She didn't like it when I smiled without her knowing why. I realized I was still holding the phone to my cheek, even though Jill had already hung up. Before lowering the phone, I said, "Thank you. I look forward to our discussion tomorrow."

Rhonda did not comment. After refilling her wineglass, she went back upstairs with time to spare before her next show started. I marveled at how I'd gone from giddy schoolboy one minute to guilt-ridden husband the next and there was no logical rationale for either emotion.

* * *

The following morning, I arrived at Jill's office and found her receptionist swiping on his phone while snacking on a light green slab of something approximating a pastry along with a bag of dark green chips. To the side, what looked like miniature body parts floated in a jar of clear liquid.

"I didn't know they still sold Pop Tarts. Loved them when I was a kid."

He glared at me. "If I say 'OK, boomer,' will you think I'm being rude?"

It surprised me how perceptive he was. I did think he was being rude. "Actually, based on my age, I am considered part of Generation X depending on which arbitrary demographic boundaries you choose." I was not fond of distinctions with no practical use other than on click-bait headlines.

He ignored my correction. "It's my usual breakfast—a healthy breakfast pastry, Swiss chard and kale chips, washed down with high antioxidant, fruit-infused water. You should try some. You'll live longer."

He turned a brown bag so I could see the "Avocado Poppe Tarte" label which I thought was clever but due for replacement soon. Surely there were lawyers in a conference room somewhere racking up billable hours as they prepared a lawsuit for trademark infringement.

I took a single chard/kale chip and bit down, expecting a crunch. Instead, it was like biting into a slightly soggy kitchen dishrag after it'd been used to clean out the forgotten vegetables at the bottom of the fridge drawer. My mother never let me spit out my food, so I swallowed just to get it away from my taste buds. If this is what it took to live longer, I questioned the return on the effort.

He went back to staring at his screen and swiping.

The door to Jill's office opened. She waved me in with one hand while holding her iPhone with the other. She had a Bluetooth earbud in one ear so I could only hear her half of the conversation but it was clear she was dealing with the same father trying to see to it that his idiot son did not face any consequences for being an idiot. I was just guessing, but it was a reasonable assumption the condition was hereditary.

"Mr. Adams, I don't care what you read on the internet. There is no legal basis for claiming your son is a 'sovereign citizen' and therefore not subject to the government's laws."

She closed the door and stepped behind her desk as I took a chair in front of it.

"I'm sure the YouTube video was impressive, but the court here in Rhodes is not a 'maritime admiralty courtroom' and the court actually does have jurisdiction over your son's case."

She closed her eyes and pursed her lips as the voice on the other end of the call rambled on.

"My advice? You and your son should beg the judge for forgiveness for wasting her time and hope she shows you the mercy you don't deserve."

She tapped her screen to end the call and then continued to poke at it. "Do you know how to block a caller on this thing?"

"Scroll down and you should see 'Block this caller' in red."

She pushed so hard on the screen that I could see her finger tremble with the exertion. "What is it about your visits here that coincides with his calls? If he gets through this block at your next visit, I might have to drop you as a client."

She was smiling, but the threat of losing her help prompted me to stumble through an apology—though I wasn't sure what the apology needed to cover. That behind us, she had me tell her everything I had done since I was last in her office, including who I was with and every conversation. Her smile faded as I ran through what happened at the special HOA meeting and my visit to confront Vanessa Hershey with the detectives. To me, it seemed her growing frown was not just aimed in the general direction of my case, but at me personally. I was determined to give her a better impression. Perhaps if she could understand my reasoning, she wouldn't need to frown so hard.

"I just want this to be over. When I saw the picture of Ms. Hershey's tennis bag, I got the detectives involved. I knew I shouldn't confront a suspect—and a potential killer—by myself."

She tilted her head and stared at me. "Yah think?" Dealing with Mr. Adams must have flipped on her sarcasm setting. "I know this doesn't match what you learned on Career Day in kindergarten, but the police are not your friends. At least, not when you're the prime suspect in a murder or two."

The rebuke and reference placed me squarely back in my childhood. I couldn't look her in the eye. Looking at the ground would have been too timid, so I looked at the front of her desk as a compromise.

"I realize the detectives are not my friends. Their goal is to solve the crime."

She sighed. "That would be nice if it was true. No, they're measured on clearing cases. They only need to come up with a halfway believable story they can sell to the DA. That moves the file off the pile on their desks and onto the pile at the DA's office. The DA will try to get rid of it with a plea bargain. If they can't work that out, they'll try to convince a jury you're guilty."

I nodded. This fit in with what I'd seen in countless legal dramas

She continued. "The prosecuting attorney is going to tell one story built around motive, means, and opportunity where you're clearly guilty. My job is to tell a different story where you might not be guilty."

"Might not?" I said. That didn't sound as strong as I'd hoped.

"It's the DA's job to prove you guilty beyond a reasonable doubt. I only need to give the jury an excuse to hold some doubt." I knew all that of course, but under pressure we all tend to forget some things.

"The prosecution will tell the jury you had the means—your father's gun that had recently been fired as well as the readily available garden stakes. Then there's your motive—both women had been a thorn in your side. And we can't forget the opportunity—both houses were a short walk in the dark of night. Unfortunately for you, a wife who sleeps with the help of a mask and white wine would not provide a solid alibi."

"But you have a way to prove my innocence?"

She shook her head. "I wish I did. I was hoping you could tell me the police had made some mistakes along the way. Something we could use to create that doubt for the jury."

I could only shrug. "Everything they did seemed proper to me. I was there when the agents found my father's gun, and I could tell someone had recently fired it."

She held up a hand to stop me. "You said the *agents* found your father's gun. Don't you mean the *detectives* found it?"

I explained my first visitors from law enforcement and my first "interview" was with the FBI. The local police came later.

"Why the FBI? A simple homicide doesn't fall under their jurisdiction, so what do they have to do with Miss Oskarsdotter's murder? Are you sure you didn't get confused under the pressure of that morning?"

"Stewart and Maloney weren't the aggressive types. It wasn't really until my second interview with the local police that some of the discussion was hostile. The FBI were professional by comparison."

"I still don't understand. Why would the FBI get involved?"

She waited for an answer. It was difficult to concentrate when my head was full of the "thinking music" from *Jeopardy!* I ran through the events of that morning when it came to me as the music conveniently ended.

"The police captain wanted to know that as well. Scully—or maybe it was Mulder—said it had to do with a criminal enterprise, or it might have been organized crime."

"They're saying there's organized crime in The Estates?"

"They didn't exactly say that. I thought they were just making up a reason for them to be involved. Does it matter?"

"I'm not positive, but it is out of the ordinary. We need to understand why they were there and if their involvement can point us to some other explanation for one or both murders."

She began making notes on her ever-present legal pad. I guess lawyers have to use them. As I watched her write, it came to me. I slapped the desk; Jill jumped.

"I've got it. The connection is the Shumakers. They could be the ones with a link to organized crime. They'd been informers and the criminals were getting close to finding them. The hitmen just had the wrong address so, they killed Miss Oskarsdotter and then Edith as they narrowed in on their real targets. The Shumakers haven't just disappeared. They've been transferred to a new location for their protection."

Jill gave me a smile, but I couldn't tell if it was meant to be reassuring or just patronizing. I opted for the former.

She outlined an action plan for the next couple of days. She would contact the FBI to learn why they had interviewed me on that first morning. While she was following the official angle, she'd have Dix try to work some of her contacts to see what they could learn. My role was to go home and write down anything else I recalled about my early encounters with the FBI and police. Jill also made the point that I should stay home once I got there, but it sounded to me like a suggestion and not an order.

As I left her office, I searched my pockets for a breath mint, stick of gum, or anything to take the chard/kale taste out of my mouth. The search halted when my fingers wrapped around the two shell casings in the plastic bag. For the hundredth time, I had to ask myself, what kind of idiot kept these in his pocket?

Chapter Eighteen

Once I got home, I didn't spend any additional effort considering what kind of idiot would continue to carry the shell casings. I had a pretty good idea who fit the profile.

Instead of belaboring that, I followed my lawyer's advice and wrote down everything I could remember about the first few days of Brad's Not-So-Excellent Adventure. I had to use a lined 8.5 by 11-inch pad, since I didn't have any legal-sized paper. I figured Jill could have it transcribed later if the format mattered to her.

As for what I remembered, it wasn't much. My visit to the FBI office was a bit fuzzy, and there was that small—and hopefully insignificant—gap when Rhonda's ersatz Xanax put me under. I couldn't blame her, since I was the one who took them all at once. On the positive side, she'd done me a favor, and I slept better for those few hours than I had since.

I followed those paragraphs with a summary of my conversations with the city of Rhodes detectives. Then there was my attempt to recover surveillance footage from the Shumakers' house, but I didn't want to put that in writing. It had not been my proudest moment in what had become a series of nonproud moments. I had to consider the chance these notes would somehow fall into the hands of law enforcement. Some might consider this paranoid, but decided I'd only make a verbal report on those events inside my lawyer's office.

Finally, I documented the failed attempt to prove Vanessa Hershey had been the one to take out Edith. I hoped it would be useful to Jill, because the whole exercise was making me depressed as I recalled my series of missteps and failures.

After filling three sparse pages, I hit writer's block and couldn't think of anything to add. If this had been a school assignment, I would have rewritten it with wider margins and larger printing to make it stretch to four or more pages, but I guessed Jill would have seen through that ploy. Not to mention, my life was on the line here. I needed to keep that in mind while doing this particular bit of homework according to GFI best practices. When it comes to documentation, quantity beats quality every time.

In college, my classmates seemed able to easily write volumes when I could only fill a portion of one of the standard blue exam books. My history professor told me I "wrote like a mathematician." I think he meant it as a slight, but I took it as a compliment. His opinion trumped mine, however. On the final, I got a D along with a handwritten question, "You do understand these are called *essay* questions for a reason?"

In those days, I wasn't good at adding superfluous text just to burnish a narrative—though I've picked up some skills in my years at GFI. Working for an insurance company had taught me there are times when burying key points under mountains of detail is called for. When you don't want to lie—but also don't want to highlight certain facts—obfuscation can be your friend. You could watch any Sunday morning political talk show for a short course in this skill set.

To fulfill Jill's request, I hoped the parts I left in my written document would be enough to help her produce a miracle. I could not count on Georgia prisons having walls that would fall to a Shawshank rock hammer, and I doubted the warden would value a convict skilled in fraud detection.

I kept at it until early evening when my homework was interrupted as the doorbell rang. I checked the porch camera, but something was blocking the view. I opened the door, and Dix was standing there with her finger pressed to the lens of the camera. She was wearing a light blue skirt and white blouse. I identified her look as falling under suburban casual, which I'd learned is the same as business casual but with brighter colors and no briefcase.

Removing her finger from the door cam, she said, "I don't enjoy being on the other end of surveillance," and walked past me into the house.

I followed her in just as Rhonda and Prince came from the kitchen and into the living room. For the first time in my memory, Prince did not bark at a visitor.

"Brad, you're being rude. Introduce me to our guest."

Rhonda apparently didn't recall briefly seeing Dix when she delivered me home after the neighborhood meeting. Before I could speak, Dix stepped forward and held out a hand to my wife.

"You must be Rhonda. I'm so pleased to finally meet you. I'm Cassandra Dixon. I work with Ms. Richards, and I'm here to help your husband prepare some materials for his defense."

Rhonda and Dix/Cassandra gave each other a brief hug that displayed a warm openness without actually requiring any but the slightest physical contact.

"Brad, honey, be a dear and get some sweet tea for Ms. Dixon."

"Please, call me Cassandra."

"Only if you'll call me Rhonda."

I stood there looking on in amazement at another demonstration of Dix's chameleon capabilities. She seemed able to change her appearance and behavior to fit into whatever environment she encountered. It was more than the costume change. She altered her carriage, her accent, her facial expressions, and language. I wondered if she was actually more than one person. Perhaps I was seeing identical twins who'd been raised in different environments. Then I remembered that theater degree.

I returned with two glasses of iced tea and sat to wait until either Dix or Rhonda tired of their conversation so I could get to the task at hand with Dix's assistance. I had no intention of hiding anything from Rhonda, but I'd already tried to explain the details of my current dilemma. She'd made it clear she wasn't that interested.

I was glad when their conversation wrapped up five minutes after the tea delivery, but then it took another five minutes for the back and forth of so-nice-to-finally-meet-you, this-has-been-lovely, we'll-have-to-have-lunch-real-soon, and I-am-so-looking-forward-to-it. Rhonda got in the last word with, "I'll leave you two to work on more important matters."

When she had left the room, I said, "Well done. You almost had me believing you were sincere."

"Well, *Brad, honey*, let's be clear. It doesn't matter what you believe. Only what those who can help or harm you believe. We'll start with the FBI. The issue before us is in three parts. What do they believe about you and what can they prove?"

"You said three parts."

"You can count. That's a useful skill to have. Can you listen as well? The third question is the big one. Why do they care? A murder—even two—should not be on their radar unless, for some reason, it somehow fell under their jurisdiction. For example, did Miss Oskarsdotter rob banks?"

Dix went through a list of other federal crimes Miss Oskarsdotter might have been implicated in, including Medicare fraud, counterfeiting, and hijacking an airplane. When she'd run out of specific examples, I shrugged.

"I really don't know," I said. "But most sound unlikely."

"Do you know *any* reason the feds would be interested in Miss Oskarsdotter?"

"She was mean as a snake, but I don't think that's enough, is it?"

"If that was all it took, half my ex's family would be under investigation."

Dix paused. Somehow, I had the impression she knew more than she was saying. Or perhaps she thought I knew more than I was saying.

She let the silence last for what seemed a long time. "Think. Do you know anything unusual about Miss Oskarsdotter—other than her weird-ass name?"

I don't know why I felt a need to come to the defense of the deceased, but I had to correct Dix on this. "Her last name is a normal construct for a Scandinavian surname. It means 'daughter of Oskar.'"

"Thank you for telling me what I learned from my inquiries yesterday." She pulled an iPad out of her bag and flipped it around to show me a full-face photo of Miss Inga. "Now I don't want to fall into racial stereotypes, but does this look like your idea of a typical Swede?"

I assumed Dix had enlarged the picture from Miss Inga's driver's license or other ID. She was staring straight into the camera lens and attempting a smile but hadn't managed to get both sides of her mouth to cooperate. Her raven hair was pulled back as always, though it seemed there were a few more strands of gray than she usually allowed. Her eyes stood out on either side of a prominent nose. Under heavy eyebrows, the whites of her eyes—with streaks of red—stood in contrast to the surrounding olive skin creased with dark lines.

"Now that you mention it, no, but I doubt all Swedes are blonde."

"No, they're not, and you get ten points for demonstrating cultural sensitivity and lose fifty points for missing the obvious. Did you ever examine Miss Oskarsdotter's face?"

"Not closely. I mean, it was tough to make eye contact with her when she was wound up at an HOA meeting. It's the same with bears. You never want to look them in the eye because it makes them think you're being aggressive, and that's when they attack."

She flipped the tablet back to her and made an adjustment before swinging it back in my direction. She had zoomed out so I could now see the orange jumpsuit covering Inga's shoulders and a small nameplate centered at the bottom of the frame. It had some digits but no name.

I asked the logical question. "This is Miss Inga?"

"Was Miss Inga," she said. "To you and the other residents here in the valley of happy chestnuts. To people in the Garden State, she was known as Angelica Del Luca."

I took a stab at a translation. "They called her 'Angel of the Devil?'"

"Nice try, but no. Angelica does mean angel, but from what I can find, 'Del Luca' just means 'of Luca' and Luca is either the title of a Disney movie or refers to a town in central Italy. I'm betting on the town. Either way, it seems your neighbor had something in her past that attracted the attention of the FBI. Something she wanted to hide."

I slapped the table and leaned back. "Of course. Angelica Del Luca. That explains it."

"Explains what? You know who murdered her?"

"No. It explains her killer fettuccine alfredo."

I'd gotten a little loud and glanced to see if Rhonda would come into the room to check on us.

Dix turned to see what I was looking at before asking, "You think Angelica or Miss Inga or whoever she is. . . . You think she poisoned someone with a pasta dish?"

It was my turn to treat Dix like the amateur. "No. I just thought it strange that this little old Scandinavian woman was so good at making Italian dishes. Now I get it, and I sure could go for one of her cannoli right now."

I stood and paced the room, waving my hands as I explained all the strange things about Miss Inga that now made sense. It wasn't just that I'd never heard her even attempt to say "y'all." The Estates were full of people that weren't "from around here." When I'd first met Miss Inga, I assumed she'd moved down from Minnesota or Wisconsin or another state where ice fishing was a thing. I'd expected her to offer up an occasional "dontcha know" or "you betcha." Instead, she would say she liked to *tawk* with the other ladies while enjoying a cup of *cawfee*.

As more anomalies came to mind, I continued pacing and waving. It was not normal for me to communicate with the help of my hands, and it occurred to me I might be unconsciously channeling Miss Inga/Angelica. Then I realized it could not be unconscious if I was thinking about it while it happened. My next thought was that channeling a dead person was creepy.

As I continued to circle the room, Dix stopped me by standing in my path and snapping her fingers inches from my face. "Calm down and sit down. You marching around and flailing your arms is not helping."

Dix might have been in suburban casual attire, but she exuded as much authority as she had the first time I met her. I sat.

"Now that we're both back on earth, can you focus?" she asked. "People don't move a thousand miles and change their name for no reason."

I pulled out my phone and did a quick check. "Actually, it was probably seven hundred and forty miles if she flew and another hundred and sixteen if she drove. Both estimates are based on a one-way trip from Newark to Atlanta."

Dix didn't respond, and it seemed the room got colder. I looked up, and she stared at me as if asking herself what she was going to do with me—or more likely, to me.

"What difference does that make?"

The need for precision in an investigation was clear to me. I couldn't understand how anyone with Dix's experience would not know that. Still, I didn't want to rub her nose in her amateur status compared to my years with GFI.

"If we knew how far she traveled, and by what means, we could tell which part of the Northeast she lived in before relocating to the Atlanta area." I wondered how much more mentoring Dix would require.

"Or we could look at the arrest record that accompanied the mug shot."

I nodded. "Sure. That would be another way."

Every time I imagined I had some level of expertise or skills greater than Dix's, she came up with something to prove me wrong. I changed the topic before I spent any more time feeling inadequate. "Where did you get the arrest records?"

"It's better if you don't know. That way, my contact is safe, even if the police beat a confession out of you." She drained the last of her sweet tea and smacked her lips. I wasn't sure if it was in appreciation of the beverage or in anticipation of the police roughing me up. "Let's just say that in my business, it helps to have friends. I scratch their back and they give me a nice massage when I need one." With that, she stretched and rolled her shoulders.

"Fine. I don't need to know the source, but what else do you know and why grill me if you already had all the answers?"

She chuckled. "I needed to know what you knew. Well, not really 'needed,' but I was curious how far your investigation skills had taken you."

"I've shared everything I know," I said as I focused on the floor. I wasn't in need of her pity, but if loading in a bit of guilt helped, I was willing to use it.

And it worked.

"I apologize, Brad. It's my turn to share a few things. It seems in Miss Oskarsotter's previous life as Angelica Del Luca, she was a bookkeeper for a small construction management firm in the northeast. At least the company was small in terms of employees—there were three—but a bit larger in terms of revenue—over ninety million in the previous calendar year."

"Whoa. What kind of construction did they manage?"

"None. They got their revenue from providing 'project management and related services' to other companies that did the actual construction work. Apparently, the feds had reason to suspect something illegal was going on but could never prove it. They prompted the state to audit the firm's books. Their fees were exorbitant, but—on the surface—not illegal. The FBI caught a break when they looked at Angelica's personal financial situation. She'd faithfully filed her 1040 and paid taxes on a sixty-two-thousand-dollar salary and five-hundred-dollar Christmas bonus. The problem arose when her local parish dutifully reported her half million dollars in charitable donations." Dix grinned. "As they say, no good deed goes unpunished."

"So, it's like Al Capone," I said. "They got her on tax evasion."

"Yeah, but she wasn't the actual target. The feds wanted to get something on her for leverage so they could build a case against her boss, Robert Cunningham, also known as Robbie."

"Robbie? I thought criminals had intimidating nicknames."

"It turned out Robbie wasn't an old school criminal. Along with his Gen Z posse, he started bringing in a steady revenue stream by stealing and scamming NFTs and crypto currency before hiding his profits inside more traditional income streams like construction management."

Dix explained that Miss Inga had been a good friend of Mr. Cunningham's maternal grandmother and, as I was aware, made a heck of a good cannoli. Robbie had hired her to keep track of the flow of the digital and real currency that flowed through his operation while he was busy managing a small army of hackers and scammers.

All was well until Miss Inga's donations came to the government's attention. She hadn't attended services in decades, until in her late sixties, and hedged her bets with the Almighty. She'd gathered more money than she could spend in the years left to her, and perhaps she figured a few dollars in the collection plate might add a little grease to things once she reached the pearly gates.

"There's one thing I don't understand," said. "I don't remember the exact date she moved in, but I'm sure Miss Inga brought her fettuccine alfredo to at least two Italian Nights. That means she had to have moved into The Estates more than a year ago. How long does it take the FBI to build a case against this Cunningham once they had her?"

"It turns out crypto scammers are not that fastidious when it comes to recordkeeping, and neither was Angelica. A court of law requires more precision, so the U.S. Marshals kept an eye on Miss Inga here while she worked through the records to make an ironclad case for the FBI."

"U.S. Marshals now too?"

"You wouldn't have noticed them, but they handle witness protection for the FBI."

I slapped the top of the coffee table, causing the empty sweet tea glass to rattle. "Now that you mention it, neighbors did talk about the number of nephews and nieces that were regularly visiting Miss Inga. She seemed to have a lot of them and they were all young, well-dressed, athletic types."

"You have nosy neighbors," Dix said drily.

"They're not *that* nosy. I mean, wouldn't you be curious if one of your elderly neighbors had a score or more nieces and nephews visiting off and on?" Dix shook her head before I finished. "And while most were white, a number were Black or Asian."

"Well, they could come from mixed race families or be adopted."

"Normal people might assume that, but that explanation didn't slow down the people posting on Folks-Next-Door.com."

I was glad I didn't need to go into more detail because the doorbell rang. Before the sound had faded, I heard Rhonda shut Prince in the guest room. To give her time to present herself, I walked slowly to the door and opened it to find one of our neighbors. Becky lived a street away on Chestnut Circle. Or Chestnut Chase. Though, upon further thought, perhaps it was Chestnut Court.

After the formal introductions, Becky, Rhonda, and Dix went through a reprise of the so-nice-to-meet-you chorus as I waited patiently for the next verse to find out what brought Becky running to our house. I hadn't seen her running, of course, but she hadn't fully caught her breath since walking in, and her face was flush and slightly damp. I assumed she'd been caught by a lawn sprinkler. As with my wife, I couldn't imagine one of her friends actually perspiring.

After Rhonda brought a fresh round of sweet tea, Becky got to the news that had brought her to our door. "I can't believe it could happen again in this wonderful neighborhood." She turned to Dix. "I call it a wonderful neighborhood, but we're more like a family here. Even if some people who don't know better are saying the most terrible things about Brad, this really is the perfect place to live and raise kids. Do y'all have any children, Cassandra?"

Dix replied that she had not been blessed with children, which sent Becky into a protracted apology for her question followed by an implication Cassandra's biological clock was ticking. It was at that point that I jumped in before Becky experienced the conclusion of the ticking clock I could see in Dix's eyes.

"I don't mean to be rude, but you have us wondering. What has happened?"

"Well, y'all know how everyone has been worried about the Shumakers since their car was found abandoned, and no one has seen them in days now? Well, this afternoon that nice new couple over on Chestnut Heights—the ones with the baby who I am sure will not look like that forever and will without a doubt be cute in a few years, bless his little heart—they were taking a walk with that poor child in a stroller when they passed by the community garden and there they were."

She paused as if her story had come to its conclusion. I had to prompt her to continue.

"There who were?"

"Why, the Shumakers."

"The Shumakers were at the community garden?"

"Well, not 'at' so much as they were 'in' the community garden. The husband pushing the stroller didn't see it until his wife pointed to the stockinged foot sticking up out of the dirt. It wasn't until the police and fire people arrived that anyone could see that it was the Shumakers."

Chapter Nineteen

"They're sure it was the Shumakers?" I asked.

"Brianna said she was pretty sure it was them. It was hard to tell with their faces being all purple and all. Robert Clark—you know, he's got that job with the police as a foreign-sick-whatever. Anyway, he was out walking his dog and went right up to see what was going on when they dug 'em up. He told Brianna the bodies had been frozen before they were buried. They had plastic bags over their heads, and he said they must have been asphyxiated and that explained the purple faces. I had to explain to Brianna that asphyxiated meant they'd suffocated because she didn't know, which didn't surprise me at all."

I hadn't noticed her take a breath until this point before she continued.

"I waited on the jogging path but Jordan Franklin—you remember her, she was on the tennis team with us for half the season until she left just because Lisa mentioned once she knew a terrific place where they use a laser to remove the little moustache some women have. Lisa was jus' trying to be helpful, but there are always people who don't want to accept a bit of kindness. Anyway, Jordan walked over to get a better look and to flirt with one of the officers like she does. She said the plastic bag made an absolute mess of Meredith Shumaker's hair but at least the killer was good enough to freeze her body. Otherwise, Robert said it would have been all bloated and covered in blisters by now. So that's a small mercy."

"You didn't see it?"

Her bangs moved as Becky fanned herself with one hand. "Oh, I simply couldn't. The thought of seeing two dead bodies was too much for me to handle."

"You poor dear," Rhonda said. "I have some sweet tea prepared, if you'd like some."

Becky looked at our glasses and then toward the kitchen. "Y'all are so kind to offer, but I don't think I should have any caffeine right now. I'll have enough trouble getting to sleep tonight with my nerves all frazzled." She turned her arm and looked at her bare wrist. "Well, it *is* after five. I certainly don't want to be a bother, but I don't suppose you already have something open?"

"I'm afraid we're out of wine right now, but I'm sure we could find something in the cupboard. What would help settle your nerves?"

"Well, my mama always said I was an old-fashioned girl, and I could see my way to a taste of an Old-Fashioned right now."

Rhonda grabbed Becky's hand and led her toward the kitchen. "I know we have some bourbon, but I don't think we have any bitters or cherries."

"Oh, don't worry. All we Southern girls need is bourbon and ice. I've always thought that other stuff was just mixed in so some Yankee bartender could charge more." Once they were in the kitchen, we could hear her continue. "I don't want to be a bother. If you're out of ice, I can make do without it."

Cassandra looked at me after the other two were out of the room. "Do all of your neighbors 'get the vapors' like that?"

"More than I'd like to admit. Though in Becky's case, I think it makes a convenient excuse to ask for something stronger than iced tea."

"Yeah. I caught that."

With Becky and Rhonda busy in the kitchen, I suggested to Dix that we go over to the community garden and see what we could learn. It seemed like a good idea to me but not an adventure where I was comfortable going by myself. She hesitated, but relented when I reminded her it wasn't every day one had a chance to watch the police remove two frozen bodies from the ground. It might be a good addition to her investigator's resume.

With her changed appearance from the HOA meeting, I didn't think anyone would recognize Dix, but I didn't want someone to identify me at the scene of yet another crime. So I ran upstairs to my son's room and grabbed another of his caps and the Harry Potter glasses he'd worn long ago on Halloween.

Dix looked up as I came back to the living room. "You are a master of disguise. A cap and a pair of glasses, and you think people won't recognize you?"

"Glasses were enough for Superman."

She shook her head. "The more I'm around you, the more I'm convinced you're innocent."

She hadn't meant it as a compliment, but I chose to take it as one.

Once we were out the door, Dix asked, "So, where's this community garden?

"It's a small flat area on one side of the lake."

"You mean that large puddle?"

"That's unfair. It might not be on the scale of a real lake, but it at least ranks as a pond."

I wasn't sure why I felt I needed to defend the lake's title. If I'd had my way, we would have filled it in just to lower the cost of the HOA's liability insurance. I'd suggested that at one point, but Edith pointed out how expensive it would be to change the name of the neighborhood on every physical sign and legal document. If that weren't enough, Herb reminded me the county took a dim view of anyone messing with what they considered a "natural wetland."

As we walked, I explained to Dix that only a handful of ducks and geese bother to visit our little "lake" while large flocks routinely fly past us to the neighborhoods nearby, where no doubt the water is better—or at least bigger. Still, the county had declared our lake to be part of a wetland area and would not allow us to change a thing. If a tree fell, we had to leave it to lie there and decompose in God's own time. As far as anyone could tell, there was nothing worth protecting in our little patch of nature. Nothing that could be considered an endangered species unless it was a strain of algae with a particularly unpleasant smell.

Though she hadn't asked for that level of detail, Dix listened quietly as we walked. We had to backtrack once when I mistook Chestnut Prairie Road for Chestnut Plains Drive. That experience provided an opportunity for Dix to take her turn and expound on the malevolent individual who'd named our streets. That took up the rest of our walk.

We finally came around the last corner. The police had cordoned off an area surrounding the small garden and brought in two mobile spotlights to illuminate it. Off to the right, twenty or thirty individuals stood in a group with cell phones raised like they were livestreaming a rock concert. I guessed they were showing their followers what they were missing by not being there. Personally, I'd never seen the attraction in standing in the middle of a crowd while staring at a 6.5-inch screen held high over my head. Then again, that might have been one reason I only had twenty-six followers on social media.

Dix and I took a spot further away on the left. With the bright lights pointed toward the garden and the crowd, we were in relative darkness.

"Your neighborhood isn't exactly in the middle of a food desert, so why do you have a community garden?"

"A few people thought it would be a good idea to start one so we could provide food for some of the less fortunate in our county."

"Nice thought, but how many people can you feed from a garden that looks to be about twelve feet square?"

"It was much larger in the beginning. Fifty people signed up on the work schedule and the HOA paid for a company to bring in a Bobcat to scoop the red clay out of a quarter acre and backfill with good soil. A local nursery provided all the seed and supplies for the first season. It was quite a spectacle. The volunteers wore matching T-shirts and a TV camera crew filmed the first planting."

"And then?"

"Most of the boomers found all that bending and kneeling was not good for their artificial joints. The Gen X and Y folks realized they had no time on the weekends after golf, tennis, and their kid's soccer games."

"You left out Gen Z. I suppose they found it was hard work?"

"No. They were the most honest and never signed up in the first place. That left us with one retired couple still on their original knees and hips who manage to take care of the little bit that's left."

We stood there in silence, and I realized the frogs were not croaking their usual nightly performance. The moment seemed to call for something, so I took off my cap and placed it over my heart. "First the garden died, and now it's turned into a cemetery."

From behind me, a voice growled, "I don't suppose you'd like to tell me how that happened?"

My first reaction was to turn to Dix. The current situation and threatening tone in the voice seemed to call for active measures, which was not on the list of my GFI roles and responsibilities. I hoped Dix had some experience there. Unfortunately, she must have wandered off and was no longer to my left. She apparently didn't know the real reason I wanted her there was to be my backup in case some strange person accosted me. Like I feared was happening at that moment. I started to turn to see who was behind me, but the person growled,

"Don't move, if you know what's good for you."

I froze in place.

His impression of Batman talking to the Joker—vocalizing with the back of his throat and sounding like he had a mouth full of gravel—definitely gave the whole situation what my kids would call a "bad vibe." I imagined the growl, though effective at disguising his voice, had to be wreaking havoc on his vocal chords.

To be honest, at this point, I didn't want to turn around. I was not sure if I was a hostage or something else to him. All I knew was that once you see the face of your captor, they have to kill you. They can't leave you as a witness. It's in the kidnapper's code or something. Either way, I didn't want to give him any excuse to get rid of me permanently to make sure I wouldn't talk.

That's when he pressed something into my back. With no experience in having a gun shoved against my vertebrae, I was just guessing at the source of the pressure, but my imagination filled in the gaps. Probably a .44 Magnum based on the impression it made even as I tried to curve my spine to get away from it.

The voice asked, "Ware *mumble mumble*?"

When I hesitated, the gun—which I swear had grown in size since the last time he'd pushed it into my back—probed further into my spinal cord. I had no option but to guess at the meaning of his question, so I gave him my best answer to "Where are we?"

"Nah, dummy. Wire *mumble* hair?" As he grew more frustrated, a few words came through the rumble. Thinking he meant to ask, "Why are you here?" I decided to give him an abbreviated answer, while leaving out any reference to Dix in case she was still in the area and might yet come to my rescue.

"Just seeing what the commotion is all about."

"Wadda-u tell cops?" he said. At least it sounded something like that. Since he explicitly mentioned cops and not agents—I started with my first interrogation in the Rhodes police offices.

"The day after the murders, I went to the police station, but it was nothing like you see in the movies. I was looking for 1950s Steelcase desks, typewriters for writing up reports, rotary phones, and full ashtrays. It took me a while to get past the sign-in kiosk, but then they took me to a small room—"

"Stop babbling," was followed by another sharp poke.

"Ouch. I know this is kind of stream-of-consciousness, but I'm nervous and not used to being taken hostage. Unless you count the FBI and police as hostage-takers, which they could be considered, and—ouch."

From there, I tried to compress my narrative down to just the important bits, but the gun jammed in my back made it difficult to concentrate. My assailant must have realized the jabbing was just slowing things down so he backed off a bit as I provided as much detail as I could remember. The entire time I searched for any sign of Dix.

I assumed, like me, my assailant had a reason to remain unobserved by the crowd around the makeshift graveyard. Up to that point, we'd both kept our "conversation" at a low level, but he seemed to grow impatient after I was a few more minutes into my narration. His weapon slipped off my spine and jammed into my right kidney. I let out an involuntary scream—which is the only kind of scream I ever let out—and the faces in the mobile lights all turned to look in our direction.

When a few plainclothes officers left the group and headed toward us, my inquisitor shoved me. I crashed forward, hitting my knees. I heard him clearly say, "Oh, fudge" as he ran away. Well, if he had the vocabulary of Marge, the HOA president, he would have said "Oh, fudge."

I know poets and my sister's friends on social media are fond of nature, but I doubt they've experienced falling on top of a bunch of broken tree limbs and having their nose buried in a four-inch layer of compost. The trees looked lovely from a distance, but beneath them they left sharp sticks and rotting vegetation. I'd read that healthy compost wasn't supposed to smell bad. If that were true, then I had found myself in a really unhealthy batch. Or perhaps it was just a result of dog walkers who thought they did not need to pick up their pets' deposits when they left them in nature.

I got to my hands and knees, which limited the areas where I had bits poking into me. My back and kidney still hurt from my ordeal at the point of a gun, and my throat tightened as my allergies reacted to the countless varieties of mold and fungi that covered my face and clothes.

I'd lost track of the time but was convinced my day could not get any worse when, through my reddening and watering eyes, I saw detectives Jackson and Williams walk up. Detective Jackson looked down at me and asked, "Are we on field maneuvers with the neighborhood watch program?"

I leaned on a small tree and got to my feet as bits of organic debris fell to the ground around me. Both detectives had disposable gloves on from their work in the garden. Standing in front of me, they pulled out disposable face masks and put them on. Apparently, I smelled worse than the two corpses they'd just examined.

Williams shook his head. "This is too hardcore for a neighborhood watch group. Maybe he's trying out for a prepper militia."

"Or are we overlooking the obvious? Is this just a case of a criminal returning to the scene of a crime? I've seen it before, but never understood why they do that."

"Maybe they want to see if the police are discovering anything that could point to them," Detective Williams said. "I also read somewhere that if the killer is a narcissist, it could be they're proud of their handiwork and can't resist the urge to view it again."

"Which is it, Mr. Hanson? Are you here to see what we might discover on those two bodies, or are you getting off on watching your handiwork come out of the ground?"

I tried to keep from trembling as adrenaline washed through my system. Where was this chemical boost when I needed it a few minutes ago? I decided a shaky voice might add some authenticity to my story.

"As usual, detectives, you've got it wrong. I came here tonight to see what was happening with all the lights and vehicles. It's not something we see in The Estates on a regular basis." A tremor passed through me. It was involuntary but positioned me for the next part. "I was standing here—keeping out of the way—when someone came up and stuck a gun in my ribs. Well, he stuck it in my back really, and I don't know what he would have done if you hadn't walked over and scared him away."

Williams brought out a notepad and pen. "And this man with a gun is what made you scream?"

"I couldn't help it. He jammed his gun into my back. And I think he might have injured my kidney." I rubbed the spot to reinforce the message.

Williams took notes while Jackson continued to smirk. "When you start pissing blood, let us know. That might make this fairy tale believable."

Williams looked up. "What did this man look like? I know the light isn't good here, but can you tell us his height, weight, skin color, clothing?"

Jackson took his turn. "Maybe he was covered in leaves too? Or did he go all-out with camo?"

"He came up behind me in the dark. I didn't know he was there until the gun was in my back, and he told me not to turn around."

Jackson nodded. "Convenient for both of you."

Williams looked at his partner. "You might not believe us, but if you were attacked tonight, we want to find the guy who did it." He flipped a page in his notebook. "You said he spoke to you. Did he say anything that might help us identify him? Any accent or unique vocabulary?"

I didn't want to hesitate, but I had to consider how to answer his question. I could say there was nothing unique about his speech, which wouldn't help them catch him. Or, I could tell them I'd been at the mercy of Batman, and they wouldn't bother trying to catch him.

They already believed I was a killer and who knows what else. I decided to take a risk that fully ignored what the actuarial tables might have to say on the topic.

"You know, in the movie, *The Dark Knight*, where Batman interrogates the Joker in the police station? Well, this guy tonight talked just like the Batman did in that scene. A deep voice. More of a growl than anything. And he had a gun in my back the whole time."

Neither detective spoke for a moment until Williams said, "I don't believe a thing you just said, but I gotta give you props for picking my favorite scene."

Chapter Twenty

I walked home from my latest unproductive and humiliating encounter with the police. It had become a routine. Each visit caused me stress, and I got nothing positive out of the meetings. At least the detectives were getting paid for the time they spent harassing me. My only solace was they still didn't have enough evidence to arrest me, or I certainly would have been in jail. But I'd been noticing that sentences that begin with "my only solace" don't really deliver on the promised comfort.

In the back of my mind, I had to consider that the police were just toying with me. They might have left me on the loose so they could watch what I did, hoping to gather additional evidence against me. Did I mention I was feeling paranoid? And stressed. Could anyone blame me?

From the detectives' reaction at the community garden, I knew I smelled bad. When I walked into the house, Rhonda confirmed that and told me to take a shower while she would handle my clothes. I dumped the contents of my pockets on the kitchen counter and panicked for a moment when I didn't see the .22 casings I'd been carrying around. Then I recalled

Rhonda had placed them in a plastic bag, and they were safe—though not secure—in my dresser drawer upstairs.

Rhonda handed me a towel and sent me to the back porch to undress. I lowered the shades to protect my modesty, but more importantly, to keep from having pictures of me show up on Folks-Next-Door. As I removed each item of clothing, she placed them in a plastic garbage bag. At her request I did not remove my underwear. I think she would have applied a hazmat sticker to the bag if we'd had any available.

After my shower, I put on a set of sweats and took a beer out to the backyard. My wife was already outside, standing next to the firepit, which was putting out a great deal more smoke than usual. As I got closer, I could see the reason. She had fed my filthy clothing to the flames.

Though it was perfectly obvious, I yelled, "What are you doing?" as I slapped my beer on a side table and ran to the storage shed to grab the fire extinguisher.

"Calm down," she said. "You don't think I was going to put those rags in my new washer?"

I stopped halfway to the shed and looked back. Dousing the fire would be a waste of time. The wad of clothing was beyond recovery.

"Isn't that the function of a washer?" I shouted. "To wash dirty clothes?"

"Don't be ridiculous. You're always thinking of extremes. Of course, a washing machine is to wash dirty clothes, but only clothes with an acceptable level of dirt . . . or light food stains."

I didn't know what to say or at least couldn't think of anything that she would not see as mansplaining. It had become her favorite word since one of the daytime talk shows had made it the topic of a weeklong series. She closed the door between the kitchen and the back porch and returned to whatever she was watching.

I returned to the fire pit to watch my clothing take its final earthly form. Rhonda had insisted we get a firepit after Carlos and Jenny Mendez had one installed two years ago. The first time she knew Carlos and Jenny were out of town, Rhonda took a tape measure and found theirs was thirty-six inches across. The following week, we had a forty-eight inch firepit installed. It was placed much too close to the house, but she hadn't asked my opinion.

Since then, whenever the topic came up, I would ask her if she knew how many housefires each year resulted from an improperly installed firepit. She had no response and would change the subject, which was lucky for me since I did not know either. I'd searched for the information but GFI did not even track that specific cause but lumped it under "other" and below my dad's favorite threat—oily rags. As far as I could tell, no one had kept oily rags in their garage since the mid-'60s, but that did nothing to diminish the real threat of our too-close firepit.

Over the years, Rhonda and I had let most of our family traditions drift away but retained this argument as it filled a shared need. She was proven correct each year when our house hadn't burned down, and I was proven correct every time I learned of a house anywhere in the world that was consumed in a firepit tragedy. To this point, the number was three, but it demonstrated that it *was* possible. I hadn't told Rhonda this because I was almost positive that such incidents were underreported.

After the ordeals of the day and my brief abduction, I decided to throw caution to the wind and let go of my obligation to water down the premises. Instead, I sat and closed my eyes to relax to the sound of a crackling fire and the gentle scratching of mice in the woodpile. At least I hoped it was mice. Not that I favored the disease-laden vermin, but I didn't want to consider what other pest might make the noise. Any four-legged creature bigger than a mouse would be a problem. I'd heard of neighbors discovering snakes in their wood piles, but snakes would be silent. From that point, the thought of snakes hiding a few feet from where I sat was more of a concern than the scratching.

I tried not to think of what might be lurking in the woodpile and, instead, attempted to wrestle my focus back to the investigation. For example, what if the police had planted a listening device in the woodpile? If it was shorting out, that could explain the scratching sound. I realized—not for the first time—my brain was hardwired to constantly worry about something. There were days I worried about what it meant that I had this innate need to worry.

However, I did not get up to investigate the woodpile, for the time being. Even if there was a listening device, the most interesting thing it would be picking up was the sound of my breathing. And there was always the possibility of something alive in there.

The light on my closed eyelids flickered. To minimize the sparks thrown off the fire, I kept a minimal amount of wood in the pit. As it was consumed, it gradually threw less light on the backyard. A silence descended. It was too quiet. That's always a sign that something is about to happen. Even the mice had stopped doing whatever it was they had been doing. Maybe the snakes had eaten them. I worried about what other causes might be behind the sudden lack of noise when I heard a low growl from behind me.

"You wanted me? Here I am."

Another man might have been afraid at this point. But I'm not another man, and the interruption distracted me from my fear of snakes in the woodpile. Plus, I recognized Tony's voice and realized it was the same voice that had said, "Oh, fudge" as he ran off when the detectives approached. Tony had disguised his voice by impersonating the Caped Crusader, but I finally saw through, or should I say I heard through, his deception.

"You son of a B," I said. There weren't many situations that called for me to quit self-editing.

Tony must have stopped at his house before coming over because he carried a half-full beer bottle of the local grocer's store-brand. He sat down next to me and put his feet up on the edge of the firepit. That put the soles of his sneakers close to the flames—in total disregard of their melting point—which he probably didn't even know. And after what Tony had pulled, I wasn't about to tell him.

"I had you going pretty good," said Tony, "until your cop buddies showed up and spoiled my fun."

"You think it's fun to put a gun in my back and scare the you-know-what out of me?"

"Calm down, Sherlock. I was just playing with you. Anyway, I didn't have a gun. I know any amateur dirtbag can carry in this state, but I'm not going to get caught packing unless I gotta good reason." He downed the rest of his beer for emphasis.

"It sure felt like a gun."

I didn't mean to time it that way, but he spit out some beer and then laughed, snorted, and coughed. The beer and saliva sizzled where the drops fell on bits of hot stone. "Don't do that, dummy. I haven't had beer come out my nose since I was twelve." He coughed into his sleeve a few more times. "It was a freakin' stick." He followed that with more snorts and laughs. "But don't worry." He wiped his nose on his sleeve and paused to get the timing right before he said, "It wasn't loaded."

"Then why'd you panic and run off if it was just a stick? There is nothing illegal in imitating a person with a gun. Unless it was in the commission of another crime like attempted robbery—"

"Enough. I didn't panic. Barney Fife and his partner don't scare me, but I've told you before. I don't like cops. You never can tell what they're going to plant on you."

"But planting evidence would be illegal."

He ignored my comment. "Anyway, what'd they want to know?"

"They wanted to know if I'd buried the Shumakers' bodies in the garden. I assured them I hadn't and besides, I'm not stupid enough to bury bodies in a couple of inches of loose dirt."

"I'm not saying it was the best place to hide stiffs, but maybe the guy was in a hurry. You ever tried to dig something the size of a grave in this damn red Georgia clay? The garden at least had real black dirt you can break up with a shovel."

"Whoever did it should have disposed of the bodies up in the North Georgia foothills where nobody would've ever found them, or if they had found them, no one would have cared. They would assume it was the result of a justifiable homicide.'"

He nodded. "Maybe you got a point. The killer got lazy and took a shortcut. Even Tommy DeVito got careless when he had a body in the trunk of his car."

"Who is Tommy DeVito? You mean Danny DeVito?"

That drew another snort-laugh. "Tommy DeVito was the guy Joe Pesci played in *Goodfellas*. First time I saw that movie as a kid, I wanted to be just like him, except Pesci's too short. So, I decided I'd be like Jimmy—the Robert De Niro dude. He was better looking too, but in the movie, Jimmy is half Irish, so that didn't work."

I asked the obvious question. "What about the guy Ray Liotta played?"

Tony shook his head and replied through clenched teeth. "He was part Mick too. Worse'n that, he was a rat." He stood up, walked into my house, and returned with the last of the craft beers I'd been saving. I thought it would be safe hidden behind Rhonda's kale and avocados. Healthy foods were like kryptonite to Tony, but he'd somehow gotten past them.

When he sat down, he was silent for a moment. One might almost say he was pensive, but that would give him credit for a depth of thought I was not prepared to accept.

"You don't know how rough it was for me as a kid," he said with an intense look at the fire.

I didn't know what to say. I was honestly surprised. Not to mention, the conversation was getting uncomfortably close to the topic of his feelings, and I had not consumed enough beer for that. I was not sure there was enough beer for that.

We both sat staring at the fire, which I guess—in the end—is what a firepit is for. They're not big enough to change the ambient temperature in an unenclosed space, and there's no grill for cooking anything. I once thought we could make s'mores at the firepit. After it was first installed, I'd suggested it to Rhonda. She said s'mores were nothing but carbs and sugar and went back to sipping her glass of rosé.

A minute passed before Tony spoke again. "I didn't have a positive male role model until *The Sopranos* came on TV."

It was my turn to have beer come out my nose.

My reaction had been involuntary, but as I wiped my nose on my sleeve, I realized it hadn't been the most supportive thing I could have done in response to Tony's sharing. Without a good idea how to recover—and not really wanting to return to talk of his childhood—I tried to redirect the conversation to address the immediate problem of solving the string of murders.

"With the Shumakers dead and no actual evidence against Vanessa Hershey, I'm out of suspects. I had almost convinced myself the Shumakers committed the first two murders."

Tony sighed. "You could still be right. The Shumakers might've offed Edith and Angelica and then someone else had a reason to murder them."

I tilted my head. Something nagged at me. "What did you say?"

"Like people say here in the South, maybe they just needed killin'." He followed this with a laugh at his own joke as he walked away.

I continued to sit and stare at the dwindling fire. While "they just needed killin'" might have been a sufficient explanation in some mythical corner of the state, I doubted it would work with detectives Jackson and Williams, not to mention their FBI counterparts. It also irked me that, as a Yankee transplant, Tony was so eager to poke fun at Georgia and the South. After all, no one had forced him to give up the joys of long winters, high taxes, and cars that turn to a pile of rust before the loan was paid off.

To be fair, I've told a few redneck jokes in my day, and I'm a Yankee by birth. But it's a different thing when an unrepentant outsider like Tony makes fun of the South. In the same way it's OK for my wife to complain about her family, but I've got no right to say anything bad about them. Even if I'm just repeating what she said about her sister hiding wine bottles behind the corn flakes. That's why I've never told Tony that New Jersey is only called "the Garden state" because of the glow-in-the-dark flowers that flourish over the toxic waste dumps.

Of course, according to the locals, I was no true Southerner either, even though my family moved to Georgia when I was a toddler. When it came to eligibility as a True Southerner, being born north of the Mason-Dixon line was considered a congenital disorder.

I would always fall into the category of "not from around here." That was something I needed to consider if the time came to choose a jury.

I'd never investigated a murder before, but it didn't take a genius to realize I'd been flailing around over the last few days. I had made no actual progress other than to convince the cops that, if I were the murderer, I was more of a bumbling fool than a cold-blooded assassin.

It was time to make better use of the tools I knew best. After quenching the fire, stirring the ashes, and dousing the remains again, I went inside and downstairs to my war room. Before settling in to work, I went back upstairs and outside two more times to make sure the fire was out by pouring more water into the firepit and stirring the ashes. There was a time when I was concerned about my need to check, recheck, and triple check some things. I'd since come to accept it as a part of me. And there were benefits. The extra trips up and down the stairs helped to keep me in shape. Turning a compulsion into a positive attribute was another of my skills.

Satisfied at last that I had not missed any live embers, I returned to the basement and jotted down a few notes from the firepit conversation. For the next half hour, I stared at my whiteboard, waiting for some magic to happen. I had not made many additions since I first set it up, but now I had to move the pictures of the Shumakers from the line of suspects and make room for them on the top line of victims. I'd just finished redrawing all the lines when it occurred to me that while they were now victims, that didn't mean the Shumakers could not still be suspects in the first two killings. As my imagination ran wild, I had to sit down.

What if Edith dispatched Miss Inga, but was then, in turn, attacked by Mr. Shumaker? Then his wife might have killed him in some kind of social-media inspired murder-suicide pact. Though it would have been tough for the one committing suicide to tie a plastic bag around their own neck and then bury themselves in the community garden. So, the Shumakers must have worked together to kill Edith, and then they could have been murdered by another killer who might or might not be on my list of suspects. I attacked the whiteboard until I had dozens of new color-coded lines with arrows indicating who might have killed whom. It was so much simpler on TV where there were only two suspects and you knew the actor you actually recognized was always the one who did it. I had to figure out who were the bit players in The Estates and who was on the "also starring" list.

When I completed reworking the connections, I returned to staring at the whiteboard—now labelled version 2.1. While I'd put a lot of effort into collecting and organizing the contents, something was missing. The whiteboard wasn't to the point where I could dramatically circle a picture five times with red marker before slapping it and saying, "There's the murderer."

I needed help. Tony was good for an occasional useful observation, but his contributions had not been of the highest caliber so far. I had to face facts. I'd be better off if I went Watsonless. I was my own Watson from this point forward. I was sure my notes would be more useful and my handwriting was better.

As for Rhonda, she had not seemed interested in helping me work through the details that morning. While I would have preferred to wrap up the case myself, it was time to visit Jill and Dix for their assistance.

For a moment, I considered taking the whiteboard off the wall so I could transport it to Jill's law office, but that seemed excessive, even for me. In the end, I used my iPhone to capture a picture of the entire board, closeup shots of each suspect and/or victim, and the various lists. It was the sort of thing a Watson would do in this century.

As I glanced through the images, it occurred to me that what I needed was to get this information into a spreadsheet. I might not have Tony's "particular skills" but I could use *my* skills without setting a house on fire. As any good hammer-owner would do, I molded the images into nails. The obvious next step was to assign numerical values to everything on the whiteboard.

I used a ten-point scale for the trust I placed in each piece of information. If I thought a note was completely untrustworthy—-e.g., "they just needed killin'"—I would give it a 0. Any verifiable facts—e.g., "Miss Inga was shot from behind with a .22"—would get a 10.

Next, I added an "annoyance factor" connecting each suspect to the victims that annoyed them. When averaged along the rows, I could see that—with seven—Edith annoyed more individuals, while Miss Inga only annoyed three. However, the people annoyed by Miss Inga tended to be really annoyed at an average of 9.00 compared to those annoyed by Edith at 4.14. After another hour spent refining the model, it told me exactly nothing. I found no comfort in the fact it told me nothing with two digits of precision.

"What are you doing down here?" boomed a voice.

I jumped like a twelve-year-old caught watching a late-night offering on Cinemax. Not that I'd ever experienced that. I'd been so absorbed in reviewing my spreadsheet, I hadn't heard the footsteps coming down the stairs.

I turned and saw Rhonda standing on the bottom step with her hands on her hips. It was the power pose she'd started using after reading *Fifty Things You Can Do to Piss Off the Patriarchy*. By virtue of a Y chromosome, I knew I was a member of the patriarchy, but I didn't feel like one since I was never invited to the meetings.

"I'm trying to work through what I know so I can get the detectives off my back."

She pursed her lips and walked over to examine the whiteboard. "And you think this mishmash is going to help you do that?"

"If I organize everything, I might see something the police are missing."

While it was always cooler in the basement than in the rest of the house, Rhonda used her hands to rub her arms like it was the middle of winter.

"Did I ever tell you that at times you remind me of Prince?"

I'd never seen myself as a corgi, so I shook my head.

"The way he'll chase after his tail for hours." She turned and climbed the stairs. "I don't like any of this. I wish it was over so I could get back to my life."

I nodded. "Me too, honey. Me too."

Chapter Twenty-One

The following morning, I texted Jill to ask if I could drive to her office to discuss my case. A few minutes later, I received a message from her assistant that I had an appointment set for 10 AM, and to be prompt because she had another appointment at 11 am. Thinking of Jill's office, I realized I hadn't seen Dix since she disappeared at the community garden. I wanted to follow up with some variation of a "Where's Dix?" text, but didn't like any of them. In the end, I decided to wait and find out when I got to Jill's office.

That gave me time for three essential functions before the visit—reviewing the spreadsheet three or four more times, checking once to make sure the firepit was still dormant, and picking out the right clothes. On any normal day, it didn't take any time at all to decide on my wardrobe. I had six business casual shirts and rotated through them based on an app that ensured I wouldn't wear a specific shirt-pants combination for another six days. The attendees at the Monday morning staff meeting would not see combo #1 for another six weeks. Just as the Wednesday quality task force would not see combo #3 repeated until week seven. Steve Jobs might have had the luxury of always wearing a black mock turtleneck, but didn't have the genius—or arrogance—to justify that.

My challenge was I couldn't recall what I'd worn the last time I visited Jill's office, and I hadn't logged it in my app. Fortunately, I kept a new shirt on the top shelf. It had never been in the rotation. I matched it with a pair of khakis and made a note to buy another shirt for the next emergency.

After a quick trip to use the hose on the firepit, I spent the remaining time reviewing my spreadsheet and tweaking the numbers, but the end result was the same. It was useless in helping me decide who had committed the murders. Hoping that fresh eyes would see what I was missing, I packed up my laptop and drove to Jill's office.

As before, Jill's receptionist/assistant remained focused on his phone's screen and waved me toward the open door to her office. I was relieved to see Dix was there, leaning her chair back against the wall. Jill waved me to the other chair in front of her desk. Dix was dressed in what I would call "upscale casual." I did not know if this was her real persona or a disguise but was glad to see her in any case. Jill was wearing the same navy-blue business suit that she'd worn on my last visit. If I hadn't spent time that morning fretting over my wardrobe, I wouldn't have noticed. Average people like me need the right clothes to look good. I was certain Jill would make any outfit look stunning. I considered telling her about the wardrobe scheduling app, but an inner voice suggested this might not be the right time, and I should understand the right time might never arrive.

We exchanged the usual pleasantries, but I was eager to learn where Dix had gone. She said, "I understood you wanted to hide in the shadows, but I wanted to get closer. Even up close there was not much to learn so I headed home to get ready for the rest of my evening. Do you want details on that?"

I could feel the blood rush to my cheeks as sweat glands I hadn't used in years decided this was the moment to show what they could do.

While I walked to the side table to prepare for my Show and Tell, I said, "That won't be necessary. You're not the suspect here." When they each finished their polite laughs, I asked Jill if I could use her TV. She said, "Sure," so I opened my laptop and ran an HDMI cable to the flatscreen TV mounted on the side wall. I kept one of these cables in my laptop bag and another in my car's trunk for emergencies. You never know when you'll need one, and I can't understand why others don't do the same.

"I've been doing some work at home. It's not finished, but I wanted to get your input."

With that, I scrolled through the images I'd captured of my whiteboard and paused for questions when I got to a full-screen view of the Excel spreadsheet. Jill was looking at me the way I imagined she'd look at someone just diagnosed with a terminal disease. Her brow had acquired a set of horizontal worry creases, and she held her lips in a perfectly straight line. It was a very serious look, and in that moment, I wanted nothing more than to see her smile again but didn't know how to make it happen.

"If you disagree with any of the numbers, I'm willing to discuss adjustments. Or I might have overlooked something."

Dix was looking at the floor while her body shook—starting at the shoulders and down to the toes. When she got control of herself, she asked, "You think this is something normal people do?"

Jill dismissed the comment with a wave of her hand. "I can see you've put a great deal of effort into this, but I'm not sure it's the best use of your time."

"But I'm trying to find the real killer."

"Do you remember what I told you during our last meeting? We talked through how the DA would try to prove that you had motive, means, and opportunity. Based on that, they would try to convince the jury that you were guilty 'beyond a reasonable doubt.'"

Dix had stopped shaking with her entire body, but her shoulders continued to vibrate, and she held one fist to her mouth.

"Dix, you can step outside if you can't control yourself," Jill said, then turned back to me. "My job is not to prove who killed who, but just to give the jury that reasonable doubt concerning the DA's case against you."

As she reviewed the basics of my situation, I remembered what she'd told me. The prosecution would claim my motive was my desire to rid my life of an irritant—Miss Inga and her constant complaining. The means was my father's .22 that someone had recently fired. My opportunity had come in the middle of the night while my wife was sleeping soundly and could not swear under oath that I hadn't left the house. I bet the DA's office already had this one posted in the win column.

"But there's no witness," I argued. "No direct evidence. Everything they have is just circumstantial evidence and relies on an inference to connect it to me." I dedicated a moment of silent thanks to *Law & Order* for the inspiration and Wikipedia for the specifics.

Dix had stopped shaking and was finally able to speak. "I'll take this one, boss." She turned to me. "You saw in the news a man was just put to death in a neighboring state?"

I nodded.

"They convicted him based on circumstantial evidence."

I made a mental note to read past the first two paragraphs on Wikipedia articles.

"But don't they need to prove I'm guilty beyond a reasonable doubt?"

Jill rubbed her forehead. "Brad, I like you, but what makes you think every jury is full of reasonable people? Citizenship is the only requirement, and that's not a high bar. Every jury contains people who believe what they hear on talk radio. If we don't build an alternate version of events in the jury's mind, then I'm afraid the circumstantial evidence is going to send you away for a very long time . . . or possibly worse."

After letting the "possibly worse" sink in for a minute, she continued. "We also need to face facts. A jury in this county is not going to look favorably at you. It might be easy for them to see you as the killer if the prosecution does a halfway decent job of laying out their case."

I'd always prided myself on being likable, or at least, not being offensive. "Why would any jury look at me unfavorably?"

Jill raised her right index finger.

"First, half of the jury will be the folks who aren't clever enough to get excused from jury duty. And people who are not clever dislike anyone who is clever. When they learn you are a fraud investigator, they'll peg you as someone clever and that means you could easily be cunning enough to commit the murders."

She lifted the middle finger on her right hand, but not in an offensive way. She paired it with her index finger so it looked like she was doing a Cub Scout pledge. It might have been a Girl Scout pledge. I wasn't sure if they did that the same way.

"Second, the rest of the jury will be made up of people who really want to sit on a jury—particularly on a murder case. They'll be the ones who listen to true crime podcasts for entertainment and binge-watch Court TV. You'd like to think that would mean they had some expertise and would be impartial jurors. You'd be wrong. They can't wait to get into a courtroom to see how the sausage is really made and get their chance to turn the grinder. Sorry for changing the metaphor, but these fanboys and girls want to watch the wheels of justice as they crush you and roll over your body. They don't give up weeks of their life to see someone get off with an innocent verdict. Where's the fun in that?"

"But what about those cases where the podcast or documentary proves someone didn't commit the crime?" I said. "Don't these people love those shows just as much as the ones with a guilty verdict?"

"Sure. But the instances where a verdict is reversed are only interesting after the accused has already spent decades in prison. Only then do people cheer when a guilty verdict is overturned. Do you want to spend years in prison while you wait for the true crime junkies to get interested in proving the DA goofed and overturning your case?"

I shook my head, and she held up a third finger. Was it still called a ring finger if it was on your right hand? I made a note to check on that.

"Third, you work for an insurance company."

"I don't know why that matters."

"Have you ever met anyone who likes an insurance company?"

I was going to argue, but then I remembered when I'd overheard my mother tell a friend that I just "worked in an office doing something." It was on that same trip to visit my folks where my dad asked if I'd ever thought of changing industries. He'd heard that used car sales was a booming business, and they were always looking for talent.

A few things were starting to make sense. "I guess this explains why my kids never brought home the invitations when it was time to let us know about Career Day," I said.

"It's amazing how perceptive children can be," said Dix.

On the one hand, I was proud of my kids for their early understanding of society's prejudice against a specific industry. On the other, I had to face the fact my company was ranked somewhere below payday lending on the trust and likability scales.

By that point, I had perceived the pattern and was not surprised when Jill held up four fingers.

"Fourth, you're not from around here."

"Wait a sec. I've lived here almost my entire life. Longer than most of my neighbors."

"When was the last time you ate grits? How long since you attended a gun and knife show? Where should the Dawgs focus recruiting this year?"

I hesitated. "What? Why would any of that come up in court?"

"It won't, but just like a predator can smell your fear, somehow the jury will sense that—no matter how long you've lived here—you haven't made a commitment to be a Southerner."

I might not have killed anyone, but Jill was right. I hadn't admitted it to myself, but deep in my heart, I retained a kernel of Yankee. I preferred *A Prairie Home Companion* over the

Grand Ole Opry, I'd never acquired a taste for sweet tea, and each year I prayed for the Vikings to win the Super Bowl. And somehow, I knew in the pit of my soul that Jill was right. The jury would know.

I sat in silence while Jill spent the remainder of the hour going over what she and Dix had been doing since our last meeting. Since I hadn't been charged with anything, it was too early for Jill to file any discovery motions. She'd had to fall back on having dinner with an assistant DA who talked a lot after a couple of cocktails. I could understand why he would say anything to keep the conversation going and prolong the dinner. His careless chatter was to our advantage, and I couldn't blame him. If I was in his place, and not happily married, I would have done the same.

The gist of it was that the police wanted to put more pieces together so they could wrap up all four murders in one package. I wasn't considered a flight risk, which was a little insulting. Not that I had any intention of fleeing, but I would have liked to have been taken more seriously in that regard. Maybe they would have been more worried if I hadn't let my passport expire.

As for Dix, she'd posed as a potential buyer interested in a home in The Estates. Her realtor had brought her as a guest to several neighborhood functions to help close the deal. She'd gotten the most information from the group that played mah-jongg every Wednesday.

"Your wife didn't recognize me, although that might not have been the quality of my disguise. More the fact she never actually looked at me when we met the first two times. Anyway, the ladies at mah-jongg knew quite a bit about the background of Miss Oskarsdotter, aka Angelica Del Luca."

"Why would she tell that crowd about her past life? She was supposed to be in hiding."

"She didn't tell them. At least not directly. She was lonely living here so far from her old neighborhood. When she found out Edith also had an accounting background, they became friends. Edith's eyesight was better than Angelica's, and she started helping Angelica go through the books to prepare for court. The more Edith looked at the books, she realized she was now one of the few with knowledge of how the scam worked."

"I can see where this is going."

"Yeah. Edith was a member of the mah-jongg crowd. There is something about playing with tiles for hours while sitting on top of a really juicy secret. Since her life depended on it, Miss Oskarsdotter had every reason to keep quiet and she'd only told one person."

Dix looked from side to side as it she was the one sharing a closely held secret.

"Unfortunately for her, Edith's only motivation to keep the secret was the promise she'd made to Miss Oskarsdotter. When she balanced the benefits of keeping her promise with the almost insignificant risk posed by telling just a few close friends, she decided it couldn't hurt."

I nodded. "This was exactly where I thought it was going."

Dix finished her tale. "Edith shared with her mah-jongg table one week and swore them to secrecy. From what I can tell, the other ladies were true to their vows and kept the secret. That lasted until the next Wednesday's mah-jongg game. They rotate the players between tables to keep things fun. Edith was now sitting with her secret while playing with a new group of confidants. And everyone she'd told the last week were also at fresh tables. By the end of that day, twenty-some ladies were all sworn to secrecy. Half of them went to Bunco the following Friday."

"We can assume that by the following week," Jill broke in, "hundreds of individuals knew that Miss Oskarsdotter had worked for this crypto crime family and was in some sort of witness protection program. This had to be something no other nearby subdivisions could claim. It was, we can conjecture, a better claim to fame than winning the city-wide mixed doubles championship."

Dix finished my thought. "Any one of those individuals could have shared that information with someone who spoke to someone who whispered in someone's ear and the result was Miss Oskarsdotter/Angelica was marked for a hit. Since Edith had a look at the books, she must have been a target as well."

I was silent as I absorbed this barrage.

"I know this is a lot to take in," said Jill with a compassionate look at me. "It complicates things, but on the positive side, we have a good opportunity to raise doubt when we tell the jury how both ladies might have been targeted by Robbie Cunningham or one of his associates."

My mind was racing as I ran through the possibilities and what this could mean. First, this was an opportunity to get a bigger whiteboard—maybe two. Second, Jill had said she liked me. As I left her office, I thought that had to be a good sign for my defense.

I was almost to my car when I saw Dix waving her hands and running to catch up to me. I was impressed that she wasn't even breathing hard when she got to where I had parked.

"Jill cleared her calendar. You need to come back in and discuss the latest development."

"What development?"

"The police obtained a warrant to search your premises. From what we know, they've only seized one item so far, but it was enough for them to think they now have probable cause. You can assume your next meeting with the police will end with you in custody."

"Oh, fudge."

I followed Dix back into the building, and we took our seats.

Jill looked furious. "What do you think they found, and whatever it is, why didn't you warn me this was coming?"

I felt like I had when Miss Swanson scolded me in fifth grade. I don't remember what I'd done to make her mad, but her rebuke was burned into my memory. She'd been my first serious crush. Just out of college, she was new to her job and the first teacher whose perfume didn't make my eyes water.

I tried and failed to look Jill in the eye. "But I didn't kill any of those people."

"That's good to hear, but that's not what I asked you. Let me rephrase. What did the police take from your house, and why did you keep its existence from your lawyer?"

"I can only think of one thing that they might have gotten excited about. I did have two .22 casings in a plastic bag that I was keeping as sort of a souvenir."

Jill just looked at me and slowly shook her head while Dix let loose with a string of words that would have put big bucks in a swear jar if they'd had one. I got up from the chair and headed for the door. Quickly.

As I ran through the outer office, I heard Jill ask Dix, "Where do you think he's going?"

I told the receptionist to let her know I was going to my house to clear things up before the police jumped to any conclusions. Though to be honest, I thought that ship had sailed.

Chapter Twenty-Two

I pulled into my driveway and almost hit Tony. "Slow down, Sherlock. For a corporate drone, you do know how to liven things up around here."

I saw an unmarked car and a conspicuously marked car sitting at the curb. Neighbors were already gathered on the sidewalk. A few were crouched behind the cars as if they thought a gun battle could break out at any moment. Most had their cellphones out. No doubt they hoped for something that would go viral.

Standing to one side, there were three well-dressed individuals who bore all the signs of being realtors. By that, I mean they literally held yard signs for their respective agencies ready to post in my yard if the opportunity came to them. This was turning into the suburban version of vultures circling in the sky.

Tony walked next to me as I headed to my front door. "The uniformed goons wouldn't let me in to see what's happening. Can I tag along with you?"

During the drive over, I had hoped I would find a way to bring Tony into this confrontation. "Absolutely. I'll need you for what's about to happen."

I opened the front door only to have it blocked by a uniformed officer's black boot. I had to stick my driver's license through the four-inch gap to convince her it was my house, and she should let me in. Tony almost climbed on my back to make sure he also made it inside. The realtors tried to follow but the officer closed the door on the one at the head of the line. There was some scuffling on the porch as a half dozen business cards poked through between the door and the frame.

I could hear someone walking upstairs and at least one person opening and closing drawers and cabinets in the kitchen while Rhonda tried to convince them there was nothing to find there. With Tony on my heels, I walked into the kitchen to find Detectives Jackson and Williams rearranging the contents of our pantry.

"I'm glad you're finally here, Brad. Can you convince these gentlemen to go detect somewhere else? They're making a mess, and you're going to have to rewash every kitchen item they've manhandled."

Jackson closed the pantry door. "Ma'am, I said we were almost done, and we're being as careful as we can with your things. Now that your husband is here, he can save us time if he'll just point us to any other evidence he's been keeping from us. Anything other than what we've already found, that is."

With that, he pulled a plastic evidence bag from his jacket pocket. Inside that plastic bag was a second bag I recognized and inside *that* bag were the two .22 casings I now regretted keeping.

"I can explain."

"I'm sure you can. And we'd like you to accompany us to our office where you can explain in detail and on the record."

"My client will not explain anything at any level of detail without his lawyer present. I'm certain he was about to make that clear."

I could not see Jill, but I heard her from where she stood behind Tony and Detective Williams. She and Dix had arrived like the cavalry and shouldered their way into the increasingly crowded kitchen. Jill held a hand out toward the senior detective. "And now that I'm here, I'd like to take a look at the warrant you used to justify this invasion of my client's home."

Jackson pulled a folded set of papers from his breast pocket and handed them to her. After flipping through the pages, she handed them back.

"Nicely typed and almost legal. This warrant is for searching the property of Bradley Han*sen*, as in 'H-A-N-S-*E*-N.' You are standing in the kitchen owned by my client, Bradley Han*son*, as in 'H-A-N-S-*O*-N.' You can leave now, and please place Mr. Hanson's items on the table as you go."

Detective Jackson looked at her as if he'd just learned his winning lottery ticket had expired the day before, and he'd have to take his new Corvette back to the dealer. Soon, anger replaced disappointment, and he made several contributions to the swear jar's invisible account before he noticed his partner holding his palms out and fingers spread wide. Jackson stopped his tirade and asked Williams what he wanted.

The younger detective raised his hand as if asking permission to speak before impressing the rest of the class. "Miss Richards is correct in saying the warrant has the wrong spelling. However, as I'm sure she will agree, the Supreme Court case *U.S. v. Leon* says the results of a search are allowed if the police officers had a good faith belief that the warrant was valid."

Jill smiled. It was a this-is-going-to-be-fun grin.

"I didn't know there was a first-year, night-school law student in the room."

Williams' smile faded as he realized he'd stepped into the trap he'd intended for her.

"It's remote-learning. Not night school."

"Forgive me. That's my mistake, just as your mistake is trying to apply *U.S. v. Leon* where it doesn't fit."

She went on to explain that it applied to situations where the judge granting the warrant was in error. In this instance, the error was with the officers who had typed the wrong name. There was more to it than that, but I watched as one by one the audience lost focus on her explanation. This used to happen to me when I went into detail on an insurance policy's fine print. My solution was to use a set of slides to clarify subtle points. I was sure it would also improve her elucidation of relevant case law, but she hadn't thought to bring her laptop, and so, missed the opportunity.

When she ended her impromptu lecture, Jackson raised his eyebrows and looked at Williams. "I covered your ass and wrote up all your reports for a year so you could study for that damn class."

"I'm afraid—"

"And don't tell me again how you're continuing your education, and I should have learned to type."

This went on for a while. It felt like I was seeing a real-life version of every buddy-cop movie ever made—just without the laughs. I was not surprised when Jackson wrapped things up with the appropriate and expected closing line. "I'm too old for this. I've got one month to go until I can retire and go fishing." He followed it up by holding out the evidence bag with the two casings and giving it a little shake. "The thing is, if we leave here without these casings, we all know they won't be here when we come back with a fricking S-O-N warrant. And while I'm not a lawyer or working to become one, I have a warrant here signed by a judge. If you feel the warrant is invalid, you may bring it up to this judge, or another. If you get them to agree, any evidence we collect will be ruled inadmissible at trial."

When I worked a case for GFI, I'd learned it helped to keep something in reserve. A little secret or two that I could drop on a suspected fraudster at the right moment. Sometimes, a surprise disclosure could shock them into revealing a critical detail. Maybe even a confession. Other times, it was just fun to see their face as they realized I knew what I knew and might know even more. This seemed to be a good time to drop a small bomb.

I pointed at the bag with the two casings. "I assume you are interested in those because you think they're related to the shooting death of Miss Oskarsdotter."

Jill's eyes widened, and she mouthed the word "no." In the rest of the room, other eyes narrowed, accompanied by small smiles.

"You'd be wrong, in that case. Follow me downstairs, and I'll show you."

The smiles tightened, and Jill glared at me. It looked like I would receive a lecture on the wisdom of surprising the person hired to defend me.

Once we were in the basement, everyone except my wife crowded into my still-unfinished office. Rhonda stayed two steps from the bottom of the stairs and looked from one pile of my crap to another. I had led her to believe I was making progress in cleaning things out, and she was not happy to see how little progress there was. The smell of fresh-cut pine mingled with the scent of erasable markers and a tinge of laser printer toner. The two detectives wanted to examine my whiteboard. I couldn't blame them, but that was not why I brought them downstairs.

"You can see I've been framing the walls to make this into my home office. I'm not as handy as some of my neighbors, but I'm proud of it."

I bent over to pull a black and orange tool out of a bag along with a small container.

"This device is called a powder-actuated tool and here are the .22 'blanks' it fires. With it, I can drive nails through the bottom plate and into the concrete. I carried around those casings as sort of a souvenir from my first big home improvement project. I'm pretty sure your lab people will confirm that these shells did not play any part in the death of Miss Oskarsdotter."

Jackson resumed his NSFW rant and kicked one of the two-by-fours I'd nailed into the floor. His foot lost that encounter, which added some additional invective to his monologue. It was sad to watch someone so close to the end of their career come face to face with failure. While I hadn't felt anything positive toward Jackson up until then, I didn't like seeing the older man shuffle out with slumped shoulders.

Thankfully, I had one last surprise that might buck up his spirits.

"Would the trip be worthwhile if I told you I know who killed Miss Oskarsdotter?"

Everyone who had started toward the stairs turned around, and Rhonda joined the rest of us between the unfinished walls of my office. The setting wasn't quite what I'd hoped for. To be faithful to the wrap-up of a murder mystery, any gathering to reveal the killer should have included all the suspects. The suspense builds as more and more heads swivel to see if they can spot the guilty party.

It would have been nice to bring in Vanessa Hershey, Mr. Price, and the others, but I was sure I would have lost some of this crowd if I made them wait while I summoned the rest. Perfect was the enemy of good enough, and this would have to be good enough. It was time to drop my second bomb of the night.

The framed space was crowded, and the group moved back into a semicircle around me as I walked to my whiteboard. It would have been nice to use my laptop and a projector, but there wasn't time to pull the equipment together. Again, good enough would have to do. I took the eraser and dramatically erased the "Unknown neighbor" tag from the suspects line and replaced it with a short blank line.

I tapped the first two photos and said, "Let's start with what we know about the initial killings. According to the police estimate, at 10:20 PM on the night in question, Miss Inga Oskarsdotter was killed in classic execution style with two .22 bullets that might or might not have come from a pistol that was stored in my unlocked garage."

From her position on the steps, Rhonda added, "I told him to get that lock fixed, but he never gets around to anything I want done. My friends all felt it was a shame the way I had to settle for some things."

I used the red marker to draw a circle around the now-unfilled spot in the suspect list.

"As my wife has just stated, she had made it known that the garage lock was broken. Most of our neighbors had also heard we had to store the pistol after my father shot it in the retirement home. Any of those neighbors could have learned of this, taken the gun, used it to commit the first murder, and later returned it to the garage to place me under suspicion."

As I spoke, I drew a rough map of our house relative to the crime scenes and added a note that read, "This map not to scale." I thought my attention to detail would impress the group, but when I turned toward them, I found most were examining the partially finished walls, the scattered content on the top of my desk, or their shoes.

"Moving on, the second murder took place twenty minutes later at 10:40 pm when an assailant, conceivably the same one, lured Edith Skinner into her backyard, and struck her from behind, possibly with a nonstandard tennis racquet, causing her to fall to her death on strategically placed stakes."

Two minutes into my presentation, and the group was already looking at their watches. That was nothing new to me, so I continued with my next point.

"Briefly, that describes the means, but what of the motives? Both women were disliked for different reasons, but surely any animosity was not enough to incite someone to kill them. On the other hand, sinister forces were at work in the background."

I checked my notes. At this point, I had written "dramatic pause for effect," so that's what I did. Also, while "sinister" wasn't a word I got to use when dealing with auto repair shops overcharging for replacement parts, I thought it set the right tone for this presentation.

"Miss Oskarsdotter was under federal protection as a key witness in a government prosecution of crypto crime. She had copies of financial records that could jail the boss of the operation and all his minions."

That last bit might have been an overstatement, but I wanted to regain the attention of those now checking their phones.

"And Miss Oskarsdotter shared some of those records with Edith Skinner, sealing her fate as well. Once the criminals discovered where their errant bookkeeper was hiding, they marked her for execution, along with anyone unlucky enough to have looked at the records."

Detective Jackson let out a puff of air. "I'm sure the FBI had a copy of the accounting records, so why'd the scammers need to whack these two old ladies?"

His partner answered. "I'd guess the books are just lists of code words and amounts. Alone, they wouldn't be much use in court. The FBI needed Miss Oskarsdotter as a witness on the stand to tie the entries to specific individuals and their crimes." He received a scowl from Jackson as a reward.

Tony was leaning against the frame of the other side wall. "Am I the only one getting tired of pronouncing 'Oscars' daughter?' Those feds can't be that bright if that was the best fake name they could come up with. She couldn't have liked it when she was alive. Now that she's dead, can we just start calling her Angelica? No good Italian should have to go through the afterlife with a name no one can say."

I drew a second circle around the blank spot I'd left for the killer's identity.

"I'm glad you mentioned that, Tony. Along the way, we did learn Angelica Del Luca was the real name of Miss Oskarsdotter. I didn't know that until Cassandra, the investigator working with my attorney, shared that information when I met with them in Jill's office. Then, in my backyard one night, you and I were kicking around ideas and you told me the Shumakers might've killed *Edith and Angelica*. I thought it was a dumb idea to put that on the Shumakers, and still do, but something kept nagging me about our conversation. It wasn't until today I realized what it was. See, I'm sure I didn't tell you that was her real name, so where did you hear it?"

While I provided this dramatic revelation, I casually walked to my desk and removed the scissors and letter opener and locked them in a drawer. The last thing I wanted was for Tony to panic and use them to grab a hostage.

Tony laughed. "I heard it from you, Sherlock. Where else? You've been pretty stressed, and it must have slipped that big brain of yours."

"No. I'm sure I didn't tell you. That realization got me to look at the complete puzzle and the pieces finally came together."

Though it wasn't very original, I thought the puzzle reference made for a nice metaphor. I'd held it in reserve for a moment just like this one.

"Several of the pieces fell into place when I realized that with your gangster fetish, you'd see this as the perfect way to gain street cred with Robbie and the crypto kids back in New Jersey. You planned to solve a problem for them by eliminating the FBI's star witness and cleaning up the only other loose end with Edith's death. It was important to do the first one like a real hit man, but you were somehow clever enough to use a different method on your second victim, so they'd appear unconnected."

With that, I wrote Tony's name on the whiteboard. I followed that with more red circles around it and tapped the board. I had a moment of regret for insulting Tony by saying he was "somehow clever enough," but since I was accusing him of two murders, I thought he might not catch the minor slight.

When I looked at Tony, I was surprised to see he was just smirking at me. I'd just laid out my reasoning that he should be the number one suspect, and he seemed pleased. That almost made me lose track of things, but a glance at my notes told me it was time to wrap things up with a flourish.

I tapped the whiteboard again and said, "Motive, method, and opportunity. It all fits. The man who did his best to foil my investigation is, in fact, the man who murdered the two women."

Jackson and Williams didn't look convinced, but I'd raised enough doubt that they moved to where they stood on either side of Tony. I was glad of that. While I hadn't seen any suspicious bulges in his T-shirt and slacks, I hadn't thought to look for an ankle piece. With the detectives positioned to either side, I didn't think he could bend down and grab it if he'd thought to wear one.

The room was quiet. It might have been my imagination, but I thought I saw respect in Dix's eyes for the first time since we'd met. Jill was smiling at me with her head slightly tilted to one side. I hoped that was meant to be encouraging. I took it that way.

When I glanced at Rhonda, she was scowling. "How can you accuse your best friend of something so terrible? What is wrong with you?"

"We don't have time to go through the list of things wrong with him," said Tony. "When I moved here, I became his friend 'cause it looked like he didn't have any. Maybe that was my mistake."

He took a step in my direction. The detectives on either side visibly stiffened until he returned to his previous position.

Tony hung his head down toward his chest for a moment before he looked up and scanned the faces in the room. He ended his visual tour by staring at me.

"It's sad it had to come to this," he said. "I didn't know myself if you were guilty or not. I was going along for the ride and figured the truth would come out sooner or later. Now that you've tossed me under the bus, that tells me everything I need to know."

He winked at me and continued, "Tell me, Sherlock. If I knew Miss Angelica Oscar-whatever was a rat, why'd I wait until now to do something about it? I've been here for over a year. Why'd I take so long to make a move? You know me and how patient I am."

I looked at my notes, but I hadn't thought to cover possible objections. I'd assumed he'd confess or make a break for it when I got to this point. It never occurred to me that he'd argue with me.

"And speaking of opportunity, you say the killer did the deeds at 10:20 and 10:40?"

Tony reached into a back pocket and the detectives moved back slightly to have room to pounce if needed. Jackson and Williams relaxed when he came up with his phone and started tapping and swiping before showing the screen to them.

"Here's some good shots I took of me at the game the night the of the murders. Every time the Yankees added to their lead over the Braves, I took a picture of me with the scoreboard there in the background. Look at the timestamps and tell me how I got from the stadium to The Estates and back in time to knock off a couple of senior citizens and still watch the Braves get beat up by my Yankees."

The detectives studied the pictures for another minute. Williams pulled out his phone and tapped on the screen. When he looked up, he said, "The time stamps match what happened at the game."

"You spun a nice story, Mr. Hanson," Jackson said grimly. "Almost had me convinced. But even if we toss the casings, looks like you're still going to need your lawyer."

Tony folded his arms across his chest and grinned. On my whiteboard, it all seemed so simple. But I hadn't counted on ballpark selfies messing up my carefully crafted whodunit. I'd had people rip apart my reasoning before, but I'd never seen people so happy when it happened. It made me sick to my stomach.

Between the office and the neighborhood, I knew plenty of people. But, as Tony had pointed out, I didn't have any real friends. In fact, despite his flaws, Tony had been the only one to rise above "acquaintance." The weight of years spent on the outskirts of every circle hit me hard. In that moment, I felt profoundly alone—worse still when I had to admit I'd been alone my entire life.

Chapter Twenty-Three

The next morning, I stayed in bed. There was no reason to rise when I didn't feel like shining. Without a job, there was no need to get in Atlanta's stop-and-crawl traffic. I didn't feel like working on a home office that someone else would use while I was rotting in prison—like the once-fresh fruit and vegetables in the bottom drawer of our refrigerator. I don't know why that image kept coming to mind. At first, I thought it was because I really hated cleaning out that bottom drawer. I could see now the contents of that drawer were a metaphor for my unfulfilled dreams. If there was one good thing about staying in bed, it gave me freedom to think of metaphors. Or it would have been a good thing if they'd been good metaphors.

Since Tony hadn't followed the script I'd written in my head, my investigation had gotten turned upside down, and I was still a suspect in the murders. I saw no reason to leave my cocoon.

I'd scored points when I showed everyone the nail-driving tool. It was one of the few dramatic moments in my life that I could say I initiated. Why didn't I quit while I was ahead? What made me think I could put all the pieces together on my own?

All I wanted was to avoid the start of a day that would only bring further humiliation, when the doorbell rang. Knowing I was not getting out of bed, Rhonda answered the door, and someone spoke a few sentences before I heard it close and the sound of one of those pull tabs being ripped off a package. Without mentioning the exact contents of the delivery, Rhonda talked to herself as she climbed the stairs. Based on her monologue, the delivery had not been welcomed.

She came into the bedroom and handed me a large DHL envelope while she clutched another. The letter inside my envelope was an invitation to a meeting tomorrow at the law offices of Jill Richards, attorney at law, for the purpose of "resolving questions surrounding the participation of her client"—that would be me—in "the crimes currently under investigation"—that would be what I most definitely did not do.

Rhonda shook her copy in my direction. "What have you and your lady lawyer been up to now? It wasn't enough to embarrass me in front of all those people yesterday? Now you have to drag me into another spectacle? Can't you just tell the police what they want to know so this can all be over?"

"They don't believe me when I say I'm innocent."

"Maybe those old ladies annoyed you one time too many. Something in you snapped, and now you can't remember because you've repressed those memories. I've read about that happening to people. If that's it, then you weren't responsible for your actions. You should get a reduced sentence. Wouldn't that be better than this dragging on for weeks and you end up in prison for life?"

"I didn't repress any memories because there was nothing to repress."

"So, you can't remember anything about that night? Don't you think that's a sign something did happen and you are repressing it?"

I always lost arguments with Rhonda when she used circular logic, because she had more stamina than I did when it came to repeating herself. Once we got on that merry-go-round, we would spin and spin until I got dizzy and fell off. Then she would proclaim victory. I decided that day I would skip a few revolutions and get off before my inner ear failed me again.

"You might be right. I was dreaming about that night just before you woke me. I'm going back to sleep and see if I can get back in the dream. Maybe that'll unrepress something."

She smiled as if I'd just told her we were going to not only redo the kitchen in the fall but renovate the sunroom at the same time.

I must have programmed myself to dream because that's what happened soon after I pulled the covers back over my head. The programming was a little off, however, as when I woke up, the dream had involved me winning a lawsuit against the city for false arrest. They had to pay me a million dollars for my pain and suffering, along with tickets for a two-week Caribbean cruise for me and my lawyer. Don't judge me too quickly. The dream ended before I had decided whether I was going to go on a cruise with a woman I wasn't married to or would try to talk the booking company into giving me a refund.

I looked at the alarm clock, and it was almost noon. As much as I wanted to slide back into that dream, it was time to get up. I couldn't remember the last time I'd slept in past seven and made two resolutions. One, I would throw off the covers and the funk I'd fallen into. And two, when Rhonda asked if I remembered anything from my dream, I was definitely going to repress it.

After my morning, now afternoon, cleanup, I went down to my office-in-progress to make some calls. First, I called Jill's office to learn what was going to happen at the meeting the next day. Her assistant told me Jill was with a client and could not be disturbed. I asked for Dix, figuring she'd know what was up, but was informed she was out doing "research."

Since I'd effectively burned all the bridges between me and my Watson, there was nothing to do but work on my own. While I was in my extended horizontal, eyes closed, solitary brainstorming session, UPS had delivered the new—significantly larger—whiteboard I'd ordered. I struggled to get the huge board down the stairs and then hung it on the framed wall orthogonal to the first one. Sometimes the most mundane action can illicit profound ruminations.

Like my brain including the word "orthogonal" instead of thinking the second wall was simply at a right angle. I'd looked up the word after watching a video of an astronaut on the moon. He told Houston he was setting a pole "orthogonal to the surface," and I didn't know what he meant. Once I discovered its meaning, I still wondered why he hadn't just said it was perpendicular or that he was sticking the pole straight up in the moon dirt.

I decided he used orthogonal because it sounded cool, or at least it would sound cool to the nerds in NASA's core demographic. Once I'd learned orthogonal, I tried using it and discovered that while it might be a very good word, it wasn't one that I should use around normal people. And by normal people, I mean everyone else. Through experience, I'd come to understand there were words and phrases I shouldn't say out loud. Phrases like, "mundane action can illicit profound ruminations."

As I sat staring at the blank whiteboard, it occurred to me that if I ended up in prison, there would be many of my usual words and phrases I would be wise to never speak out loud.

* * *

Rhonda and I arrived at my lawyer's office a few minutes before the scheduled start time of 11 AM. I dropped my wife off at the front door and then parked around on the side because all the spaces in front were occupied. As expected, I saw the unmarked—but with government license plates might as well be marked—car of Detectives Jackson and Williams. Next to theirs was a similarly conspicuous-by-its-plain-exterior car of my favorite FBI agents. There were a handful of other cars I did not recognize, and then our county's one and only SWAT vehicle. Several helmeted and body armor clad officers were leaning on it. Either someone expected an unusually volatile meeting this morning, or the team wanted to show they were essential in a county that hadn't had a hostage situation in this century.

In addition to the building occupants I'd seen listed before, there was now an entry on the wall for a business consultant/futurist—in other words, a fortune teller for the white-collar crowd. The assorted businesses had access to a shared conference room, and that was the site of the meeting about to start. I was met at the door by a young woman. She wore huge black-rimmed glasses that covered half her face, a T-shirt that said, "Code Like a Girl," and her hair wrapped into two buns on top of her head. She held out a cardboard box that held a small collection of phones. Catching on to her unspoken request, I placed my cellphone in the box with the rest.

After giving up my phone, I walked in and took one of the few empty seats. Just like at church, the seats in the back had filled up first, so I wound up near the head of the table where Jill and Dix were in a hushed conversation with occasional glances around the room. There was one empty spot where Rhonda had taken a chair and then rolled it back to where she was positioned by the side wall. Sitting with her arms across her chest, she did a reasonably good impression of a teenager forced to attend a family reunion and convinced she was not going to enjoy it. On the drive over, she had maintained complete silence, except for occasional outbursts where she'd cursed lawyers, the police, and me before going mute and staring out the side window.

Jill looked at her watch and surveyed the room as the time for the meeting came and went. I felt a drop of sweat roll down the side of my face and turned so Rhonda would not see it. I'd worn my wool navy blazer because I thought it would help me create a good impression. Rhonda insisted I should wear my tan summer-weight blazer, even though she always said it made my complexion appear washed out—which I assumed was not a good thing.

Glancing around the room, I saw I was not the only one perspiring. The HVAC system was having trouble keeping the room cool with this number of people. In addition to Jill, Dix, Rhonda, and me, there were the two detectives, the two not-so-special agents, and Robert Clark, my neighbor and the city's forensic scientist. The only empty seats were across the table from me and must have been for the mystery guest—or guests—Jill was waiting for.

Running through the possible candidates, I could not imagine who might be missing. I doubted it would be Mr. Price, Walter and Sally Harrison, or Vanessa Hershey. Unless some startling new information had come to light to implicate one of them, it had to be someone I'd never considered. I just hoped whoever it was, we would not have a repeat of the embarrassment I experienced two days earlier.

That was top of mind when Tony strolled into the room. In place of his usual uniform of T-shirt and shorts, he was wearing nice slacks, a burgundy dress shirt with the top two buttons undone, and a tan blazer. The open shirt revealed two gold chains that I thought had gone out with *Saturday Night Fever*, if not before. As for the jacket, I'm not the best judge of fabrics, but it appeared to be a light tan summer weight. It might have been the lighting in the conference room, but the coat didn't make him look washed out in the least.

Jill pointed Tony to a seat across from me and said, "It looks like everyone is here, so we can begin. First of all, thank you for giving up your personal devices for the duration of the meeting. We do not want any interruptions so that we can finish on schedule. As you know, Mr. Hanson is my client and Ms. Dixon and I have been working to prove his innocence. Although it was not our initial intent, in the course of our work, we uncovered evidence that will show you who is actually guilty of these crimes."

As I looked around the room, the group reminded me of an audience that had just been told Jill was a magician and was going to cut her assistant in two. Half the group was clearly skeptical and didn't believe she could deliver the miracle. The others were looking forward to the blood and screaming.

She ran through a set of introductions for the benefit of the FBI agents and Robert Clark, since the rest had all been present when I'd executed a faceplant on my basement floor. Preliminaries handled, Jill nodded to Dix, who stood and cleared her throat before addressing the group. She was wearing a pair of designer jeans, though I'm not sure they're still called that, an Oxford shirt, and a charcoal blazer. It looked like she was preparing to give a TED Talk. All she needed was a Madonna microphone and a slide clicker in her right hand. Jill rolled her chair to one side so Dix could step over to the large flat screen. Dix powered up the display and then picked up a combination laser pointer and presentation remote. While this was going on, Jill was staring at me. I'm not a believer in telepathy, but I'm positive she was sending me a message to stay seated and keep my mouth shut.

Next, Dix used the small control panel on the table and the LEDs lit up on the teleconferencing microphone array in the center. "To make sure we avoid any future misunderstandings, we'll be recording today's discussion. Now, if everyone can see the screen, I will begin."

Dix's first click brought up a timeline that covered the night of the first two murders and ran through the night the Shumakers' bodies were discovered.

"A few days ago, we had several theories of 'who dun it.' Mr. Hanson took the first step to narrow down the possibilities by proposing one theory of the initial crimes. He built his argument on some things he knew to be true and some assumptions regarding Mr. Columbo—"

Tony lifted one finger from the hand he had resting on the table and said, "After that little misunderstanding, we're all friends here. Call me Tony."

"We are all friends here, but for the recording, I will continue to refer to you as Mr. Columbo." As she said this, she clicked the remote, and the screen displayed a closeup of the timeline from the night of the murders with additional timestamps noted at 8:50 PM, 9:43 pm, and 10:37 pm. Another click, and we saw the three selfies of Tony at the ballpark—the pictures that had destroyed my carefully constructed narrative.

Tony grinned and pointed at the pictures. "Go Yanks!"

Dix clicked again before saying, "Here we see the last picture as posted on Mr. Columbo's Facebook feed."

Tony leaned back with his hands clenched behind his head. "Like I told you in Bradley's nerd cave, I couldn't have killed the old broads."

Dix nodded. "We can clearly see that when we look at this post." She scrolled down. "And this one." Another scroll. "And last of all, this one. Just to be certain, I hired an imaging expert to examine these. She couldn't find any sign of tampering."

"Could've saved that money if you'd just believed me," said Tony with a big smile.

"I believed you in that instance, but I find it best to exercise caution rather than assume anything. For example, these three posts *conveniently* demonstrated you could not have killed either woman that night. It occurred to me that I should check to see if there were other *convenient* posts for the time between the Shumakers' disappearance and the night their bodies were discovered."

She scrolled back to the top of his feed. "But there aren't any posts after the last one at the Braves game, so there is nothing for us to see."

"Sorry to disappoint you."

"That's OK. In my job, I chase a great number of hunches and only a few turn out to prove anything. The trick I've learned is that I need to be thorough and chase down every viable lead. For example, when I found there weren't any posts after the night of the game, I went to see if there were any interesting posts *before* that night."

As Dix scrolled down toward the bottom, Tony stopped smiling and sat upright.

When she had scrolled as far as possible, the screen displayed the first of the three selfies. She said, "But Mr. Columbo's Facebook feed consists only of these three posts. It's almost as if Mr. Columbo prepared this account just so that he'd have an alibi."

Tony waved his hands to dismiss the image. "So, I'm the last of my generation to get on Facebook. I thought it was just for boomers posting from the Golden Corral's Early Bird Special."

"That's one possible explanation. Another possible explanation is that you created an account just so that you would be able to prove you were somewhere else at the time of the murders."

Jackson had been scowling through the exchange so far and finally slapped the table. "The guy's got an alibi. What does it matter if the ink isn't dry on his Facebook account?"

"That's a good question, Detective. At first, I wondered the same thing. But the timing seemed too convenient. I wondered why would he work so hard to prove he was at the ballpark on the night of the murders unless he knew someone else would commit the murders and wanted to prepare his defense in advance."

"For that to be true," said Jackson, "he must have had a partner."

"That occurred to me as well," Dix said. "Do you have any thoughts about that theory of the crime, Mrs. Hanson?"

Chapter Twenty-Four

The implication behind the question did not register at first, but when I turned in my seat, I could see that even though her makeup was perfect, my wife's face was pale. I would say washed out, though it looked better on her than it did on me.

Rhonda unwound her folded arms before rolling her chair away from the wall and up next to mine. She placed one hand over the other in front of her on the table, before saying, "I am not in the business of chasing down criminals like some of you. I don't have any thoughts on the matter."

I've never mastered the art of seamlessly inserting myself into a conversation, so I raised a hand and waited until Dix noticed me to ask, "Why should she need to comment here? She hasn't been involved in any of this."

Rhonda smiled at me. "Thank you, dear. Of course, I haven't been involved in your investigations. I simply wouldn't have anything to contribute." With that, she dropped her right hand from the table and used it to squeeze my thigh. As my body reacted to the unfamiliar—almost forgotten—stimulus, I felt my cheeks heat up as blood rushed there. Next,

I got lightheaded as the blood drained from my face to respond to another call.

I might have missed the next bit of the meeting, but was able to focus again when Dix said, "You might be correct, but indulge me for a few minutes. This line of inquiry might not go anywhere, but I'd like to try, and I need Mrs. Hanson's assistance in clearing up a few things. Is that acceptable?"

I nodded before saying to Rhonda, "I trust Dix, I mean, Ms. Dixon. If she needs our help to sort through things, I think we ought to do what she asks."

Rhonda looked at me like she had last Christmas when I suggested we ask my parents to stay with us for the holidays. In both instances, I would come to understand later how I'd screwed up.

Dix took my wife's silence as consent. "I appreciate your cooperation, Mrs. Hanson. Now, as Detective Jackson noted, if we assume Mr. Columbo prepared his alibi in advance, he must have had a partner who committed the murders."

"If you say so."

"This partner would need access to a gun similar to the one we found in your garage."

Dix clicked the remote and everyone saw a closeup of my father's .22 Ruger pistol.

"Since your husband was the initial suspect, the police dusted this gun for fingerprints and—as expected—they found several of his."

Rhonda looked at the faces around the table. "But I'm sure my dear husband could never have hurt anyone, especially someone who was elderly. His parents are elderly, after all, and much older than my parents."

"I've never had the pleasure of meeting any of your parents, but I also find it hard to accept that Mr. Hanson would have committed murder." As Dix spoke, she walked to the other end of the table where Robert Clark was sitting in his white lab coat. She picked up a manilla folder from in front of him and took it with her back to the head of the table. Once there, she opened it and flipped through the top pages. "But what would you say if I told you the lab also discovered your fingerprints on the pistol?"

Rhonda froze solid for a moment and then came back to life like one of the animatronic presidents at Disney. But when she spoke, her lips were better synced to her speaking. "I remember now. Brad asked me to clean that nasty old gun; it was covered in oil. I hated to touch the thing, but I had to hold on to it while I wiped it down. That must explain how my prints got there."

I hadn't asked Rhonda to clean the pistol, so technically I suppose she had lied, but I was used to her saying things that didn't match my idea of reality. Not entirely wrong. Just different. Up until that moment, it had never seemed based on malice, but more like a small child might make up stories to avoid facing uncomfortable situations.

My wife looked at me and smiled. I'm sure it looked loving to others, but I received a clear message to keep my [expletive deleted] mouth shut. I didn't know what I would say and so followed that advice.

Dix was not afraid to use silence to give her audience time to catch up with the implications of her presentation up to that point. Unsure where the rest stood, I had the feeling I wasn't entirely caught up and wished I'd brought along a fidget spinner to give my hands something to do.

Half the people in the room jerked reflexively when Dix broke the silence. "If we continue to speculate about a partner for Mr. Columbo—"

"Hold on, I proved I didn't do it, but am I going to need a lawyer?"

Dix and Tony locked eyes and smiled at each other as each one tried to get the other would-be alpha to back down. Eventually, Tony blinked.

"I'm just a private citizen asking questions," said Dix, "so my first thought is 'No. You don't.' But then, I'm not sitting where you are."

Tony looked down at his hands and started to use his right index finger to clean the finger nails on his other hand, depositing little clumps of grit on the table. If this was intended to unsettle Dix, it didn't work.

She clicked the remote and the screen displayed a picture of a tennis racquet.

"Moving on to the second homicide, we know from the bruising on Edith Skinner's head the racquet used to strike her had a fourteen-by-twenty-one pattern. It took a while, but I discovered a racquet like that for sale at the local Goodwill. If you look closely, Mrs. Hanson, you can see your initials embossed at the top of the grip."

Rhonda took her hand from my thigh and used it to rub the back of her other hand. Her facial muscles were so taunt there were small fissures forming in her makeup. "I'm a very generous person, and I believe in sharing what I have with the less fortunate. That particular racquet was no longer competitive, so I took it to Goodwill along with some old clothes—presents from my mother-in-law that I'd never wear outside the house . . . I'm not sure why I included the racquet . . . I don't suppose poor people have anywhere to play tennis."

Dix hesitated. "That explains why I was able to purchase it for two dollars. From the strong smell of bleach, you must have given it a good cleaning before you gave it away. Is it common for you to use bleach on your tennis equipment?"

"No, but I knew the racquet would be going into that musty old building, and have you seen the people they have working there? I assumed they wouldn't so much as wipe it with a filthy rag, so I thought I'd give it a good cleaning before I gave it away."

"Very thoughtful of you," said Dix, "and it seemed very clean when I purchased it. Still, I thought it was an odd coincidence when it matched the string pattern we were looking for, so on a whim I sent it to the lab for testing."

"I don't know why you'd bother."

"Oh, it was no bother. But to be absolutely sure it was your old racquet, I asked the lab to check for fingerprints. While most were wiped clean, it seemed you missed a few spots. What would you say if I told you the lab was able to lift several clean prints?"

"I said I was just trying to clean it before giving it away. That's all."

"Yet despite the cleaning you gave it, the lab found something else. What would you say if I told you they inspected where the strings go into the grommets and found traces of Edith Skinner's blood?"

"I don't have anything to say. . . . I can't explain how blood got there . . . unless some homeless person bought it, used it to kill Edith, and then donated it back to Goodwill."

"Interesting scenario, though it conflicts with your earlier statement about poor people and tennis."

"That was just a supposition on my part. I really don't know what poor people do for recreation. I just assume they have a lot of time for that since they don't have jobs."

"If I were you, I'd avoid making any more unkind comments about the unemployed. It turns out that people who don't have a job also don't have as many excuses to get out of jury duty."

My wife turned to face me. "Are you going to just sit there and let her talk to me that way?"

I was thinking through how best to answer her question when she grabbed my thigh again. This time, her fingernails dug into me, and it took all my strength not to visibly wince.

When I didn't respond, Rhonda let go of my leg and again crossed her arms. This time, it didn't look like an act of defiance. She used her hands to rub her upper arms as if she'd just felt a blast of cold air.

Dix went over the details on the gun and the racquet again, establishing Rhonda's access to both and emphasizing the blood on the racquet. Then she asked questions about her whereabouts on the night in question. In classic fashion, she got my wife to contradict herself several times.

Tired of the back and forth, Rhonda sat up straighter. "You're confusing me now with all your questions. Days have gone by, and so what if I can't remember exactly where I was at such and such a time?"

Dix did not respond but went to the door, opened it a crack and spoke with someone outside. She returned to the head of the table carrying the box of phones. "My apologies. The young lady you met on your way in is the technical expert I turn to when I need access to data hiding behind someone's password. I had her collect the phones of everyone except, of course, for the detectives and special agents."

I knew mine was in the box with the others, but I could not keep my hand from instinctively patting the pocket that normally held my phone.

Dix leaned over her laptop and on the screen, we saw her accept an email from "girl-hackr." She straightened up and scanned the faces at the table before focusing again on Rhonda. "You know smart phones are really wonderous pieces of technology. We can use them to communicate, search the web, and even find out the number of carbs in our fast food, though that's one thing I never do. It takes the joy out of a double cheeseburger and fries, don't you think?"

My wife sniffed. "I don't eat fast food."

Dix pulled one phone from the box. It was Rhonda's unless there was another person in the room using a fake Gucci phone case. Rhonda thought it was authentic, and I hadn't wanted to tell her I got it off eBay.

Dix held it up and admired it for a moment. "I'm know we're all familiar with using our phones for directions, but we don't give any thought to the fact that, via the internal GPS, the phone keeps a record of our location throughout the day." Back on her laptop, she opened a file attached to the email and the screen displayed a map of The Estates. She zoomed in to display a trail of dots. "For example, Mrs. Hanson, what would you say if I told you my geek friend out there was able to pull location data along with timestamps from your phone and then build this graphic of your travels on the night in question?"

Another zoom and we could see the outline of the house at Angelica's address. A line of blue dots ran to the house. Dix zoomed in to a single blue dot. "I know it's not a good likeness of you, Mrs. Hanson, but this makes it look like you visited Miss Del Luca's home that evening and then went on to visit Miss Skinner's home shortly after that."

Rhonda sighed. She stared deep into my eyes for the first time in months, possibly years. I couldn't tell if it was a plea for help or forgiveness. Maybe both.

Speaking so soft I could barely hear her, she said, "It's not as if either of them had many years left anyway. I mean, you could consider these acts of mercy, couldn't you?"

Tony formed his hands into fists and looked like he was preparing for a prize fight. Others at the table looked confused until Detective Williams asked, "Mrs. Hanson, are you confessing to the murders of Angelica Del Luca aka Inga Oskarsdotter and Edith Skinner?"

She appeared to shrink as her head sank lower. "I killed the old shrews. I might as well confess since you have all this evidence . . . I used my father-in-law's gun to shoot Miss Del Luca . . . and used my tennis racquet to hit Miss Skinner so she'd fall on the stakes . . . But you don't know the whole story."

I felt sick. I thought I had already imagined all the bad things that might happen to me. That's what working for an insurance company does to you, and I came into the job predisposed to worry. All of my fears of what might happen in some tragic future had not prepared me for what I now faced.

Standing at the head of the table, Dix tried and failed to keep from grinning. "We'd love to hear your whole story. I have more to my story as well. You'll learn this in court, but I might as well tell you now. I made all this up. The bleach had removed all blood from the racquet, your prints weren't on the gun, and we never hacked your phone. This map was faked."

Rhonda pointed at the FBI special agents and the forensic scientist. "You faked it? What about them?"

"I don't mean to disparage any of these fine public servants, but for today they were basically window dressing."

Maloney and Stewart looked offended, but Robert Clark shrugged off his lab coat, and said, "It's hot in here. Can I take this off now? And Jill, you're still buying wings and beer? That was the deal, right?"

Rhonda glared at Dix. "You lied—"

"And my mother said I'd never use my theatre degree."

As what had happened dawned on her, my wife turned on Jill. "Don't sit there smiling, lady. This won't stand up in court. It's inadmissible, because she lied to me."

"I'm smiling because this is fun," said Jill. "It's the first time in my career I've seen someone fall apart and confess so quickly. You see it all the time on TV, but at law school they told us not to expect to ever see it. I also love it when an amateur tries to tell me how the law works."

Rhonda pounded the table with each syllable. "But she lied."

Dix picked up again. "Mrs. Hanson, if you had listened carefully, you would have heard me precede each question with 'What would you say if I told you.' Those were hypotheticals. It was all a 'What if I told you' exercise until you made a very admissible confession."

Rhonda dug her fingernails into the armrests. "You tricked me."

"And you killed two people and—while we're at it—are likely an accomplice after the fact in two more homicides. Yes, I tricked you, but I think I'm going to be able to live with that."

Rhonda looked from Dix to Tony and back again several times before pointing at him.

"It wasn't my fault. You don't know the whole story. He made me do it."

Tony shook his head. "Don't know what the bitch is talking about. Whatever she did, she did on her own."

Yes, that should have earned him an obligation to the swear jar, but I had a feeling he was soon going to face more serious consequences. No one calls Rhonda names without regretting it.

"Tony told me he needed to get rid of the old biddies," she snarled. "He blackmailed me into it."

Tony ran through a list of expletives I knew, interspersed with quite a few that were new to me—probably from corners of the internet I didn't visit. He paused his tirade when Detective Jackson walked up to stand behind him and placed a hand on one shoulder.

Jill took advantage of the moment of silence. "Mrs. Hanson, how did Mr. Columbo blackmail you?"

The anger left Tony's face. He seemed to enjoy watching me as Rhonda detailed how they had gone from harmless flirting to a "consensual extramarital liaison" some months before. I managed to keep my face blank, which turned out to be easy. The blood that had been rushing around my arteries several minutes earlier seemed to drain out of me—leaving me unable to control my facial expression or any other part of my body.

As you'd expect, I was hurt and wounded like anyone would be when they find their partner has been cheating on them. However, I had learned long before that suppressing uncomfortable emotion was my super power. On its own, it wasn't something that would ever rate a comic book series, but it was ingrained in my Scandinavian soul. It took four centuries for the north lands to expel all the angry malcontents the world would know as the Vikings. As a result, Norway, Sweden, etc., turned into a peaceful paradise while the rest of Europe absorbed all the fair-skinned blondes that had anger management issues.

Thinking about that helped me block out most of Rhonda's sharing, until she detailed how Tony had surreptitiously taken pictures of them and threatened to post them online unless she "whacked" the two seniors. He sat and smiled when she got to the part where she said seeing those pictures would crush me. She dabbed at her eyes and said she'd do anything to keep from hurting me like that.

Tony started to rise and the detective behind him pushed him back into his seat. "She wasn't interested in protecting her dear hubby. Sure, I wanted him out of the way, but she was the one who came up with the idea to frame him with his father's gun."

Rhonda turned to me. "I couldn't bear the thought of him killing you, dear. I thought pinning it on you would be the best way I could protect you from Tony. And I saw how those parents who'd scammed college admissions got to go to someplace called 'Club Fed.' It sounded nice, and I thought you'd like the time to yourself to sit and read. You always say you never have enough time for reading. I did it for you, honey. You have to believe me."

I didn't know what to say and based on all the stunned faces in the room, no one else did either. It seemed we'd need to wait for a true crime podcast to wrap things up neatly so we'd understand what had just happened.

My mind raced with too many thoughts at once. The sword over my head was gone—I was no longer a suspect. I would not have to face new prisoner orientation at the state prison. But returning to my old life was out of the question. My wife had not only cheated on me; she was a murderer. Somehow, I could accept that, awful as it was.

What I couldn't fathom was how to explain this to Kate and Luke. Years of parenting classes and books hadn't prepared me for this. I imagined Folks-Next-Door.com would be full of opinions on the matter—and probably archived posts from past years. Odds were, even a reality TV show had covered it by now.

Someone in the room was sobbing and then someone was laughing. Dix came over and pulled me up into a hug. With my head on her shoulder, I realized I was the someone in both cases.

Not wanting to be in that room another minute, I turned to the agents and detectives. "I assume you don't need me here anymore?"

They nodded. Somehow, I walked out of the room.

I drove back to my house, went inside, and saw five realtor cards had been slipped under the door.

Chapter Twenty-Five

Weeks later, I was up with the sun and hard at work knocking down the perimeter of the firepit. Between the fire hazard and the impact on the climate, I'd decided I didn't need a firepit even if it added to my property's market valuation.

Tony and Rhonda were both in jail, although I no longer cared what happened to them. I did care about my children, however, who had understandably taken it hard. "Why didn't you tell us this was going on, Dad?" they said, and I had the good sense to shrug and take the blame instead of foisting the responsibility on their mother, who was already down enough that it seemed unfair to deliver another kick.

Rhonda had flipped and given the prosecutors everything they needed to charge Tony with being the mastermind behind the first two murders, setting the house fire, and then kidnapping and killing the Shumakers. He was never sure if they'd seen Rhonda that night or ever looked at their security camera recordings but wanted to clean up any loose ends. He also admitted he didn't like the thought of never getting his hands dirty if he left all the killing to a woman.

Tony then tried to roll on the crypto criminals, but it turned out he'd never gotten close enough to know any incriminating details. In any case, Angelica's decoded records were enough to put them away. During the investigation, the Feds discovered that one of Robbie's hackers had breached their system and tracked Miss Inga to her witness protection in Georgia. Robbie had dispatched Tony to follow her and wait until he got the word to off her. The months of delay was the result of Robbie's indecision. Turns out he was comfortable taking people's money through crypto scams but he hesitated before taking a life. Miss Inga and Edith would possibly still be alive if it were not for Tony's patience running out. He wanted to take care of things here and get back to Jersey where he'd never have to face a plate with grits again.

As for The Estates, the neighborhood had created a small memorial shrine with flowers and cards in front of the Shumakers' burned-out lot. I thought it was touching that people now expressed such love for a couple they shunned when they were alive. Some tried to leave memorial gifts in front of Edith's and Angelica's, but the listing agents came by several times a day to remove anything that might deter a buyer or, just as bad, give a buyer a reason to think they could make a low-ball offer.

My life had settled into a new normal. Detective Williams had dropped in once to apologize for the city, and the not-so-special agents visited to "close the file," which was as near as they could come to saying sorry. I heard Detective Jackson had retired, which was just as well. He did not visit me, although he did contact the county office responsible for issuing building permits. Thanks to his efforts, my home office renovation would now have to wait until I paid the fine and filed the proper paperwork.

As for Kate and Luke, after our brief and tearful reunion after their mother's arrest, they had escaped back into their university lives as soon as they could. I'd arranged counseling for each of them, but they were tight-lipped about it. At least, based on the invoices, they were going. When we were together, there was an awkward attempt at normality, but I was used to that in other parts of my life. In the meantime, I was researching "how to text your adult children," "how often to text your adult children," and "a parent's guide to Gen Z emojis." Who knew eggplant and taco images were dirty?

I had one item left to close out this portion of my life. I needed to settle my account with my lawyer. When I entered the outer office, Jill's assistant's outstanding peripheral vision allowed him to wave me in without losing focus on his phone. Once I made it inside Jill's office, I saw Dix in her usual spot. I took the other chair.

Since Jill was on a call, I leaned over toward Dix. "I don't think I'll ever be able to say 'thank you' enough times. You did such a beautiful job of putting the pieces together. I'd be behind bars if it weren't for you."

"It's why Jill keeps me on the payroll. And to be fair, you started things off by making Tony reveal his too-perfect alibi. Criminals like him always think they're being smart, but if they were smart, they wouldn't be criminals.

One way or another, they do something dumb and get caught."

"I suppose so . . . I'm just a little disappointed."

"You could be in prison right now, but you're not. And I heard you might get your old job back. What's there to be disappointed about?"

"It's just this thing ended up a lot like the work I do on insurance frauds—the culprits get clumsy or greedy or both and trip over their lies." I shrugged. "Don't get me wrong. I'm glad it's over, but I expected a car chase or a fistfight or something exciting. I was thinking of applying to work for the FBI or some other branch of law enforcement, but in the end, this was just as mundane as working at GFI."

She let out a breath. "I've been through a couple of exciting somethings. Be thankful for mundane. Exciting things are fun to share at the bar with friends, but . . . they leave scars."

Jill was still on the phone, so I leaned in further to ask a follow-up. Dix leaned in as well and whispered, "I like you, but if you ask to see my scars, I will hurt you. Now, do you want to say anything else?"

I shook my head.

We both straightened up when Jill removed her feet from the credenza under the window and spun around to face us. She dropped her phone on her blotter and grimaced.

"Once again, when you're about to visit, Mr. Adams calls. Apparently by the grace of the almighty and a gullible rookie judge, his son avoided imprisonment on the previous charges. Now he's been arrested for an alleged money laundering scheme. He was apparently inspired by Cunningham's crypto scam, but did not study it enough to see that wannabe criminal kingpin went to jail. Once again, I refused to represent the kid, but with his life story, I'm tempted to make an offer on the movie rights."

"Funny you should mention that," I said. "I've been contacted by two different filmmakers who are interested in making documentaries based on my experience. I haven't signed anything yet. I was wondering if you could look over their offers."

"Sorry. I don't do entertainment law. I still have need of my soul."

Dix made a noise through her nose that sounded like a steam train releasing pressure.

"I understand," I said. "There is another legal issue, though. I take my marriage vows seriously, but I feel like I might be at the point where I should talk with a divorce lawyer. Just in case."

Jill nodded. "I think that makes sense. Rhonda is likely to get a long prison sentence, and then there's the whole thing about her murdering your neighbors, sleeping with another man, and trying to frame you for the killings."

Dix released more steam. "I can see how that could kill the romance."

After receiving a nasty look from Jill, Dix stood. "Gotta get back to a client who's looking for a Maltese Falcon," she said, and left the room. I was pretty certain she'd made that up.

Once the door was closed, Jill said, "I can recommend several good divorce attorneys. In my practice, I prefer to stick to criminal cases where simple things like felonies are involved and not the raw violence and anguish of marital relationships. . . . Also, I try to avoid representing someone I'm dating."

"I'm confused. We're not dating."

She smiled. "Why don't we discuss that over dinner tonight?"

Acknowledgements

No one reads acknowledgements unless they suspect they'll be mentioned somewhere. If you think you have a chance, keep reading.

My goal of finding an agent who would laugh with me was fulfilled when I signed with Jenna Satterthwaite of the Storm Literary Agency. As an author and an agent, she is exceptional. I was convinced she was the perfect fit by the end of our first conversation. While she was on the phone, she was also watching children in a playground. When she reassured them, "There's no blood, you're OK," I knew we could work together. In fact, I found this a good motto for my writing journey.

I'm convinced that editing a comedic murder mystery calls on skills that only a few possess. It's possible to make the prose better but leave the punchlines dying on the floor. Fortunately, I met Jess Verdi of Crooked Lane Books at an Atlanta Writers Conference, and she saw something in my initial paragraphs. Thanks to Jess and everyone on the Crooked Lane team who had a hand in this book, including Rebecca Nelson (design), Thai Fantauzzi Pérez (production), Dulce Botello (marketing and publicity), Mikaela Bender (marketing and publicity),

Stephanie Manova (subrights), Megan Matti (subrights), and Martin Biro (editorial). Jess and her team have guided me through the process and kept it fun. They polished my pages without sanding off the silly bits.

I would never have been able to work with Jenna and Jess without the invaluable support of my critique group. The members changed over the years but the recent players include: Gabby (G. A.) Anderson, Dan Burke, Kim Conrey, April Dilbeck, Phil Fasone, Ed Gruber, Karen (K. A.) Kirtland, Mike Shaw, Deborah (D. L.) Mitchell, Katherine Nichols, Patrick (P. D.) Scullin, and last—only due to my adherence to alphabetical order—George Weinstein. I owe a debt I will never repay to each of these writers for their honest feedback on what worked and what fell flat. I almost always listened to them and on occasion followed their suggestions.

I feel I should write a separate essay acknowledging the many invaluable contributions of George Weinstein. In addition to leading our weekly critique group meetings, George has devoted countless hours to nurturing writers across Georgia. He is an award-winning author, the executive director of the Atlanta Writers Club, and the director of the Atlanta Writers Conference twice a year. Through many channels, he generously shares his industry knowledge with everyone. Without George, this book would never have made it to publication. Don't hold it against him.

While they were not directly involved in the creation of this book, I want to thank all the outstanding people I worked with during my years at Hewlett-Packard. Some laughed at my presentations out of politeness. Most because I was in their chain of command. Either way, they encouraged me and as a result they share some of the blame today.

Finally, I want to express my gratitude to Erik, Kari, and Kristin. They endured decades of Dad Jokes, not to mention having no control over what I said about them in the annual Christmas letter. I am proud of this book, but it cannot compare to the joy I feel every time I look at them.

I could name many more individuals, but I will refrain from doing so based on the polite requests of some not to be included and the legal threats from others.